OBJECTS OF DESIRE

OBJECTS OF DESIRE

C J Emerson

CHIVERS

British Library Cataloguing in Publication Data available

This Large Print edition published by BBC Audiobooks Ltd, Bath, 2008.
Published by arrangement with Allison & Busby Ltd.

U.K. Hardcover ISBN 978 1 405 64280 4
U.K. Softcover ISBN 978 1 405 64281 1

Printed and bound in Great Britain by
Antony Rowe Ltd., Chippenham, Wiltshire

CHAPTER ONE

Taking this baby feels no different from any of the others. People move aside long before Jess reaches them; no need for a bell, she thinks, they can see I'm unclean. The corridor from the delivery room seems endless as she walks towards the nurses congregated at their station. The chatter quietens as she passes by and their heads rotate, but they avoid eye contact.

Everyone belongs, except her.

As she waits for the lift her smile becomes set into a rictus grin. The new mothers watching her know the truth—she does not own this baby, and although this is not the first time, she holds the body awkwardly, like someone else's gift.

The smile is painful and she wants to scratch the spreading red patch on her neck, but her hands are not free. Times like this, she never speaks.

In her arms, the child is sleeping her first sleep outside the womb.

On the ground floor she hurries towards the main entrance, her footsteps moving to the rhythm of the song in her head.

The yellow blanket in her arms feels hot and the baby's eyes are no more than slits below a strawberry birthmark on her throat, a

1

dark slash against the wrinkled red skin.

Jess slows, as if uncertain where to go, but then accelerates through the doors that slide aside just in time, programmed for slower steps than hers.

The blanket could be filled with lead as she walks towards the Jeep straddling two spaces reserved for doctors. The engine is already running, and she straps the tiny body into the car seat that's permanently fixed in the back. Before she shuts the door, she pulls the blanket away to keep the baby's face clear and runs a finger down its cheek.

The car is already moving as she fastens the seat-belt. This is when the tears always come, no matter how she tries to hold them back. No sounds, no sobbing, just hot, heavy drops that spread slowly to cover her cheeks in a stinging film. The driver is silent, but he squeezes the woman's arm before accelerating down the ramp towards the main road, swerving to miss an ambulance hurrying towards the warehouse doors of A & E.

*   *   *

Even though the legal department do most of the legwork for an Emergency Protection Order, it's gone eight o'clock before Jess Chadwick leaves her office on the edge of the forest and drives home. The light has already flattened as the Jeep bucks down the rutted mile-long track to her farmhouse, a grey stone complex a couple of hundred feet up the side of the valley. She takes it slowly, dodging the larger potholes as the car climbs along a hidden corridor in the patchwork of oak, beech and yew that sprawls down the steep hillside.

The sun is half hidden behind the ridge on the other side of the river as it begins to set amongst the Welsh hills, but she's warm from the drive and wants some fresh air to clear away the smell of hospital and new baby that's clung to her clothes all day. The beer bottle is slippery in her hand, and she feels the alcohol unlock her body as she leans on the stone wall that separates her garden from the fields all around. Across the valley is another country. Before she moved, she always thought Wales would be the wild place but it looks more pastoral there, fields of pale green and yellow above the lines of trees spilling down the steep lower slopes. Over here, across the river boundary on the edge of England, her house feels isolated, standing alone in a small clearing in the surrounding forest that advances and retreats along with the light. A breeze blows up from the west, carrying the stutterings of sheep in the fields opposite; their cries reaching across the river sound for all the world like babies crying for no reason.

Jess shivers suddenly. The breeze has strengthened and the trees lining the edge of

3

the lower field are swaying to a slow rhythm of their own. She finishes the beer and goes back inside. On evenings like this she's glad that she keeps the range burning all through the summer; silent company, as if the house itself was alive. 'Lares and Penates,' she thinks, 'perhaps the Romans had something there.'

She forgot to buy food today. The loaf has turned green and the fridge is empty, except for beer and a half-empty tin of cat food. In London she could have phoned for a pizza, but no one delivers here; a small price to pay. Under a cushion on the sofa she finds an open bag of tortilla chips and a half-eaten shrew.

'Wagner! Where are you, you furry bastard?'

She shrouds the headless body in kitchen paper, throws it in the bin, tries one of the chips. Soft, but acceptable.

She wonders if she should have a bath, but can't be bothered. Music, maybe. Something jagged. She stands by the wall full of discs, twisting her head to read the spines, but then the phone in the study starts ringing. She doesn't want to talk and lets the answerphone kick in.

No one calls these days. It's the Welsh Marches, she told her friends, not the rainforest. I'm one hundred and fifty miles away; I can be back in a couple of hours. But she hasn't been to London since she moved here seven months ago, no one's come down the M4 to stay, and in a way she's glad.

All the same, she pushes the study door open with her foot to hear who's calling.

'Hi Jess—it's Ed. Just wanted to see how you were.' The voice on the phone is light with a gentle Forest drawl, and there's a pause as if he could see her hesitating.

Maybe he has the right to call. She picks up the cordless and wanders back outside.

'Sorry, Ed, I was hiding. Thanks for being my driver this morning.'

'The modern police, always at your service.' He pauses for a moment. 'There's another thing. I was asked to give you a heads up on a message I got from CID. Seems a body was found up on the Dyke late this afternoon. It's a young boy, nine or ten years old, no identification. Ring any bells?'

Jess has always wondered when this call would come, about the one that got away. She's never had a death before, not one of hers, and she runs through a film strip in her mind of all her clients, the children she's supposed to protect. There are so many she can't picture all their faces, and she says a silent prayer to anyone who might be listening before she replies. 'How did he die?'

'No details yet. I'll call when I've had sight of the path report.'

'Where was he found?'

'You know that parking area on the back road between Gwenstow and St Brevels? It

5

was a few hundred yards from there, just off the path into the woods.'

Before she moved, Jess had a fantasy that working in the country would be different from London. No more baby-fathers trying to knife her, no more heroin mothers forgetting to feed the kids. But as Ed talks she pictures the scene he describes, a section of the trail just a few miles from her house. It reminds her of a Hackney squat rather than woodland scene, a litter bin of used condoms, roaches and the occasional needle, and she shivers to think of the dead child lying there.

When Ed rings off she goes back inside, closing the door behind her. Beyond the study window the trees have become moving shapes in the dusk, and she wishes she'd put up a blind.

*   *   *

That night Jess dreams of her daughter, as she knew she would. A girl whose name she's never known, a faceless child crying in a dark forest.

1986—1

She's still flying from the gig, the last of the tour. They cracked the States—New York, Chicago, LA and then the towns in between. Climax, Colorado; Mars, Pennsylvania; Noodle, Texas; Enigma, Georgia. Then back to London for the finale.

Neither her mind nor her body knows that it's time to stop. A month off, then back to the studio for the next album. Eighteen years old, fucking superstar.

The room's too loud; even the walls are talking. She wants music, she wants a beat, she starts to sing. She can't stand still, wants to hold the mood. Jamie's got some gear but she can't see him anywhere. The crowd is a slurry of punks and sluts, painted and hungry. Older men with fake piercings and no muscle tone.

Older women stay away.

You could get stoned just standing here.

A clutch of wannabes are huddled in the corner, coughing over a spliff and watching her. They could be from another dimension; not quite identical, all wearing skewed versions of her own face and clothes.

Which one do you want to screw? she thinks. Me or Jamie—I guess it really doesn't matter.

She's isolated, under observation, and every

person she looks at turns their face away.

She needs that gear. Too early to come down. Where the fuck is Jamie?

'Hey Chad—want some of this?' One of the girls from the corner, a dog sniffing a stranger. It's like looking in a mirror except that the hormones don't seem to be working; her breasts have yet to swell and her hips are narrow and sharp. But the look in the girl's eyes is ageless. She's older than she looks, skeletal, on a diet that keeps food at a distance.

The girl smiles as she presents her tribute, wet cardboard and exploding seeds.

'Weed's no good to me, honey. How about some charlie?' She hears her voice, charred and ridged, ageing too fast.

The girl shrinks. 'Don't know him—what's he look like?'

'Jesus!'

Raised voices and breaking glass and red wine climbing the green velvet curtains. Twenty feet high? Whoever this place belongs to, he can afford to have them cleaned. Why should she care? Whatever, it will be trashed by morning; all for the thrill of having her and Jamie stay for a while, do some gear, get screwed. Maybe they'll put up a plaque.

Almost every person she passes reaches out, and she dodges their fingers with a swaying dance. Don't look in their eyes—they think it's permission.

8

When they can't reach her with their hands and their fingertips they use voices. Chad, Chad, over here, over here.

It's *my* turn.

She thinks, if I stood still for long enough they would strip me bare, pull the skin away from my flesh, polish my bones.

She thinks, maybe they'd like to eat me.

She wonders, what would that feel like?

She needs to find Jamie.

The house is a stranger to her, a private hotel of corridors and overflowing rooms. She finds the hall with its Hollywood staircase winding down in two graceful curves. A Filipino woman, dressed like a maid, is garnering a pile of vomit: goujons of beige sauced with red wine and bile. Chad wonders if it hit anyone on its way down and then the smell reaches her.

Must be over twelve hours since she ate.

Jamie, then food.

He'll be outside somewhere. Touching leaves, talking to flowers, screwing a stranger.

The paths down to the river front are discreetly lit, winding through beds of manicured shrubs and small copses. It's quieter out here, although the music from the house vibrates the earth and there are other, more primitive sounds. Chad recognises one of the roadies propped against a tree, his fingers locked through the red mohican of the bass player from the support band. The roadie frees one hand and pulls on the neck of a bottle of beer, letting some of the froth run down his chin.

Someone's untied a dinghy; it floats just out of reach, making its way to the swift currents in the centre of the river. One of the men on the bank wades after it but slips and falls to laughter and applause. They're too far away to be sure, but one of them looks like Jamie.

Her stomach has shrunken to a small, hard rock.

Downriver she sees the lights of a bridge—Kew, Richmond?—and the amber glow of London beyond.

More sounds, off the path in front of her. One of the wannabes is lying a few feet away, almost submerged under the bulk of an exec from the record label. The girl's face is pale as chicken skin and her eyes are as wide and dark as a frightened deer.

'Should be more careful what you wish for, honey,' Chad mutters as she passes by.

A couple of people have reached the rowing boat and climb in but there are no oars and they seem undecided as they pick up speed, drifting past the edge of the grounds and away towards the distant bridge.

No sign of Jamie.

She tries the house again, upstairs, lost in the labyrinth of shagpile corridors. The spliff girl comes out from a bedroom and sidles past Chad, sniffing and wiping her mouth with a

10

tissue, trailing the mixed salts of sex and sweat.

He's sitting on the bed, leather trousers concertinaed above his boots.

'You're a fucking nonce, Jamie, you know that? How old was she—fourteen, fifteen?'

'Lighten up, Chad, it was just a blow job. I was doing the wee girl a favour—I'm no' a fucking monk.'

It's a woman's bedroom, a glass-topped dressing table over by the window. A space has been cleared in the centre and a small piece of silver foil is open and empty. Jamie sees her glance.

'Sorry, babe—she said she was looking for Charlie. I would'a saved you a line or two, but you know how it is. We'll find Raoul, he's carrying. If you'd been here we could'a had a wee party, just the three of us.'

He has the most beautiful smile she's seen.

'It was just a bit of fun—I didn'ae even take the boots off. I save ma wee toes for you, only you.' He starts to sing, and she can't help laughing, falling on the bed next to him. She could do with a screw.

CHAPTER TWO

The nightmares never change, and Jess is awake long before the sun crests the ridge that rises from the fields behind her house, evaporating a thick roll of mist rising up from the hidden river. The valley is like a world apart, with its own laws. A few months ago, on one of the tracks running down from the Dyke, she found a small shrine of candles and feathers, eggshells and woven straw. There was something comforting about gods who didn't want to live in the sky, she thought. Each time she returns to the shrine the objects have changed, although she's never seen anyone. Maybe one day she'll leave a token of her own.

Going into the office is like moving from myth into reality, the workspaces squashed to fit the contours of an old red-brick Victorian school with windows that are narrow, high and unwashed, framing a mosaic of grubby sky. In summer the windows jam, and in winter pockets of air and water chase each other through the heavy antique radiators, providing atonal symphonies but no heat.

At the desk opposite hers, three towers of green files frame a woman wearing brittle, blonde hair sprayed into a rigid helmet. From halfway down the office, Jess can smell the dust from the archives. The woman circles a hand in the air as Jess approaches.

'Kettle's hot, don't talk—court report late, writing like buggery—file's a complete tip.' Her head dips even further.

'I've told you, Else, write it straight on to the computer—it'll save you time.'

Now she looks up and smiles. 'Jess, you're

12

twenty-five years younger than me and a damn sight more intelligent. Use your computers, leave me to my quills. This time next year, I'll be painting watercolours and you have some trainee here, all computers, no common sense.' The rolling Bavarian accent of her childhood is still strong after forty years.

Jess realises that the pattern of her desk has been disturbed. Last night she left the usual empty surface and precisely placed phone, but someone has placed a new file in front of her seat, off-centre.

'Does Joe have any idea how many cases I'm working on? The man's a complete moron.'

She takes the file and runs up the back stairs to the next floor but her supervisor's fishbowl office is dark and Jess can see nothing but her own reflection in the glass walls. It's the first time she's looked at herself today, an angular creature with short pale hair like wilted spikes. She is colourless, shadowed, a featureless geometry.

This is fine.

Back at her desk, Jess sips some of the coffee she made to share with Else and opens the file. It's thin, two standard forms inside the jacket, a referral from a teacher. A new case then, no known history. She likes this, to be free of the burden of other people's judgements and preconceptions. There are families that stay with the department through generations, their case notes ragged with the handwriting of her predecessors—some eloquent, some barely literate. Through it all the clients twist in and out of focus, but the shape of the case workers is clear.

Jess checks the name on the front of the file; Bryony Pearce. The name has no resonance, no baggage. A new family, making their first tentative steps through the one-way gate into her world.

She scans the transcript of the duty worker's conversation with the teacher. Bryony is a quiet girl, nine years old, good in class. Enough friends. Normal.

Until she stopped talking, stopped joining in, stopped playing. Nothing was wrong, said Bryony. Everything OK at home. Nothing at all to worry about, except for the bruising that the teacher saw on her legs, just under the hem of her skirt. The bruising in two wide bands around her thighs. The bruising that reversed time, mottling from grey to cabbage yellow and then back to purple, a dull rainbow. And there's something else, hiding among the words. Something hinted at, but evaded.

A droplet of coffee baptises the file jacket. Jess checks Bryony's address, the Chellacote Manor estate on the outskirts of Gwenstow, about three miles from the office. There are other clients there. Low-rise, low-income social housing alongside privatised council houses with primary-colour front doors. Low expectation, but better than the sink estates further out along the mouth of the estuary towards the maw of Uskmouth, all ramp and underpass and urine stains darkening the concrete.

Bruises fade quickly on a child. They set the agenda, injecting a new visit into Jess's day. It could be something or nothing. Time was she would call in at the school, see the girl and close the case before it started. If nothing was wrong. Now there are rules and flow charts; Human Rights. Sometimes she wonders whose.

Number one—strategy discussion with the police Family Support Unit.

Even after seven months, Jess has made few contacts and counts herself lucky when Ed answers the FSU's duty phone. After Jess outlines the case he checks the databases, humming a hymn tune that Jess remembers from her childhood. After a minute or two Ed confirms that there's no record of the family, no previous history. Virgins.

They go through the routine; no officers available, but no imminent danger to the child. Ed asks if she's OK to make the visit alone. Of course, says Jess, if there's any trouble I'll let you know. She prefers it this way, working light.

Number two—the visit. Should she make an appointment or call unannounced? Neither guarantees success. Option one can mean twitching curtains and unopened doors as if social workers were irremediably contagious. And so we are, thinks Jess. One word, one visit, and you belong to us.

A fly is preening on the handset of her phone. Jess lets him—her?—decide. How do you sex a fly? If it stays for the count of five she'll call round unannounced. She's never seen a fly like this before. Its body is striated like a butler's trousers, black and cream, moving to a swift, digital beat.

It stays.

*   *   *

The houses are about thirty years old, built in long low terraces with arched openings through to communal gardens at the back, littered with the detritus of children. The front yards are tiny and mostly paved, furnished with pots of dead flowers and rusting pieces of domestic machinery. One has an old armchair, the seat grey with a peppering of mildew.

The concrete steps to the first-floor flat are steep and the walls are layered with graffiti and the occasional graze of paint, like tribal markings scraped from pushchairs that came too close. There are wires hanging loose from the plastic bell push and Jess knocks on the front door, the chips and splinters painted over recently with pillar-box red. The woman who answers is smaller than Jess, perhaps five five,

16

but hamburger fat, the skin on her face glossy and smooth as it stretches to keep up with the swelling flesh underneath. She wears stale cigarette smoke like scent.

Jess introduces herself; would it be 'Fuck off' or 'Come in'? Sometimes it's too close to call, but this time she's lucky.

'Bryony, I suppose. What's she done now?' Cigarettes have already deepened her voice which seems to belong to an older woman, the Welsh-lite of the border made even more musical by a tremolo of worry. She leads Jess into the flat; a couple of bedrooms and bathroom on the other side of the living space, more than enough for a small family. The whole apartment could fit into her farmhouse kitchen. They sit facing each other and Jess runs automatically through the checklist—no roaches in the ashtrays, no dog shit on the floors. Pass. Yet who am I to judge? she thinks.

A curling, unframed photo is propped up on the window sill. Two girls, dressed for a party, squinting at the lens.

'Which one's Bryony?'

The woman looks up from her search for the TV remote. 'The dozy one, on the left. Rhiannon's her little sister.' She turns down the volume on the oversized television but talks half to the screen, half to Jess.

'I took Bryony to school myself, this morning, like I always do. They'd have called me if she wasn't well, wouldn't they?' The

17

cigarette she'd been smoking when Jess came in is still alight in the ashtray next to her feet, but she lights another and sucks on it noisily.

Jess explains about the referral from Bryony's teacher, watches for a reaction.

'Miss Happs? She don't know her arse from her elbow, that one. What's she said?'

'She was worried that Bryony's been very quiet over the last few weeks. Maybe something's on her mind? Arguments at home perhaps?'

'Bryony argue? You must be joking. She's a good girl, my daughter. Always does what she's told, no tantrums, nothing.'

'Have you noticed any change in her, Mrs Pearce?'

'The name's Carwen, and it's not Mrs. And what business is it of yours? Or that bloody teacher. I can look after my own kids without you sticking your nose in.' She blows a thin jet of smoke directly at Jess but there is uncertainty in her voice.

'The teacher saw some marks on Bryony's legs, like bruises. Has she hurt herself in any way recently?'

Carwen stubs out the cigarette with a sudden ferocity, screwing it into a mangled worm in the ashtray.

'Are you saying I beat up my own daughter? You're mad, you are. Come in here and accuse me, you don't even know me. Bloody social.' But she doesn't move from the chair.

18

'I'm not accusing anyone.'

Carwen stares at her for another moment then sits back heavily and lights another cigarette, closing her eyes as she inhales. On the television, a woman with a microphone is interviewing someone in a studio audience.

The handbag at Jess's feet judders a couple of times, almost imperceptibly; a new text on her mobile, she'll check it later. The sound, slight though it is, rouses Carwen who squints through a cloud of bitter smoke.

'You're not from round here.'

'London—I moved down this year.'

'Thought this would be easier, did you? Green fields and sheep shaggers, that's what you thought.' The smile lasts no longer than a second. 'You got no idea. Anyone can see you ain't had no kids—but you got some piece of paper says you know more about being a mother than I do. Fucking joke.'

Bullseye, thinks Jess. Bigger joke than you know. She shrugs, stands, collects her bag.

'I need to see Bryony today. Now. But I need your permission. You can come with me but you don't have to. If there's nothing wrong, then the whole thing can be finished today. No more fuss, no more visits from Londoners who think they know best. It's up to you.'

The woman in the television audience is chopping the air with her hands and shouting silent words while the people around her laugh.

'Can't say I've noticed no bruises. So how did this teacher see them—she been pawing at my Bryony? Bloody disgrace, that's what it is. You're all sick, all of you.' Find another scapegoat; the first rule of blame management.

'I have to go now, Carwen. What's it going to be?'

*   *   *

A grey drizzle mists the air as Jess leaves the block of flats and makes her way across the street. A couple of teenagers are scanning the interior of her car, and the cut-down bikes they straddle are too small for their unwieldy legs. As they hear Jess approach they push themselves a few yards away; one of them looks familiar, a lopsided face with no front teeth and a home-made tattoo on his neck. He jabs towards Jess with his finger.

'You're the social, aren't you? You took our Kelly's baby away. You're dirt, you are, that's what my sister said.' He hawks onto the road, a child's gobbet, then backs away still further as Jess walks towards him.

'Have the school holidays come early, Darren? I'd get back to class if I were you, or you'll be seeing even more of me.'

The boys pedal away, hunched like clowns, their obscenities fading as they turn into the next street. The drizzle has turned to heavy rain and Jess decides to check her phone somewhere less sullen, where there are no faces at windows watching to see which family she'll visit next.

On the road back to Gwenstow she pulls into a small lay-by overlooking a field. Two small ponies, the colour of mud, wander over to the gate and watch as she checks the text message.

'*? Nu sng? Wnt 2 upld tonite if pos. D.*'

New song, she says, what new song? As if I had the time. She's about to reply to Denny when the phone buzzes in her hand. Ed.

'Jess? I just had a call from CID about that child on the Dyke. Sorry, it's bad news—they identified the body as Perry Stiffley. Remember? We worked the case together back in February.'

How could she forget her first case after she moved. Blurred photos of a little boy, on his knees in front of a man.

She remembers Perry; a scrubby little mite with spiky black hair and a smile that made her want to take him home every time she saw him.

She remembers his father, unbelieving and distant, always in his studio. She can't think of him without seeing the hairs on his arms, filmed with the pale sawdust from his carvings.

She remembers Ed, arguing that the case should be closed for lack of evidence and ignoring her concerns, laughing at her

21

intuition. A system failure, Denny would call it, and now Perry's dead.

CHAPTER THREE

The day's started to overflow and it isn't even lunchtime. Jess checks her watch, then her diary. Bryony now, an hour at least. If the girl makes a disclosure of abuse she'll need a medical examination and God knows when that would be, always assuming that a suitable doctor can be found. And all of this before the child-care meeting in Uskmouth about another of her clients.

Please let it be nothing, thinks Jess. Please let this be an overzealous teacher protecting her back. She turns off at the roundabout and heads a mile round the ring road to the school serving the estate. The buildings are low, geometric shapes in stained concrete, squatting at the edge of fields and surrounded by high metal fences. As she parks her car the doors of the different blocks swing open in unison, and in a second she is surrounded by a whirlpool of children in grey and red.

She finds Melanie Happs in the staff room, a stringy creature with naked eyes that miss the protection of a pair of glasses. A piece of filling falls from her sandwich onto the book she is marking, and she bends forward to pick up the fragment of egg with her teeth.

'Hi Mel. How are you getting on with the lenses?'

The teacher wraps her sandwich in a piece of foil, arranges it inside a plastic lunchbox and presses the lid on firmly, working around each side in turn. Only when she's satisfied does she look up.

'Bloody awful. Like walking around with razor blades in your eyes. I suppose you're here about Bryony?'

'What do you think—something or nothing?' says Jess.

'That's your job, not mine, thank God. I'll take you to the classroom and find Bryony. Want me to sit in?'

'She doesn't know me; probably best if you do.'

They walk outside, across the crowded playground and into one of the other blocks. The walls of the classroom are covered with paintings in bright slabs of colour, family groups in Victorian clothes. 'We're doing a history project,' says Mel. 'It's one of the other things that got me worried.'

'Are we still talking about Bryony?'

'I'm not saying there's anything wrong, see? I want to make that clear. But you can't let anything go these days, can you, not with all the trouble there's been. I don't want anyone saying I don't look out for the children in my class.' Mel speaks quickly and her gaze flicks

23

backwards and forwards across Jess's face, catching her eyes on every other pass. 'She's always been a quiet girl, see? No trouble in class, good at her reading and writing and loves painting. Well, they all do, don't they, at this age? Anyway, about three weeks ago I noticed that she wasn't playing with her friends at break times. Standing by herself, she was, next to walls or corners. She stopped saying anything in class, just seemed to want to disappear. And then she did this.'

Mel opens a cupboard behind her and takes out a painting.

'I like to put up all their work but . . .' Her voice trails off as Jess looks at the sheet of paper.

The painting is good. Better than I could have done at her age, thinks Jess. Carwen and Rhiannon have been painted with flair, every feature detailed, their faces almost alive, and Jess runs her finger over the crinoline dresses, almost expecting to feel silk instead of pigment.

Bryony is there too, standing apart from the others. But she's shown herself in everyday clothes, dowdy by comparison. And it's not just the clothes.

Jess checks the other paintings on the walls again. All the children, all the mothers and fathers and stepfathers and carers, all the brothers and sisters; all of them are smiling. And when she looks back at the paper in her hands, Jess feels her heart skip as she sees that Bryony painted herself without a face.

'I'm no psychologist,' says Mel, 'but I don't think that's right.'

No, thinks Jess, not right at all.

She tries to remember if any of the children at the school have a sexual history, already moving along the cycle from abused to abuser. Children without a childhood. She thinks of Perry and his smiling face, and she remembers the photographs; he wasn't smiling then.

'What about the bruises on Bryony's legs? When did you notice those?'

'I first saw them two weeks ago, it must have been. On her legs, high up so they're mostly hidden under her skirt. I saw them when she tripped over a bag one of the boys had left sticking out from under his desk—did it on purpose, the little bugger.'

'Why didn't you call us at the time?'

'Because they weren't like a slap or anything, more like stripes across her legs. She said she'd hurt herself climbing over a gate. I should have thought then—Bryony isn't the sort who climbs over gates. Anyway, two days ago, when she painted this, I made sure to look for anything out of place and sure enough, there are fresh bruises just where the others had been. Same shape, same place, everything.'

While the teacher goes to find Bryony, Jess studies the painting as if looking for a pattern, an explanation, and then replaces it in the cupboard.

Nine years old.

She suddenly feels tired, as if there had been no sleep last night, and massages the back of her neck as she stands by the window, looking out at the children in the playground. She can't remember being that age, no longer tries. Nic had said—don't worry about it, what we call memory is nothing more than stories we invent to explain why we're here. Be mindful, stay in the present, you won't get lost that way.

She remembers Nic.

A few moments later the girl comes into the classroom. She seems too small for her grey pleated skirt and baggy red school sweatshirt, the school name, 'Chellacote', across the front in white plastic lettering. The clothes are as clean as they can ever be on a nine-year-old, without the patina of dirt and dishevelment that Jess has seen on so many children whose lives hold secrets. Bryony looks at the floor, her long, bunched hair just skimming her shoulders. She looks lost.

Jess takes it slowly: who I am, why I'm here. Do you like school? Who are your friends? Tell me about Steffy, what you do together. What about at home?

Tell me about your games.

Tell me about your dreams, the monsters under your bed.

26

All the time Bryony's been talking Jess tries to catch a glimpse of the bruises, but the girl is sitting on her hands, pulling the edges of her grey skirt tight across her legs.

Show me your wounds, Bryony. Tell me how they happened. I'll understand, really I will.

She uses different words.

'Come on now, Bryony, stop messing about,' says the teacher. 'Show Miss Chadwick your bruises and then you can get back to lunch. I know I want to get back to mine.'

Jess doesn't know what she was expecting. She'd recognise a slap, sometimes the shape of a whole adult hand is branded for a while into a child's skin. Or the bruises from fingertips that clutch too hard, too long. But this is different. As the girl lifts the hem of her skirt in a slow revealing, Jess sees two thick mottled bands, one around each thigh. The bruises are maybe two days old, the purple already fading to the yellow of rotting cabbage.

'You say these happened climbing over a gate?' says Jess. The girl nods, keeping her eyes on the floor.

'What does your mum say about these marks?' Bryony pulls the skirt tight around herself again but says nothing.

'I believe you,' says Jess. 'Accidents happen—it's OK.' She changes the subject before the catch in Bryony's voice turns to tears, and wishes she could reach out to hold the little girl and bring a smile to her face.

27

Mel sends Bryony back to the playground and asks Jess what will happen next.

'If she made a disclosure I'd arrange a medical and involve the police, but she's given us nothing. And the marks are borderline, they could be anything. Maybe she's telling the truth, but . . .'

'But you don't think so?'

'You said it earlier—can we afford to take the chance? But I can't do anything unless Bryony accuses someone or there's really clear evidence of something wrong. The picture and the bruises just aren't enough. I'll talk to someone at the Family Support Unit later, but we're all so stretched I know what they'll say.'

      *   *   *

The child-care conference is in the main council block in Uskmouth but the car park is full, as usual, and Jess leaves the Jeep behind the supermarket at the bottom of the hill. The earlier rain has stopped as she walks past the small, single-fronted shops that line the main street. People move in herds here. Right now it's large women with double pushchairs and old men with flapping trousers. Everyone seems compressed, as if they sleep in beds that are too short.

When she reaches the Poundshop a man walks out carrying a yellow plastic bucket with a Jack Russell sitting inside, the dog's tongue fluttering in the breeze. She's not sure who looks most proud, the bent old man in his grey suit and trilby or the grinning dog tasting the air, and she swears as she scrabbles for the small digital camera hidden at the bottom of her bag. She doubles back down the road a little way and runs off nine shots as they waddle towards her; only the dog notices.

She keeps her main camera in the car: an old Nikon, black-and-white film and a telephoto. That's real power, reducing people to line and shadow, capturing them in secret. Severing them from their reality, inserting them into hers. But needs must; the man and his dog will probably never see their images on her website but already she's thinking of words that will form the germ of a song. For a while at least, the dead boy and the bruised girl are a world away.

*   *   *

In the council building a woman stops Jess as she's about to enter the room they use for child-care conferences.

'Excuse me—is this the right place for the Eskell meeting?' Her voice is pitched low, with a soft Bristol accent barely masked by received pronunciation. She seems out of place, dressed for a boardroom in the City rather than a child-care meeting in Uskmouth. She smells of money and musk. She has the kind of beauty

29

that owes nothing to fashion; café latté skin, Egyptian eyes and cheekbones you could sharpen a knife on. And it looks as if someone's tried; from her left eye sweeping in an arc to her chin is a thin pale line of scar tissue. On someone else it would look ugly, thinks Jess; on this woman it's a design feature. She wants to capture her in the camera.

'Sure. You are?' asks Jess.

'Parvati Randhawa, detective sergeant. Pav. I've just joined the Family Support Unit. From Ed's description I guess you're Jess Chadwick?'

Voice, clothes; all the wrong register for a DS. And her skin is so perfect that it invites a touch, just a fingertip to trace the scar. Jess tries not to sound too defensive.

'He didn't mention you.'

'I should have let you know I'd be coming in his place. Just seemed like a good opportunity to get my feet wet—and meet you. Ed was very complimentary.'

'Did he brief you on the case? I can give you a heads up before we go in.'

Jess thinks—I don't know who you are.

'Isn't it one of the victims of that swimming coach?' says Parvati.

'Too right. The coach taught Mikey Eskell more than how to backstroke. The boy was put on the Child Protection Register last year after the case blew up.' Jess talks quickly to fill the

30

space. 'Really disturbed behaviour; swearing, acting up at school. Bad personal hygiene—you know the score.'

'How old is Mikey?'

'Fourteen. Trouble is, he was grooming his own little flock—mostly boys at his brother's school, nine- and ten-year-olds—so we placed him with his grandmother for the time being. But he needs to be in a therapeutic unit; that's what the meeting's about, to see what can be salvaged.'

The last time she saw Mikey his eyes never left hers, never blinked. 'Wrong,' he said, 'what's wrong? Just a bit of fun, no one got hurt, not much, nothing lasting. Nothing you can see.'

'You get used to it,' he said.

And then you look forward to it.

*　　　*　　　*

'This isn't Starbucks.' Parvati pushes the cup away after one sip.

'This is Uskmouth—they think Gold Blend is exotic here. The tea's OK.'

'Happy with the meeting?'

Jess shrugs. 'We're talking containment, not cure. He'll be back, our Mikey—when have you ever seen therapy work, really work? He doesn't even want to change. But I guess we have to try.' The rain is back, clattering on the café window and Jess signals for the bill.

31

'No way,' says Parvati. 'I asked you so it's my treat, if you can call it that. Promise I'll do better next time.'

'I still don't understand why you gave up Bristol to work around here—what was the attraction?' asks Jess. 'And why FSU? I didn't think there were any vacancies.'

'They wanted to boost the team, I was available. And what with the murder of the Stiffley boy . . .'

Jess sags, even though the news comes as no surprise. 'Murder? Ed told me they found a body but he didn't say anything about murder.'

'I still don't have all the details, but it seems pretty clear that he died somewhere else and was dumped up on the Dyke. Naked and not in a good state, what with the hot weather and all the wildlife . . .'

'For fuck's sake . . .'

'Sorry—I forgot he was one of yours.'

Jess flicks at her face unconsciously, as if brushing away an insect.

'What about you,' says Parvati. 'Ed tells me you haven't been down here too long yourself.'

'Since February. I was in London before that, Hackney. If you have to work there, you know that you did something really bad in a previous life.'

'But you served your time?'

Jess pauses before she answers, trying not to look at the policewoman's scar. 'A guy tried to knife me when I went to take his child into care. One strike too many—there was nothing to stay for so I got out and moved down here. End of story.' Of that story; she has so many, she loses track.

*　　　*　　　*

It feels more like six weeks than six hours since she last parked outside Carwen's block, and the streets are busier now the schools have turned out. The chat show on the television has been replaced by a cartoon, watched by a smaller version of Bryony sitting cross-legged on a cushion in front of the screen.

'You saw Bryony then. Crying, she was, when she got home. Thought I was going to have a go at her.'

'Did you see the bruises?' says Jess.

'Don't look too bad to me—load of fuss about nothing.'

'So why didn't she tell you about them before?'

'That's down to Marty. Thinks girls should be girls, not go throwing themselves all over the place like the lads.'

'Marty—is he their father?'

Carwen sniffs. 'Father? Don't make me laugh—won't find many of them round here. No, her dad buggered off just after Rhiannon was born. Lives in Lydford now, over in the forest. Couldn't be arsed to bring up his own kids. Hasn't seen us since, not once. And don't

33

think he gives us nothing, neither. I ain't had a penny off him for six years.'

'So what about Marty?'

'Met him in a club, four years ago now. Brings in some money, don't drink too much. He's not Brad Pitt but he does right by us. Puts up with the girls.'

'So you're lucky to have him,' says Jess.

'You ain't got a fuckin' clue. Bloody social.' She shakes her head. 'And they let people like you tell me how to look after my kids.'

Rhiannon turns and stares at Jess, her mouth stained pink from a sweet she's been eating, until a burst of noise from the cartoon calls her back; and Jess thinks of the painting in the classroom, Carwen and the two girls. No one else.

'Where's Bryony now?' says Jess. No point in arguing.

'Round at Steffy's. Might as well live there, these days.'

'I have to talk to the police before I can close this. The Family Support Unit. I'll tell them what's happened, and then we think about what happens next. Maybe they'll want to talk to you and Marty, or see Bryony themselves.'

'Do what you like. Just don't try any of your tricks, try to take my kids away or anything. Nothing's wrong, understand? We ain't done nothing.'

Jess takes the back road home that evening, via Abertrothy. The 'Closed' sign is showing on the door to Denny's shop, but she knows he'll be somewhere inside, surrounded by a litter of circuit boards, polystyrene packing and computers that are gutted but still alive, humming and flickering, wired up like victims of an electronic Dr Moreau. He opens the door eventually, dressed in the same sweater as always. A few more stitches have dropped this week but Jess doubts if he's noticed; one day the whole construction will finish unravelling and collapse around his feet.

'I planned a few changes to your website,' says Denny. 'If you've got time we could look at them on the test server, then go live with them tonight.' He moves a half-eaten pizza from a chair and pulls it next to his, in front of a monitor. 'Look—I changed the home page. Makes it easier for people to find their way around the songs and lyrics. And I simplified the way they can download. *And*—I collected all of the images that go with the songs into, like, a gallery.'

'But someone listening to one of the songs would still see the right image on screen, yeah? They're meant to go together.'

'Sure. I didn't make any changes to that. But now they can see all your photos in one place. A lot of people emailed saying they'd like that.' He runs through the screens to reassure Jess. 'See? No changes—one link to listen to the song, another to download it, a separate frame with the lyrics and then the image, the photo.'

'Cool. It's looking good. And I got your message about the new song—it's just not ready yet. If you could see how busy I am at work . . .'

'I still don't know why you do that job. It's like, you're famous, right? When I recognised you, the day you walked in here to buy a new computer, it did my head in. Chad, lead singer with Hacksaw, in my shop. Man . . .'

'I keep telling you Denny, the name's Jess. Jess Chadwick. Chad was someone else, a long time ago.'

'But you're still a musician, right? Deep inside, that's what turns you on. Look at the songs you write—sure, they're different from most of the stuff in Hacksaw, but they're brilliant.'

Jess smiles, gives Denny a hug. 'If it wasn't for you and this bloody website, I probably wouldn't even bother to write them. Hacksaw was fifteen years ago—I left all that behind.' Another story.

'So that's why I had to help you set up a studio at the farmhouse? Come on . . .' He jumps up suddenly and rummages through a pile of papers on the floor next to the desk. 'See this magazine? They got a Web version as

36

well—I know the guy that edits it. Real geek, but OK. He saw the website and said he wants to do an article on you. You know the sort of thing—"where are they now?". It could be really good—ex-rock star becomes social worker. How weird is that?' He hands Jess the magazine but she lets it fall to the floor. 'What do you think?'

Her face is white and clammy. 'Are you OK?' says Denny. 'You want some water or something?' He finds a can of warm Coke but she waves it away.

'No way, Den. No interview, no article—understand?' She pushes herself away from the screen, stands up and then sits again as if unsure of where to go. 'I should never have let you set the site up in the first place.' She could be talking to herself.

'OK Jess, no sweat. I'll tell the guy. Just thought you would have been pleased.' He picks up the magazine and throws it across the room. 'It's like, if I'd been in a band like Hacksaw, I'd want everyone to know. But you don't even mention them on the site, you don't have any of their songs.'

'I do—"Last Surrender".'

'OK, one song out of five albums.'

'The best song though . . .' She's smiling again now.

'Definitely the best. Sorry, Jess, I didn't mean . . .'

'Forget it, Den. Just let me do things my

way.' She pauses by the door. 'I should have the new song finished by the end of the week—I'll give you a call.' She blows him a kiss, shuts the door quietly, and when she's gone the shop is too empty to work in.

*   *   *

Back at the farmhouse there are just three emails, all via the website. Two from people she's never heard of, asking questions about Hacksaw. She never answers these, feels uncomfortable just reading them. Times like this the site is a burden, a stick stirring a stagnant pond. Delete, delete, all gone.

The third calms her down again; Spider. Why she reads his messages, she doesn't know. Maybe because he doesn't ask about her, only talks about himself. She sees a younger Denny; no job, no girlfriend, a bedsit she could draw from the details of his descriptions. So far there's been nothing to shock, no sticky revelations, only the small idlings of a lonely man trying to share his life. That's what she tells herself. Reality email. She feels pleasure at her complicity, knows that he writes only to her. Three times a week, a new episode—she's never spoken to him, never seen him, but he could almost be a friend.

He makes her feel safe in her anonymity, her hidden voyeurism.

She never replies.

38

She checks out the photos she took earlier; the dog in the bucket, the grinning man. She would have liked to follow them and find out where they lived, where the bucket would end up. She wants to know if they live alone, or if the triangle is completed with a grinning old lady, her print frock fluttering in time with the old man's trousers. She sees them dancing, holding hands and turning in circles with the dog in the middle, his tongue flapping in the stir of their steps. They seem incomplete and she wants something to file away, to make them real; a thread, a hair, the clipping of a fingernail. She'll write a song tonight.

She answers the phone before remembering not to.

'Twice in one day, Denny?'

'I should have mentioned it earlier. Listen Jess—have you been editing anything on your Web pages?'

'You kidding? I wouldn't have the first clue—I just do the music.'

'I was checking the site earlier, before you came round. Some of the links are slow and I wanted to redesign a couple of the pages and frames.'

'Whatever you say—always seemed OK to me. So what's happened?'

'One of the files was edited this morning. Not one of the songs but one of my programs. But I didn't do it.'

'You're losing it, Den. I keep telling you,

acid fries the brain. You should stick to dope and stay mellow.'

'I'm being serious. I couldn't find any changes on the file when I compared with the backup version, but the edit date had changed to today, this morning.'

'So you're worried about nothing changing. You sure you're OK?'

'Someone got through the firewall, and *no one* should be able to do that. Someone hacked onto the site.'

'You told me you used to be a hacker. What's the matter, wounded pride?'

'Someone's having a laugh. If they got through the firewall, they'd have enough skill to change the edit date on the file so I'd never have noticed. Whoever it was wanted me to know he'd been there.'

'I never knew you're important enough to have enemies, Den. I'm impressed—no, really. Maybe you should call in the spooks, MI5. On the other hand, I'd let it go. My website's hardly a matter of national security.'

*   *   *

That man is a serious anorak, she thinks, as she throws the curry in the bin, pours another beer and goes upstairs to the studio. The Gibson is a best friend; heavy and immediately warm as she fits it over her thigh, like the missing piece of a jigsaw. A tarantella is called

40

for, a suitable dance for the man and his dog and his possible wife. She lets her fingers find the tune, listening to herself play fragments of other people's music until the notes mutate into something new. But the rhythms are wrong, the beat is too slow. The melody seems fixed in a minor key and all the chords are unresolved; the improbable dancers have disappeared and in their place all she can see is a small, dark-haired boy, lying in the woods.

CHAPTER FOUR

It's gone nine the next day before Jess empties the carrier bag full of case files onto her desk; she took them home yesterday with good intentions, but this morning they're still unworked. She hadn't left the studio until the sun had risen, and then slept through the radio. In spite of a shower she feels slightly worn.

'You look horrible this morning, Jess. And you smell of deodorant; very English, very unappealing. I buy you scent for your birthday and you never use it. You should trust Else— she has a good nose for this.'

'Tomorrow, I'll wear it tomorrow.' She sorts the case files into alphabetical order and stacks them on the edge of her desk. 'You ever come across the Pearce family? Chellacote estate—mother, stepfather, couple of girls?'

Else shakes her head slowly.

'What about kids with bruising on their thighs?' Jess stands and demonstrates, drawing a wide band around the top of her leg. 'Very unusual, like strap marks perhaps.'

'Not that I remember. You got something?'

'Maybe, maybe not.' She straightens the stack of files, centres it between her phone and the corner of the desk, giving herself time. 'Remember the Stiffley case? Perry's dead— the body was found up in the woods yesterday.' Another pause. 'They think it was murder.'

The woman opposite closes her eyes for a second. 'Oh, Jess, I'm so sorry. You were fond of that boy, I remember. What happened?'

'They didn't have many details.' She doesn't want to think about what Pav told her in the café.

'And now you got this girl to worry about. So call Ed, call him now—put your mind at rest.'

It's a bad line and they shout at each other in short, punctuated phrases over the sound of traffic that drowns every other word. Ed sounds submerged, but they manage to agree to meet at lunchtime.

*　　　*　　　*

The hotel bar in the centre of Gwenstow is full by the time Jess arrives. She expected Ed to be alone but he's with his wife, sitting in the bay

42

window overlooking the gatehouse in the old town walls. Neither of them notices her as she pushes her way through the smoke and the smell of chips and boiled vegetables. Ed smiles like a vicar as he leans forward to hear what his wife is saying, and his magnified eyes bulge behind the tortoiseshell glasses. He wears his hair in a style that Jess wants to call well groomed.

Liz gets up as Jess reaches the table. 'You've got fifteen minutes while I check out the bookshop next door. He's got a half day so I'm taking him shopping in Bristol—what a lucky man.' She edges out from behind the table and disappears into the crowd.

Ed pushes a glass towards her. 'Liz was drinking white—hope that's OK.'

Jess lets the sweet wine wet her lips.

'Shopping? Bet you're looking forward to that.'

'We're having dinner with my cousin afterwards—the clever one in the family, not like me.'

'What does he do?'

'GP—small family practice in Clifton.' He sips carefully at his beer. 'Sorry about the phone call earlier, I could barely hear you. Was it about that girl you saw yesterday, Bryony Pearce?'

Jess pushes the glass away. She feels uncomfortable; this isn't the place to discuss a client, but although there are people close by no one

43

can hear them through the undercurrent of noise. All the same, she keeps her voice low, almost a whisper.

She tells Ed about the teacher's worries. She tells him about Carwen, she tells him about Bryony, she tells him about the bruises. She tells him about the picture in the classroom.

She wishes that he'd stop smiling.

'Come on, Jess.' His voice is so soft she can barely hear him. 'There's no disclosure from the child, no family history, nothing from the mother and an explanation for the injuries. You won't get away with a medical—seems pretty clear-cut to me.'

'What about the picture?'

Ed takes another sip of beer and leans a little closer. 'There's an officer in traffic—never stopped talking about his daughter. Little Miss Perfect, photos all over his desk. Then as soon as she was sixteen she fell pregnant and went to live with her bloke in a basement in Cardiff. That's reality, Jess. No one's made of sugar and spice.'

'So Bryony's messing everyone about and we should drop it? What is it—you don't trust my judgement? If you did you'd agree to a video interview with Bryony.' She takes a mouthful of wine, swallowing quickly to avoid the taste. 'I didn't press her yesterday because I didn't want to screw up any evidence—you guys hate it when we get disclosures off-tape.'

'We don't make the rules. CPS only prosecute if they're pretty certain of a result.'

Jess hates his certainty. 'I saw your new DS yesterday. She told me Perry was murdered. We worked on that case together, Ed. You and me. I never wanted to close it down—now look what's happened.'

'The Stiffley case was different. We don't know what happened yet, but even if the boy was murdered there's absolutely no connection between this girl and what happened earlier in the year.'

'People die while you wait around for proof! And now you're prepared to take a risk with Bryony Pearce?'

'Don't get angry with me. Take it up with my superiors—I guarantee you'll get the same decision.' No one would mistake him for a vicar now.

Liz is back already. 'Can you believe it, not a single new book in the shop. The whole place smelt of dust, including the man behind the till. And he'd never even heard of Raymond Carver!'

*   *   *

Back in the office Jess goes straight to the filing cabinets at the far end of the room, but the Stiffley file is missing.

Else waves a half-eaten McDonald's. 'Joe was looking for you—not a happy man. And

45

the big cheese is with him.'

'Who, Beth? Didn't think she knew the way here from County Hall.'

'This is your Director—you should show respect.'

'I've worked here for over six months, I've seen her once.'

'Busy woman. And if no respect, then pity maybe. You want Joe to work for you?'

'Better than me working for him. Where are they—Joe's hutch? Pray for me . . .'

Halfway up the back stairs, Jess stops and perches on the edge of a concrete step. It never gets warm here, not even in the height of summer, and the air is stale. The corners of the steps are filled with dust and small debris; someone's been smoking recently and Jess reaches out for a newish dog-end on the step below hers. The imprints of lipstick around the filter match the shade she wears, when she bothers. When was the last time? She doesn't have the energy to remember. Without thinking, without realising, she wraps the dog-end in a tissue and tucks it carefully into the pocket of her jeans, wipes her fingers on the denim and continues upstairs.

Joe never looks comfortable in his office, his legs and arms sticking out at odd angles as if his desk had survived from the days when the building was still a school. Opposite him, on the other side of the desk, Beth could be a small headmistress; flat heels, a buttoned-up suit and a perm. Joe starts speaking even before Jess has sat down—he talks to her ears, to her shoulders, but never to her eyes. His voice carries the tone of a revelation, but it's old news—the Stiffley file is open on his desk. He starts to tell her about the body but Jess interrupts to describe her conversations with the police.

Silence. She's moved away from the script, and they don't know how to respond. Joe looks unwell; white and soft like something uncooked. Beth sits with her knees together and her ankles crossed; we're different species, you and me, thinks Jess. We come from different worlds.

This is a not-belonging day.

Joe starts to unravel himself as if he wants to tower over Jess, but subsides at a look from Beth. Scared, shitting himself.

The press are all over this, says Beth, all over us. All over me, Joe—you. We have to watch our backs. We have to get the story straight.

She takes a piece of paper from the file in front of Joe. 'You're not the only one with contacts. I spoke to the head of FSU less than an hour ago; the pathologist's report shows that Perry died from a pulmonary embolism brought on by a heroin overdose. A blood clot in the lungs.'

Jess can't listen to this sitting down; goes over to the glass wall of the office and looks down the empty corridor. Ten years old. Fags and cider maybe, and the kids at the Comp get E's and dope, but heroin?

'I thought heroin overdoses were a myth.'

'So did I,' says Beth. 'But apparently if your bloodstream's already full of alcohol, and especially if you've never had the drug before . . .'

Jess wishes she could read through the case notes, remind herself of what happened six months ago. So many cases, sometimes the details swap places.

'What does it matter how he died,' says Joe. 'The press will make any connections they want. We'll get the blame, just like we always do.'

Jess can smell him, suddenly, sour and damp.

'Have you come across anything?' says Beth. 'Any younger kids getting mixed up with heroin?' Jess shakes her head. 'Well, it's out of our hands for now. But one way or the other, we'll all be in the spotlight soon.'

*   *   *

Jess stops on the stairs again, as if they are a staging area. There's no one to talk to, no one that belongs to her—but this is normal, this is familiar. Best friends are for other people. The closest she got was Nic, and the thought of his name after so long is like returning to a

48

familiar house after a decade away. Yet what was he? One hour a week in a book-lined room in Belsize Park that smelt of the memory of incense. An hour spent talking to a man who was paid not to judge.

When she closes her eyes it's as if she's back in the doorway of his room, looking onto a stage set where everything was placed for a purpose, where there was an underlying code. She remembers his eyes, on a level with hers. And his hands, made to play the cello; and his eyelashes, so dark and long that they seemed filmed with soot. Thirty-six weeks of intimacy without a single touch; a torture and an epiphany.

The images are surfacing without control and she opens her eyes to focus on her surroundings. It was one of Nic's lessons; live in the world, not your mind. It's like stepping back from an edge.

She calls Carwen to tell her that there'll be no follow-up on Bryony, but the phone rings without answer. This is good. She wants to be there in the flat, to tell Carwen face to face, to watch the way her eyes and body move as the words are said. She wants to judge whether there's anger at abandonment, or relief at being left alone; how else can you know the truth?

Tomorrow she'll tell Joe about the case, and he'll order her to cease contact with the family. So she'll have to drive to the Chellacote this evening; the opposite direction from her farmhouse, but she can't face another sleepless night.

*   *   *

'You want me to bring a camp bed for you, Jess? Go home now, eat properly, rest, stroke the cat.' Jess looks up from the report she's entering onto the computer and checks her watch—six-thirty. She and Else are the only two left in the room; the other screens are dead and the desks are clear.

'Just one more visit, Else, then I'll take your advice. As long as I can add a beer or two to the mix.'

As Jess walks across the street on the Chellacote estate she sees a man's face in the front window of Carwen's flat. By the time she gets to the bottom of the concrete stairs he's waiting for her, blocking the way.

He can't stand still. His frame seems too small for his clothes, moving about inside them like a weasel in a sack, and he runs his hand across the freshly cropped stubble on his head.

'You're the woman from the social.'

'And you must be Marty.'

'They ain't here. Don't wanna see you.' He's almost dancing now, grinning at a private joke. 'You got anything to say, you say it to me.'

There should be a switch somewhere, to turn him off.

50

'I brought some good news—we're closing the case.'

'Never was any *case*,' he says. 'Just a kid messing about. If it hadn't been for that nosy bitch of a teacher you could have saved yourselves some trouble.' His jeans are thick with stains and there's a scent rising from him, of oil and rotting fish. He should be in the Tate.

'I hope Bryony's bruises get better soon . . .' but Marty's already turned his back and started up the stairs.

*   *   *

Jess takes the long road back via Abertrothy to pick up beer, chips and some cans of food for Wagner, but the smell of vinegar makes her feel ill; she dumps the greasy paper and its contents in a bin at the bottom of her lane and opens all the windows to flush the polluted air. The track is still damp from yesterday's rain and the first few leaves have already fallen in patches of yellow.

There's no post and just two emails when she gets back to the farmhouse. She reads Spider's first; the immersion into someone else's world is a welcome escape.

'hi—love the latest track, "Beaten". can't work out the chords—your too good for me. you got great photos—i'm a photographer too —maybe

51

one day you'll see what i do. i think i could be a film director maybe—i got this idea for a wicked video—gotta get that video camera—i am a camera—someone said that. might go to London this weekend and see that girl i told you about. she looks like your picture. i don't like black tea but the milk was off—I should of used it anyway.'

How old did he say he was? Jess always pictures him as eighteen or seventeen but today he seems even younger. Or spacey? The email has unsettled her. Spider only ever talks about himself, never about her, and yet today he seems to have moved closer. She doesn't want him to know someone who looks like her.

She closes his message and looks at the next, from a sender she doesn't recognise. Just one name, Gina. What's she offering, thinks Jess. Pay off all my debts? Sell me a tropical holiday? Enhance my sex life?

She's about to delete the message but opens it by mistake, a double-click too far. It doesn't take long to read; two years too early and a lifetime too late.

'Dear Jess Chadwick

Mum told me not to do this, and I'm sorry to bother you, but I'd like to know if you want to meet me. I thought about you a lot, ever since Mum told me about you a long time ago, when she had a baby of her own. She calls me number

two, even though I was here first. She thinks it's funny. When I got my own computer I found you through your website. You can email me on this address, no one else will see it. I set it up just so I could write to you. I'm sixteen years old and I'm your daughter. Please write back soon.
Love, Gina.'

CHAPTER FIVE

There's no gap between waking and remembering the email, and Jess runs to the study, scared that it was nothing more than a new dream. But the message is still there and Jess runs her fingers across the words on the screen as if they were Braille.

Too much, she's not ready for this. A last look at the screen and then she gets herself ready for the day in silence; it's not until she's in the car that she hears the words 'Perry Stiffley'. If the radio has it so will the papers, so will everyone. Jess drives slowly down the valley road as if expecting reporters with notebooks to jump out in front of the car but the road is empty, as usual. The river running alongside is as low as she's seen it, the surface unmarked by wind or current, and rocks that are usually submerged are visible for the first time. She wants to stop and sit by the water's edge, walk the riverside path, anything to delay the day ahead, but a time check on the radio says she's already late and the Jeep comes close to skidding on the tight corners as the river gorge opens out just before the road reaches Gwenstow.

Before Jess reaches her desk, Else passes her a local paper, folded to show a picture of Perry, blown up from a school photograph. All the features are blurred, the eyes dark holes and the mouth a gash, but she still recognises the boy. She pushes the paper aside.

'I don't want to read it, Else. What does it say?'

'What you'd expect. I don't know where they get the details from—like they read our files or something.'

'They know about the earlier case?'

'Everything. Names, dates—what else they going to write about?' She takes the paper, throws it in the bin. 'You thought of contacting the Union? Good idea perhaps.'

'Why should I do that?' She's never seen Else look so worried.

'There was a woman here, before your time; Megan Davies. One of her kids, her clients, ended up in hospital. Beth dug up the drains, Megan was suspended. Union gave her legal advice.'

'What happened to her in the end?'

'She moved away I think. But she was waste of space, Jess; didn't go on visits, all her case reports were fiction. She fooled a lot of

54

people, not like you.'

Jess takes a coffee and sits on a low wall looking out over the car park towards the ruined castle. Gwenstow is a village, compared with London. Four tourists pose by the entrance to the castle while a passer-by takes a snapshot for them, but when he finishes they won't let him go and he takes three more, one identical shot on each of their cameras. The tourists seem happy, pointing at features on the old stone walls, and Jess wonders what they see. The tourists leave and the coffee has long grown cold when she gets a call from Pav, the DS she met in Uskmouth after the Eskell conference, wanting to talk about Perry. The policewoman arranges to come round to Jess's office; I'll be there in fifteen minutes, she says, no reason to put it off. No need for you to come in to the station.

When Pav arrives, Jess takes her through to the single interview room, a converted store cupboard without windows, fabricated at the end of the main office. It should be Ed here, her friend, not this stranger wearing grown-up clothes in browns and yellows, silk and woven wool. Jess brushes cat hairs from her combat pants and wishes she'd bothered with make-up. The room is hot and airless and her armpits already feel sticky, but Pav looks ready for a performance.

'I expect you're wondering why Ed isn't doing this. The truth is, he was so close to the original investigation we decided that an objective view would be helpful. No criticism of him intended, of course.' When she smiles her eye-teeth are daggers of ivory.

'I spoke to our Director this morning,' says Jess. 'She said it was murder.'

Pav puts her notebook on the low coffee table between them, leans forward and tucks a strand of thick hair behind her ear. Diamonds and pearls, Jess can't help noticing, but no rings. She looks more like the wife of a chief constable than a DS working on child protection.

'I thought you'd want to know, the forensic report came in yesterday, on Perry.' Her voice has the softness of someone used to giving bad news. 'We haven't found any of his clothes yet. The body had only been there for a few hours but there are a lot of animals around there. Foxes, badgers, crows.' She looks apologetic. 'You know how it is.'

I don't, thinks Jess, I don't know how it is. I don't want to know how it is.

But Pav is still speaking. 'The post-mortem lacerations made it difficult to interpret some of the marks, but there was no sign of any sexual activity.'

As if that made it OK. But maybe this is how we cope, thinks Jess, hiding from our emotions in the formality of language.

'There were drugs?' she says. 'Beth said it was heroin.'

'You sure you want to know?' Pav counts them off on her fingers. 'Alcohol, Rohypnol, cocaine, heroin. He can't have had any idea what was going on, if that helps.'

'This didn't all happen up on the Dyke.'

'No way. Perry was already dead when his body was dumped in the bushes. There was no real attempt to hide it—it's as if the perpetrator knew that he'd be found but wasn't worried, knew he couldn't be traced.' She picks up the notebook again. 'The DI in charge is a guy called John Pelham—I've worked with him before. Not everyone's ideal copper, but one of the best.'

'So what can I tell you?' asks Jess.

'The original case. I read all the files and I talked to Ed, but I wanted your views on what happened. Sometimes people remember things differently.'

It was the first case she got, the day she started at Gwenstow. Joe being pompous about contact from some outfit from the Met who were tracing a paedophile ring on the Internet and trying to identify children in some photographs. She never knew whether they had specific information or if they were trying all the Social Services departments in the UK. One of the admin assistants in the office had a son the same age as Perry and thought she recognised him from taking her son to school.

'And you were given the case,' says Pav.

'I worked mostly with Ed. We did a video

interview with Perry, to see if he would give any evidence we could use in court, but he refused to say anything. There was nothing else, no medical evidence, no disclosures. Just the photo of a boy who looked like Perry.'

She remembers the photos, taken with a wide aperture so the background to the room was out of focus and unrecognisable. For some reason the image she remembers most clearly is the man, sitting naked in a chair, his legs thin and hairy and splayed apart. The little boy is always a blur in her memory although she knows that he was clearly visible on the photo. They always know how to do that, keep the children in focus. She's seen worse, but none of them have died. Not to her knowledge. Not until now.

And then from nowhere she remembers the email from Gina, and realises how little she knows of her daughter's life. Nothing.

'Perry's father was interviewed a number of times,' says Pav. 'Looking at the files, I'm not sure why. I couldn't find any link between him and the photo, and there was never any suggestion that he was an abuser. Or did I miss something?'

'This is the Forest,' says Jess. 'They'd burn old women as witches if they thought they could get away with it. David Stiffley is an artist, and it was just him and Perry in an isolated house. No women around, if you know what I mean. He didn't fit in.'

'You'd think people would have learnt by now that child abuse has nothing to do with being gay or straight.' It's the first time that Jess has heard emotion in her voice. 'But what did *you* think about David?'

'I didn't see too much of him, left that to you guys. I guess you've already spoken to him.'

'Pelham's with him this morning.'

And you're with me, thinks Jess. Who chose whom—or did you draw lots?

*   *   *

For the first time since last night, back at her desk, she lets herself think about the email from Gina. She tries the name, says it out loud, listens to the shape it makes. She doesn't know any Ginas, there are no ready-made images to help her find a face.

She feels no ownership in this name, it was someone else's to give. She never named her baby, not even in her mind. Name something and it becomes real, a name gathers substance to itself and begins to breathe; but she wants warm flesh, not a cold label.

Constructs, Nic called them. Memories, even of flesh, are nothing more than constructs. She still doesn't know what he meant.

Gina—a soft name. Not like Jess, or Chad, or . . .

59

She should squash these thoughts. Back to Gina—Virginia, perhaps? What sort of parents would call a child Virginia?

This is too sudden. She's not ready, and then she thinks—how many years do I need? Her chest is tight and she remembers to breathe out at the same moment as a call comes in from Denny.

'Come to the shop, today, as soon as you can. Yes, it's the same problem but different, you have to see, I can't tell you on the phone.' He uses the tone of a confessional.

Jess checks her diary—a couple of visits to children near Gwenstow, then another conference but not until five. She'll make the time.

Denny's with a customer when she arrives, an elderly man with a checked cap and matching sports jacket, standing as upright as if he were still on parade. When he leaves, Den locks the door and puts up the 'Closed' sign.

'I said I'd fit it for him. Even offered to do it for free if he could bring the PC in.'

'What did he buy?'

'CD writer. I've told him what to do, written it all down. The trouble is, you never know how much they actually understand. I could speak Egyptian and they'd still smile and nod and say "thank you" at the end.' He leads her through to a monitor at the back of the workshop. 'You remember the problem I

60

found the other day? On your website? One of the files had been edited but not changed.' He clicks through the Web pages; Jess had forgotten there was a photo of her on the site. Advantage Gina.

'This is one of the first songs we put up.'

She remembers it well, a clouded lyric written soon after she moved down from London. The image on the screen is a teenage girl curled in sleep in a shop doorway. Jess can't remember where she took it— somewhere in the West End probably. Next to the image are two links, one to download the song, the other to view the lyrics. Denny clicks the second and the screen fills with her poem. 'Suffer', she called it; passable, mawkish, it meant something at the time. Denny scrolls down to the bottom, points at the screen. 'See here? This is the original line, the last line of the song: *suffering children, how blind can I be?*" Everything we're looking at here is off a backup copy of your site.' Another couple of clicks. 'And here's the line as it was this morning, on the live site.'

Jess reads the words but at first they mean nothing. Wrong, she thinks. Someone got them wrong. And then she reads them again, and then she understands. The last line of the song has been changed to something from a sick fantasy. There's a buzzing in her ears; she knows Denny is talking but can't hear what he's saying and she backs away.

'What the fuck's going on?' she says. 'Did you do this? Is it meant to be a joke?'

'Not me, Jess, not me.' He kills the screen and rubs his eyes. 'Since what happened last time I've been checking for any anomalies, edited files, that sort of thing. I found the change this morning. Same as before, a different edit date but this time it was set way back in time, even before the site was running.'

'Why do that?'

'To make sure I'd notice.'

She asks for a coffee, faces away from the screen in case the words should reappear. The first time it felt random, someone messing about. Now it's personal, targeted, as if someone knows who she really is and not just a name on the Internet. The plastic cup is hot, but she drinks the coffee straight down.

'I changed the site straight back; I shouldn't think anyone noticed the difference,' says Den. 'The site's popular but not that popular.'

'Did you find anything else?'

'Nothing. I checked every word of every song, that's why I took so long before phoning you.' She wants to believe him.

'Can't you trace who's doing this, like phone calls?'

Denny shakes his head. 'It's not that easy. Whoever did this is a real guru. He knows his stuff—the only reason I found anything was because he wanted me to. Otherwise it would have been one of the punters from the site

62

contacting us. Or maybe even the police—those new lyrics are pretty sick. How do people think of things like that?'

Welcome to my world.

*   *   *

Three days ago she was close to happy. Content, reconciled. Watching the sunset from her farmhouse. Now a little boy she used to laugh with is still, for ever, and some sick bastard is hacking her website. OK, maybe there's no comparison, but it still makes her angry. Probably an ex-fan of Hacksaw, with his brain rotted from a hundred acid trips too many and a grudge about something he can't even remember.

I'm being stalked, she thinks, *me*! It would be funny if it weren't so sad.

Without even thinking about where she's going, Jess drives towards the Dyke, looking for isolation. She parks in a clearing on the back road from Gwenstow to Abertrothy and climbs the few yards up onto the ancient ridge. It used to mark a border, now the roots of old yew trees are cracking stones. Only when Jess reaches the top does she realise that this must be where Perry's body was found.

The site is clear enough now, but just off the track all the undergrowth has been crushed, the ferns broken and browning. A fragment of blue and white police tape hangs like a banner from a branch and the dry earth has been packed hard by the trampling of official boots. The detritus of lovers and addicts has been cleared away, festering by now in a forensics lab. For some reason she expects the dark stain of blood but that isn't how he died, and the earth would have swallowed it anyway.

She walks down the trail towards the woods. The wind is soft and humid, blowing in from the sea to the south-west. The beech leaves above her rustle at the edge of hearing and a few have already fallen, as if unwilling to wait for autumn. High above, a buzzard calls with a plaintive mewing sound, and when Jess looks up there are two of them, circling on the thermals rising from the valley. She wonders if they're the same pair she sees from the farmhouse almost every day, almost friends.

Ahead on the track she hears voices, and then through breaks in the trees she sees the flashes of red from their jackets as a group of elderly ramblers chatter their way towards her. Intruders. She cuts off the main track, downhill towards the stream that runs in a hidden valley of its own, parallel to the main river. The voices fade and she tries to keep her mind blank, a walking meditation on emptiness, and when that doesn't work she focuses on the sound of her footsteps, counting and breathing in a synchronous rhythm.

Another ten minutes, and a face appears in

64

the branches of a tree. There's no body, just the bleached and chiselled features of a man smiling, the planes of his cheeks and forehead like a three-dimensional Picasso. She hadn't realised she was so close, within a few hundred yards of David Stiffley's house and workshop on the edge of the Forest proper.

She passes under the face, carved from one of the pieces of driftwood that wash up in the nearby estuary. Further down the track more faces and figures appear in the clefts of trees and peer out from behind rocks and bushes, like refugees from Middle Earth.

The trees end at a small clearing containing a rambling red-brick house and some outbuildings. The door to the workshop is open and the breeze carries the oiled scent of sawdust and shaved wood, and the sound of recorded Bach; one of the unaccompanied cello suites, a favourite of her father's.

She leans against the warm trunk of an oak, just inside the line of trees, and listens with her eyes shut until the last notes fade to silence.

*   *   *

Beer and a cat aren't enough. Tonight even the fields and trees are distant as she flips through the few pages of names in her address book. Colleagues, acquaintances, they've all been reduced to patterns of words and numbers on the page, the colour of the ink;

but only one fits her need.

She calls Chana in London, hustles an invite for the weekend. Two days of diesel fumes, voices outside at 4 a.m., the scent of weed and the smell of frying; music from every open window. The company of a friend.

But that still leaves tonight, and old impulses trying to surface. When it gets like this, Nic said, remember your anchor. She cups her elbow in her palm, presses her thumb into the soft hollow of flesh until her arm throbs.

Call it what you will, Nic had said. Sublimation, transformation: you want to collect? You want to store and classify? Do it with film. Do it with images. An urban safari without a gun; safe, legal.

She dresses down. Old trainers, combats, sweatshirt. Baseball cap. She chooses dark colours. No watch, no chain around her neck, no bracelet, no earrings. No make-up. Leaves her bag on the kitchen table. Anonymous.

Except for the Nikon; a four-roll night, she decides. Fast film, long lens, no tripod. Stay light. She enjoys the preparation, the change of identity.

She plays Linkin Park and Good Charlotte on the way to Bristol; baby punks, played loud. She needs to get there quickly, work before the light's too low. She parks on the steep rise leading to the towers of flats in St Paul's. It's too early for the clubbers and the streets are mostly empty, so she walks until she finds a crowded pub and settles into a doorway just across the street. She stands in the shadows with a clear view of the punters arriving. The skyline is becoming a silhouette; tonight she'll have bodies, preserved in her film emulsion like insects in amber.

Her mind is clear for the first time in days. The lens rests on the ridge in the corner of the wall but she doesn't need its help—times like this her body becomes motionless, she can exist without breathing. She runs through the shots, bracketing exposures; no one sees her from across the street, but each time she hears people approaching on her side she hides the camera behind her body, ready to run if she needs to, almost willing someone to stop and reach into the shadows for her so that she can release the energy that's built up. One man sees her as he stumbles past the doorway. His breath smells of meat when he asks if she's working—and then he sees his reflection in her eyes, skinless. He backs away muttering words that she can't hear, and she catches him on film, vomiting into the gutter a few yards further down.

She finishes the last roll on a group of teenage girls talking too loudly, touching each other too often, walking quickly to keep warm. I used to look like that, thinks Jess, and then— no, not me. Not me; I always walked alone.

*   *   *

67

She sleeps without dreams, and when she wakes her limbs ache with the delicious weariness of a long trek on mountain trails.

She takes the lane slowly, the dappled light through the beeches camouflaging small groups of fallow deer so accustomed to the car that they barely move out of the way in time, stopping a few yards off to watch her pass.

She checks at the bottom of the lane, then turns away from the valley road down to the motorway and cuts instead through the forest towards the old A40 and the Cotswolds, away from the Marches and into the tidiness of England. The road is almost clear until Oxford where she joins the stream of cars making its way towards London, where the North Circular is almost static. Even filtered through the Jeep's air con the traffic fumes taste of sweet poison, and she realises how long she's been away.

It's another hour before she arrives at Chana's flat in Stoke Newington, the ground floor of a flat-top Georgian house behind bent railings. The front wall is peeling with eczema, and a block further up the houses stop and the restaurants and greengrocers start. It smells like another country.

Chana envelops Jess as she steps in. 'You, girl, are one skinny bitch. You ain't worth even one cow.' She throws Jess's bag into the spare room as they pass it on the way to the kitchen.

'Beer OK? Too early for a decent drink and we got a long night ahead of us.' Jess is on the second bottle by the time Chana finishes setting out dishes of steaming food. 'Don't look at me like that, girl,' says Chana. 'My house, my rules. If I say eat, you eat. I assume this *is* your breakfast?'

'I usually make do with coffee.'

Chana shakes her head as she piles the plate with spoonfuls from different dishes. 'Ackee and saltfish with green bananas and yam. And I prepared the ackee myself, none of your tinned rubbish.'

She eats four forkfuls to every one of Jess's. 'So girl, how you doin'? Still keepin' the riff-raff off the streets?'

'I do my best. How about you—still rationing Elastoplasts and giving suppositories?'

'Nothin' ever changes here. Nurses are stable, see, not like you social workers. Load of sociopaths. If I had any sense I'd transfer back to a nice quiet hospital.' She begins to clear the table without waiting for Jess to finish playing with the food on her plate. 'Should have seen your replacement—some shit-for-brains with a degree in psychology. Lasted six weeks until one of the kids swore at her.' She brings Jess another bottle. 'And you, why ain't you dropped out yet? I thought you were gonna be some hippy eco-warrior playing guitar round a campfire, not carry on with the same old crap.'

No answer for that.

'Hey, you remember Darren Peterson?' says Chana.

How could she forget? And yet she has—the sound of his name is a surprise, as if it doesn't belong here.

'The police have started asking questions again about that psychologist, the one who ran the dodgy clinic.'

'It's got to be five years ago? I thought all of that was over.'

'But they never found the bastard,' says Chana. 'You remember, the police thought he set up the ring in the first place, but he disappeared before they could question him.'

'Do you know how many cases I've dealt with in the past five years?' says Jess.

'Modesty don't suit you, girl. If you hadn't got Darren to disclose what was happening, those perverts would still be around. You helped a lot of kids the day you got that boy to talk.'

I should have seen it before, thinks Jess, the reason why Perry is so important. He could be Darren's twin; virtually the same age, everything. And Darren wouldn't talk at first, not to anyone. How many months did it take, seeing him for hours every week until he eventually admitted what was happening, who was abusing him?

Maybe if she'd given that time to Perry . . .

70

'So who spoke to you?' says Jess.

'Police—not the FSU. All they wanted to talk about was the psychologist—Charles Goodwin. Wasn't much I could say, I never met him.'

'Me neither,' says Jess, 'but Darren talked a lot about him. He had a love/hate relationship with the man. Wasn't Goodwin married?'

'And he had a daughter. They had no idea what was going on,' says Chana. 'The little girl thought the sun shone out of Daddy's arse. I saw the family a few times after Goodwin disappeared, then they moved away. Somewhere up north, I think.' She finishes clearing the table.

'We don't get all the action, though. Didn't I hear about some poor boy murdered down your way? It was on the radio this morning.'

'Perry Stiffley. He was one of mine.'

Chana lets the saucepan drop back into the washing-up bowl and comes over to the table. 'This is serious shit. You know who did it?'

'We closed the file a few months ago. Suspected abuse, no evidence. No one was working on it, not any more. Bit late now.'

Very serious shit. You in trouble?'

Jess shrugs. 'Maybe I'll contact the Union. They'll organise legal representation if I need it.'

You do your best but shit still follows you round. And then you feel guilty for self-pity when a man has lost his only son.

She's talked enough about Perry; this is meant to be a weekend off. Chana apologises. 'I've already organised this evening,' she says. 'It's a surprise, no need to dress up; trust me, you'll love it, we won't be going far.'

It feels good to have someone else make the decisions, if only for a while. But she wants the anonymity of crowds *now*, why else did she make the trip? She wants to become background. She wants to merge.

Chana offers to drive but Jess says no, we'll take the bus, it's my treat. It takes nearly an hour to get to Camden Town, to the market bordering on the canal. But she enjoys the ride, sitting on the top deck like a tourist, making Chana laugh with stories about some of her clients, only half untrue. The place is a bazaar, a time warp, barely changed since she was last here before Gina was born, when everything was different. She finds a stall still selling the purple hair dye she used as a teenager to annoy her mother, and buys a bottle to keep as a relic. The warm air smells of patchouli and sweat, burgers and musk. Every step is a small collision with another body, every voice a different language.

Jess stops by one of the stalls selling African rugs in oranges and browns. Moroccan, the guy says, from the Atlas Mountains. My own village, I bring them over myself. My mother makes them, I take Amex, delivery no problem.

Now she knows that things have changed. Her, if not the market; checking out rugs instead of clothes or jewellery. To redress the balance she pushes through a crowd of teenage girls towards a rack of improbable clothes and buys a halter top that she'll never wear and a pair of jeans shot through with iridescent threads, then rolls them up tightly and stuffs them into her bag while a girl on the edge of the group stares at Jess without smiling, as if she's gatecrashed a party.

Past it at thirty-two; they always say that coming back is a mistake.

*   *   *

It's gone nine that night before Jess and Chana walk down Church Street to a small blues club. Jess hasn't been there for years but it's a pleasant surprise; a safe choice, undemanding. Music and beer and a dark basement with a crowd to get lost in. Jess ducks as they go down the stairs to the ticket desk. I'll get it, she says to Chana, and then skips a beat when she looks up as she hands over the note and sees a poster for the act that's playing tonight. *'Jamie Quintilia—Soft Remembered Blue.'*

Jamie, sixteen years on, singing in a cellar bar in north London.

Chana looks at her. 'If it's not a good idea you just gotta say. Seemed like serendipity when I saw who he used to play with. Your

73

band, wasn't it?'

She forgets, sometimes, what she's said to whom. The girl behind the desk pushes change into her hand and turns to the next people in the queue, and Jess walks through into the bar. The set hasn't started yet but the room is already full of people and smoke, and they manage to fit two chairs on the end of the table near the back. While Chana's at the bar, Jess checks out the audience. No one she knows; she half expected this to be a set-up, a test, full of people who know more than they should waiting for her reaction. Maybe it'll be cool. When you're on stage it's hard to see who's watching you; she'll be invisible, a face in the shadows.

She begins to relax, her back propped against the wall, pleased that she wore the new jeans. She can just see the stage, such as it is, a clearing in the tables at the opposite end of the room, and at the same time as Chana returns with the beers, a voice comes out of the speakers.

'Ladies and gentlemen. The Void Club is delighted to welcome one of the UK's biggest stars. You know him from Hacksaw, now he's playing with his own band and has come back to his roots. Give it up for Jamie Quintilia!'

Jess hadn't expected him to have changed so much. Even in this light she can see that the fire has gone from his hair and his face looks unironed, but the guitar is the same old

74

Rickenbacker, and when she closes her eyes she sees him the way he used to be, can almost taste him. She begins to tremble with anticipation, keeps her eyes closed through the shouts and applause, and then Jamie starts with a song she's not heard before, less raw than his old material. His voice was never the strongest; cracked notes in search of a melody, but he sings with deceptive phrasing and words that Jess wishes she had written; and when she opens her eyes she sees that his are closed.

There's nothing from the old days, no disruptive memories and she's about to suggest another beer when Jamie swings the guitar to one side and takes the mike from the stand.

'OK folks—hope you enjoyed that. Before the break I'm going to do one more song that you may know; "Last Surrender". I don't know about you, but I think it's the best piece Hacksaw ever recorded, written by someone I hadn't seen for a long time until tonight, but she's in this room right now and I want to ask her, I want you to *beg* her to come up here and sing it for you.' He walks forward a couple of steps, looks across the length of the room and into Jess's eyes. 'This is your song. Please?'

Everyone turns round to look at her and then they start stamping on the ground and banging glasses on the table. Chana grips her elbow and lifts her out of her seat.

'Looks like you ain't got no choice, girl. Give the punters what they want.'

75

It seems to take an hour to push her way through the tables to the small stage, and all Jess can do is focus on Jamie standing with his arm outstretched to pull her free. As he hugs her she whispers, 'I can't do this, I can't do this,' but all he says is, 'This is your song, I thought this was what you wanted.'

And then, 'B flat still OK?'

Jess lets the mike stand take her weight. She's glad of the small spotlight blinding her to the dark mass of the audience, and then Jamie starts to play the intro, slow and rhythmic. It takes a few moments for the drums and bass to cut in and Jess realises that this wasn't planned, there's been no rehearsal and they're busking from memory.

She likes that, it makes them even.

The crowd is quiet now and she starts to sing. She doesn't need to think of the words, she knows how to sing this the way she knows how to breathe. As the sound of Jamie's guitar begins to meld with her voice she knows this is one of those performances, the ones you can never plan or repeat.

The bridge is a guitar solo but Jess can't open her eyes, and as they come to the end of the final section the bass and drums fade away. She sings the last moments and waits for Jamie to close with the final major chord but it never comes, and the music fades to silence, unresolved.

Heaven might feel like this. She remembers

to bow to the applause, a last hug from Jamie and she steps back into the crowd.

CHAPTER SIX

The transition out of sleep is sudden, the small room immediately in focus, but it takes a moment for Jess to place herself. The single bed almost fills one wall, butting up against the end of a rickety table holding an old computer. Everything in the room is losing to gravity; the bookshelves piled with papers and files and ragged paperbacks, the broken mattress, the slatted wooden blind hanging from one bracket. Throughout the night the room never became dark, filled with a sodium glow from the street lamp just outside the window. But there were shadows; when Jess woke in the night she felt something moving in the room with her, yet when she switched on the light she was alone.

She reaches to the floor by the side of the bed and finds the copy of Gina's email that she read in the night; it must have fallen from her hand when she fell asleep at last. Her body feels battered and her throat is raw, the way she used to feel after an end-of-tour party. She doesn't want to move but Chana's singing a tuneless medley from last night's gig, and she can smell freshly ground coffee, a luxury she never allows herself.

Jamie, of all people. But when Jess shuts her eyes to picture him she still sees the boy of sixteen years ago, not the man from yesterday. The last time they met was in a room full of lawyers, and he couldn't meet her eyes. They were all young then; she wore loose clothes and never told him about the baby. Some secrets aren't for sharing.

Jess wanders down to the kitchen, wearing nothing but a T-shirt, holding the copy of the email. Chana pushes coffee and the Sunday papers across the table.

'Don't read these if you don't wanna know about the Stiffley case. But don't worry—they ain't got your name. Perhaps I'll just leave you the supplements. You can choose your fashions for the coming season—I ain't looked but I tell you for sure, they're all skinny clothes for skinny-arse girls like you. Sleep well?'

The coffee is heavy-scented and strong, burning as it goes down.

'Is it OK if I use your computer? I need to send a message.'

'If it's work the answer is no. If it's *lurve* you gotta tell me who.'

'I think . . . I don't know . . .' How can she say this? 'I think I'm writing to my daughter.' She regrets the words even as she hears herself say them.

Chana leans across the table and peers into Jess's eyes. 'Hey girl, you ain't kidding. I known you for how long, ten years? You never mentioned no daughter.'

Jess unfolds the email, smoothes it flat and passes it to Chana.

'This is heavy shit, girl. You gonna tell me what's happening?'

Jess keeps it short. The lure of the music business; the men, the women, the ones still choosing. The drugs that took the place of food, the periods that stopped for months at a time, morning sickness just another hangover.

She keeps it short; adoption at birth, she says, everyone thought it best.

'And you? Even your parents? You people . . .' says Chana.

She reads the email again while Jess sips a second mug of coffee.

'This could be from anyone, right? But whoever sent it knows you got a child—but that's your secret—so maybe this Gina *is* your daughter.' She hands the paper back carefully, like a page from a Bible.

Back in the study, last night's clothes are crumpled on the floor at the foot of the bed. Jess shakes her jeans out carefully as they release the air of the club, smoke and alcohol, and she wonders if the visions and sounds are captured too, locked in the fibres of material. After she's dressed, Jess folds the copy of Gina's email and replaces it carefully in her bag. For the first time it hits her, how easy she was to find. All you need is a name.

79

She can't wait any longer to reply to Gina. While the computer starts up Jess finds her notebook and checks the instructions Denny gave her, for picking up emails when she's away from home.

She tries not to feel disappointed when she sees that there's no message from Gina—it's her turn to write after all. She starts to compose a reply. *'Dear Gina . . .'* Is this how you write to your daughter? She doesn't know the rules. *'I'm sorry if this message seems formal but I'll be honest and say that, well, I don't know what to say. Of course I want to see you.'* Or does she? Someone said that the power of fantasy is inaccessibility; she knows that so well. Be careful what you wish for. *'I could come to your house, if your mum agrees.'* That sounds wrong, but what else to call her? *'Let me know when we can set a date. There's so much I want to say but I'll say it better when we meet.'* Will 'sorry' be enough? *'Love, Jess.'* She sits in front of the screen for minutes trying to decide how to sign herself. Your mother? Mum? All that is left is her name.

She wants to think about the reply before sending it and checks the inbox again. There's just one message, from a sender she doesn't recognise; another website visitor, attaching a song he's written. Chana looks over her shoulder at the screen.

'You gonna show me this lover boy's offering or what?'

'I get two or three of these a week. It'll be crap, derivative junk. It always is. They get a buzz out of thinking that I read them.'

'And you don't?'

'They should get a life.'

'Come on, girl—let me see this crap. You never know, this one might be a masterpiece.'

Jess gives in and downloads the attachment, clicks on the icon and watches the screen fill with the words of a song, line after line. She starts to read and then realises that the song is one of hers, and then Chana points at the PC.

'I ain't no expert, but this thing's damn noisy all of a sudden, and that little green light ain't usually on so long.' As she finishes speaking the words on the screen suddenly start to move in different directions, twisting and merging until they turn into a menagerie of tiny monsters that slither and slink off the screen one by one. As the last one disappears the screen blanks, and a message fades up in deep violet, flashing on and off.

'SO LONG JESS—TIME TO CUT AND RUN'

'Oh fuck.' She pushes Chana out of the way and lunges for the socket where the computer is plugged in, pulling the lead out. The disk spins down to silence and the indicator lights dim.

'This ain't good, am I right?'

'This is bad, very bad. I need to phone someone, now.' When Denny answers he sounds half asleep as he asks if Chana had a virus checker on the computer.

'Virus checker? Girl, I see enough viruses in my job. Computer is just a piece of tin, can't get no virus.'

So that's a no. Denny talks her through what to do next; she plugs in, switches on, watches the screen.

'Error—hard disk not found.'

Even Chana knows what that means.

'Sorry, Jess,' says Denny. 'Looks like a virus crashed the disk. Probably reformatted it and wiped out everything there. I could try to retrieve what's left but . . .'

Jess arranges with Den to have one of the dealers he knows in London come and fit a new system for Chana, the least she can do. Before she hangs up she asks about the website.

'No problems so far,' says Denny. 'But tell me again—what exactly did the message say, the one with the attachment?'

'It was short. Started "Dear Jess . . ."'

Before she can go any further Denny stops her. ' "Dear Jess"?'

As soon as he says it Jess remembers; the messages forwarded from the site are always addressed to Chad, not Jess. Hacksaw fans, living in the past.

'This didn't come via the website,' says Denny. 'Whoever sent that message knows your personal email address.'

82

The website is a blessing and a curse. A gateway she wishes she could close, but at least it's detached, location-less. Or that's what she thought. And now someone who knows her is sending hate mail and she wonders, what if he knows my phone number, where I live? Have I talked to him without knowing? Has he touched me in the street? Does he know the colour of my eyes?

What else does he know?

*   *   *

After the weekend the office is constricting and unfamiliar, as if she's been away for a year. She makes a list in an effort to ground herself:

1. Eskell—a visit to Mikey tomorrow morning;
2. Pearce—to be closed today;
3. Witness at a court appearance tomorrow afternoon;

And then there's Stiffley, untidy and out of her control.

At midday she takes the phone off divert and immediately gets a call from Melanie Happs, worried that Bryony hasn't turned up for school today. Shit! Jess hasn't spoken to the teacher since the school visit last week, hasn't told her that the case is to be closed.

'All the same,' says Mel, 'I still have to follow up on her. It's how it starts, see, with these kids. A day here, a day there and then they're off for weeks at a time. The head doesn't like that.' She pauses, but not long enough to break the link. 'That Perry Stiffley was one of yours, wasn't he?'

'Tell you what, Mel, leave it with me. I'll pop round to the flat, make sure Bryony's OK.' She can't let go of the case, not yet. No need to tell anyone, no need to write it up.

She waits until work finishes; at least she can argue that she went round in her own time. She remembers Marty and keeps her mobile in her hand, ready to quick dial the duty desk if there's any sign of trouble, but Carwen opens the door, filling the space like a jailer.

'Thought Marty told you to leave us alone?'

'I was passing by, thought I'd see how Bryony was. You were out when I came by the other night.'

'Well, now you've seen me you can go away again.'

'And Bryony? How are the bruises?'

'She's round at Steffy's.' Carwen's swollen cheeks are shiny with sweat and grease, and she jabs her cigarette towards Jess's face. 'Listen, if you keep bothering us I'll make a complaint to your boss. Fuckin' social. No life of your own, you got to push into other people's. Why don't you bugger off.' She tries to close the door but Jess holds it open, their bodies almost touching.

'Bryony wasn't at school today; her teacher called me, she was worried.'

'She had a virus, OK? Kids get them— thought you'd know that. She's all right now, so you can stop interfering.' She pushes Jess away and slams the door.

This is all she needs, a complaint on top of everything else. And the case is closed, she shouldn't even be here. Time to let go.

*   *   *

For the first time since she moved, the house feels empty although there's no reason why it should; Wagner's finished washing and is curled up in Jess's place on the sofa, and the radio chatters quietly in the corner while she searches for food without feeling hungry. The remains of a loaf look bruised but she cuts off the edges and toasts a slice, eating it dry.

She feels like she's failing.

The bread tastes bitter and she throws it into the bin. On the flowerbed outside the front door an early-evening slug is embracing the only pin-sized strawberry to have appeared all year. Jess watches the slow ripples for a moment and then spills a little beer next to the mollusc. She may as well get drunk in company.

Back inside she doesn't have the energy to uproot Wagner and goes into the study to check emails for the first time since leaving

Chana. Nothing, not even junk. Then she remembers that her reply to Gina never got sent, obliterated by the virus.

She tries to remember the exact words she used last time, as if they were part of a spell that would fail if not said perfectly. Approximations are no good. But when she looks at the finished message it seems too insignificant to be the first contact with her daughter. She thinks of attaching a photo and then realises there's one on the website.

It feels like Gina has all the advantages, and Jess wonders what she was told about her adoption, where she sees the blame. She wants to ask a thousand questions but doesn't. One day at a time; twelve steps to heaven and pray you don't trip.

Her hand clicks 'Send' and it's done. She's on her fourth bottle and an empty stomach, and for the first time in years wishes she had some puff. No point even thinking about it; she threw the kit away long since, a ritual disposal of the papers and tobacco, the torn fragments of cardboard and the stained, aromatic plastic pouch that she emptied from the middle of Blackfriars bridge one cold November night when she started to trust Nic.

All these years of trying and she's still not sure she made the right choice; it's like sharing her body with a stranger whose needs she's never discovered.

*   *   *

Jess drives straight to the therapeutic centre the next morning, a three-storey Edwardian house on the outskirts of Aberfelen with a front garden razed and concreted for cars. She was lucky to find this placement for Mikey so close to home, and so quickly. The centre manager offers her an office but Jess asks if the boy can be brought to her in the garden, a wilderness of small paths and over-hanging trees. He arrives a few minutes later, squinting in the bright sunlight, the white skin of his face punctuated by red and black pustules and his eyes so widely set that Jess is surprised he can focus on anything.

They walk a circuit of the garden side by side. 'How do you feel about the centre?' asks Jess, and the boy shakes his head.

'I don't understand why I'm here. There was nothing wrong, you never heard me complain. I should be at home, with my mum.

'I miss her,' he says, 'I miss my sister.'

'It's early days,' Jess tells him. 'Give them time, let the people here help you.' And Mikey shakes his head again, like a dog shaking off water.

She sees the therapist before she leaves, in his office overlooking the parked cars. Everything in the room is grey; the desk, the filing cabinets. It's a place for questions, not confidences, and even the man across the desk

87

looks out of place in his corduroy jacket and yellow bow-tie.

'You don't need to be an expert,' he says. 'Mikey was abused for so long it became the norm. In his world, this behaviour is acceptable. We are out of step with him, not the other way round.'

'But can you help him?' asks Jess.

'There are different stages of denial. Some people block out their perception of bad things altogether, either in their own behaviour or other people's. They're able to isolate themselves completely. Other people, like Mikey, know what's happening but they reframe it to become acceptable. They set up new rules. So Mikey sees nothing wrong in having been abused; it's a good protective mechanism.'

'And he sees nothing wrong in grooming other children.'

'Why should he? It's the norm in his world.'

'I guess that's what makes him so dangerous.'

'I suppose you'd prefer it if they were all old men in raincoats,' says the therapist, 'at least you'd know what you were looking for. As for Mikey, he says he'll stop abusing because he's been asked to, but we need him to stop because he understands that it's wrong. And that's going to take some time.'

*   *   *

88

It's an hour's drive to Uskmouth Crown Court, a Soviet Hall of Culture transplanted to Wales. High ceilings and wood panelling, a soulless building that doesn't fit ordinary people. Nobody laughs here. There are hope magnets in the walls and floors, sucking out optimism and leaving a vacuum of resignation. Jess sits on a bench just down from the courtroom and mentally checks her witness statement against a Schedule One offender who broke a court order and moved back in with his girlfriend and her twelve-year-old daughter, the people he'd battered every time he was drunk. Three times a week, the police reckoned, for more than two years. The last time Jess saw him he was sitting at his girlfriend's kitchen table in his underwear, eating breakfast.

Today she's lucky; half an hour's wait, fifteen minutes in the box and then she's finished. A result. Walking towards the exit she sees a woman and man outside another of the courtrooms. Pav waves her over, smiling at a shared joke as the man takes his hand off her arm. He must be six two, a big man swaddled in a suit he's owned for too long, and when he turns Jess sees a ruined empire in his face.

'Hi Jess, how did it go?' says Pav.

'I was giving evidence—Schedule One offender back at his old tricks. What about you?'

'This is DI Pelham—I mentioned him to

you the other day.'

He holds her hand a beat too long. 'Jess Chadwick—social services? The name sounds familiar.' There's a country burr hidden in his accent. 'There was a band—Hacksaw—I've got one of their albums somewhere. It's you, isn't it; Chad? I saw you at the Roundhouse, must have been '87 or '88. You look exactly the same.'

'That was a different world, and a long time ago. I'm surprised anyone remembers.' His smile already holds an invitation, and his eyes belong to a man who doesn't often hear 'no'. But all the time Jess is conscious of Pav standing beside him, her scar suddenly noticeable, a pale crescent like a zip that Jess could undo to peel away the surface and see what's underneath.

'Pav tells me that you're handling the Perry Stiffley inquiry,' she says. 'Won't that put a few noses out of joint in the local CID?'

Pelham shrugs the question away. 'It's normal practice—especially as there's an earlier case to take into account. Fresh pair of eyes, all that stuff.'

'You think there's a connection? There's a difference between child pornography and murder.'

'Sometimes the gap is very small,' says Pav.

'I'm keeping an open mind,' says Pelham. 'The trouble is there are two investigations, us and the press. The trouble is, they don't work to the Police and Criminal Evidence Act, and you know who they'll have in their sights.'

*   *   *

The local paper has the Stiffley case on the front page, and Jess buys a copy to annoy herself even further; at least they haven't used her name yet. A late lunch of Doritos and Coke in the car and she heads back to Gwenstow.

She ignores the blinking voicemail light as she reaches her desk in the empty office, pleased to be surrounded by peace for a moment. She can't believe everyone is out on visits at the same time, then notices the monitors are dead. She checks her watch—it's already past six; another day devoured and no shrinkage in the tower of case files on her desk. Sometimes she wonders if the old days weren't better; a pill for every mood, energy on tap and no need to think about tomorrow.

White Rabbit.

And here she is, alone in an empty room, barely able to keep up with the pack and about to be scapegoated. The receptors in her brain are begging to be engaged as she reaches in her bag before remembering that she hasn't smoked for a decade.

*   *   *

Halfway up the lane Jess stops the car just in time to miss a dead branch across the track. They didn't warn her about this until after she bought the farmhouse, one of the hazards of living in a place surrounded by old woods. She tries to pull the branch away but it's not completely severed from the trunk and she can't twist it enough to break the last sinews. The handsaw in the back of her car is wrapped in a blanket to keep it out of sight when she's ferrying children around, and it takes a few moments to disentangle the blade. She climbs on to the bank and starts to saw through the wood; the teeth catch in the ridges of bark and it's a while before she reaches the rhythm. The pale sawdust seems to defy gravity, misting her hands, shoes and the surrounding leaves, and the resin smell takes her back to David Stiffley's workshop just a few miles away, over in the next valley. The skin on her back tightens and she stops sawing for a moment, letting silence return as she looks into the trees and scrub, half expecting to see one of his stunted carvings grinning back at her.

The five-bar gate outside her house is swinging open across the track and a small group of deer are browsing on the roses, but they look up at the sound of the engine and escape down the slope, stopping a couple of hundred yards away to watch. Must be a new postman, she thinks, someone from a city. But there are no letters on the mat so she gets a beer and checks emails; just two, one from Spider, one from Gina.

'Hi, Jess.' So intimate and easy, this informality, and yet so anonymous. This message was typed in by her daughter and yet there's nothing of her on the screen. Nothing that she's touched, no ink on a page, no smudge or tear stains or hint of perfume; no connection. Jess doesn't know why she hasn't opened the email yet; she's scared but doesn't know why. Her hand clicks on the message; at least some part of her body knows what to do.

'Hi Jess, I was worried you wouldn't reply when you took so long. I checked my emails before school and at least twenty times when I got home each night. Mum thinks I'm ill or something. I think she wishes she hadn't told me your name. I'll be in London on Wednesday for my music lesson but I'll be back at King's Cross station by six. We could have a coffee or something. I usually get the six minutes past but I could say it's late or something.

Please come, love, Gina.'

The message is too thin, a dead thing. Jess wants the words to turn into flesh and sounds. And she feels guilty for not replying before; she can't do that again. She doesn't remember what appointments are set for Wednesday but she'll cancel them all, and then thinks—This is ridiculous; planning to see a sixteen-year-old girl I don't even know in a coffee bar at King's Cross.

Jess reads the message again, and Gina solidifies with every word. She's articulate and self-assured. Jess wonders about the lessons, the music. She's already fearful for her daughter, travelling alone, and then thinks of what she did when she was only two years older than Gina. She thinks, my motherhood gene may be damaged but some of it's still working just fine. You can sign the papers and give up your rights, but they can't cut out the DNA.

Before replying Jess goes to her spare room and pulls a long box from under the bed. It belonged to her parents; she had it in her room when she was a child. The box looks smaller and narrower than she remembers, the wooden frame covered with dark brown leather although in her memory it used to be green. In places the thin covering has dried and begun to split around the corners; the two metal clasps are tarnished and stiff, and she nearly breaks a fingernail levering one open. She hasn't looked in here for years, not even when she packed to move from London.

It's as if she's opening an Egyptian tomb, and as the lid falls back a musty smell of leather and wool rushes out, captured time. There are tracksuits and dresses for a little girl and tiny shoes, all new and unworn, and on the top a plastic carrier. It must be eleven years since she opened this bag. Inside are five envelopes; unwritten, unsealed and unsent.

94

She opens one at random and reads the first birthday card she bought for her daughter to whom she never gave a name. For the first five years of her daughter's life, Jess marked each anniversary by choosing a card, an outfit of clothes and some shoes. She takes out the smallest pair; tiny blue sandals with painted flowers on the toes, and cups them in the palms of her hands. With her eyes closed she could be holding nothing, their weight as insubstantial as a dream.

1986—2

'How many times do I have to do this?' Chad slips the headphones around her neck, sits heavily on the stool next to one of the synths and rolls herself another cigarette. The last one burnt itself out halfway through, adding to the pyramid in the ashtray.

'You wanna be the producer, that's OK by me.' The voice through the speakers meanders from mid-Atlantic to Colombia and back again. 'Trouble is, you know dip shit about it. How about you stick to the singing, I'll press the buttons. And put some bollocks into it—this is meant to be rock, not fucking dinner jazz.'

'Screw you, Raoul.' But she puts the headphones back on, listens through Jamie's recorded intro and comes in bang on cue, singing with her eyes shut. This time no one stops her.

Raoul gives her a thumbs up from behind the glass and leans across to the mike.

'Ace. We got a track. Only another eight to go. Break for ten minutes, then we'll go for the vocals on "Scarify".'

Chad looks over at the control room, sealed behind glass. Raoul and the engineer, listening to an unheard beat.

'What happened to Jamie?'

Raoul looks up from the mixing desk.

'Some chick was asking for him out front—you should go find him, we need him for the next track.'

She gets a coffee from the machine and goes outside. It's later than she thought, the sun already hidden behind the main block of Stonefield Studios. Jamie's sitting on the grass verge a few yards away, rolling a joint. Even from behind, the girl next to him looks familiar. Spiked blonde hair, sleeveless black top. A Magritte mirror.

Chad clicks a smile.

'Hey babe! Some of that for me?'

They turn in unison. Jamie takes a long draw, then passes the joint to Chad.

'This is Jax—came up from London to say hello.'

'We met.' Spliff girl, from the end-of-tour party. She looks even smaller in daylight.

'How old are you, honey?'

A beat. 'Sixteen.'

'Fuckin' aye, and I'm Princess Diana.'

'It was you she came to see, Chad,' says Jamie.

'What, like it's my turn?' She turns to the girl. 'Sorry, sweets, I don't do pussy till it's past puberty. No offence.'

There's something in the girl's eyes that she can't read. Too dark, too wide. And her body, spindle thin and unripe. There's a tattoo at the top of her left arm, a red flower growing through the links of a chain. Chad rubs at it gently, as if expecting the ink to smear under her touch, and feels the girl lean in to her.

'That's a pretty good copy.'

'I took in one of your posters when I had it done,' says Jax. 'Mum half killed me when she saw it.'

'I told you Chad, she's a real wee fan,' says Jamie.

'Whatever—we gotta split. Raoul is waiting.' Chad turns to the girl. 'And before you ask, no, you can't come in. Raoul gets really pissed if there are punters around when we're recording. Ciao kid.'

As Chad and Jamie walk away, Jax takes a clean tissue from her bag and smoothes it over the tattoo, blotting her skin.

*   *   *

Way past rush hour, and the fast train to Paddington is almost empty. Still mellow, Jax listens to Hacksaw's latest album on her Walkman, practising the words, perfecting the phrasing. If it weren't for the woman across the carriage, she'd touch herself.

The black cab drops her halfway up Bishops Avenue. She pushes the bleeper on her keyring and the main gates swing open. No cars in the drive except for Alice's—both parents are still out. Excellent timing.

The door opens before she gets to it.

'Your mother called twice tonight—I told her you were in the bath.'

'Thanks Alice.'

'Best hurry then—she's on her way back. And if she sees you looking like this . . . Couldn't you have found a shorter skirt? And clean up your face—you look like something from a horror film.' She studies the girl in front of her, an overgrown child, head too large for her body. 'I don't need to ask if you ate anything today.'

'What about my father?'

'He had to fly to Geneva this afternoon, said he would be back tomorrow.' Alice looks away as she says this, and there's a stillness between the two women, a pause.

'Is he bringing anyone back? Fabrice?' Fat Fabrice, who always smells of fish and wanders in the night. Fabrice, with his certainties, his promises and his threats.

Alice shrugs.

'He said nothing to me. Maybe you should find somewhere to go tomorrow night, stay with a friend.' Alice knows, Alice understands. 'You have to tell them, Jax. At least your mother, she'll listen to you.'

'That would be a first. And I already tried—she told me to stop being stupid and grow up. Why should they care?'

Alice takes a breath, then releases it without speaking and disappears through the far door, towards her own quarters at the side of the house. Jax watches her, but doesn't see.

Upstairs, she locks her bedroom door, showers quickly in her private bathroom and then sits on the bed. Her guitar is propped against the practice amp in one corner, fifteenth birthday presents from her father. Every wall is layered with posters of Hacksaw; Chad and Jamie singing, strutting, eyes closed, eyes open. Looking at Jax. Spotlit.

All second-hand now. She can't wait any longer; she opens her bag and removes the folded tissue on which she captured the film of moisture, the gift of skin cells left when Chad stroked her arm.

She takes an old sweet tin from her bedside cabinet, the lid printed with a picture of a small girl cuddling a dog, a golden Labrador. Trophy kit. Inside are some small plastic bags, neatly folded. All are empty except one, labelled 'Jamie'; just looking at it, she can taste him again. She takes an empty bag and carefully inters today's tissue. Number two. Chad.

The air in the room is damp and warm from the steam of the shower in her bathroom. Jax leaves the tin open, leans back, shuts her eyes and replays the day, changing the ending. Combinations; she can't decide which to try first. Her hand has found its way between her legs and she tests her fantasies, lazily; and when it's finished she captures some of her own secretions and commits them to the tin.

All three together.

CHAPTER SEVEN

The voice on the phone belongs to the same world as the long brown box under the bed. But slower than in the old days, rustier, especially when it says her name as if using an unfamiliar word. Jess wants to say—why are you calling? Why are you calling *me*? But she respects the gesture that any contact represents and says nothing.

Her mother could be making this call from anywhere; Jess runs through the list of her parents' houses: the chalet in Gstaad, the eyrie in Beverly Hills, the Venetian palazzo? Yes, Venice at this time of year, cashmere and silk and fluttering hands before the autumn floods and mists on the lagoon.

There is no small talk, no expressions of affection, just the passage of information. 'Your father's ill,' says her mother. 'For real this time. He wants to see you.' It's a request, not a command; she knows those days are over.

Jess wonders, fleetingly, how her mother knew where to phone. They have a relationship that never ended, but simply frayed away over the course of the years until they became strangers.

She leaves a message for Joe; family crisis, I'll be back in a day or so. She doesn't care what he thinks.

*   *   *

At the airport she almost misses the taxi driver holding a card with her name on it. And she hadn't expected her mother to make the journey to meet her; they walk towards each other with slower and slower steps, stopping while still an arm's-length apart. It's been more years than she thought; her mother has become old, hiding her eyes behind sunglasses and her neck within a silk scarf, and her clothes hang from a frame even more gaunt than the model she used to be.

Jess doesn't need to hear the words to know what her mother is thinking: you look terrible, you still dye your hair, where's your make-up? An old litany that she'll never forget.

Before the water taxi has gone more than a hundred yards the mist from the motionless lagoon hides both the airport and the main island in the distance. Only the marker poles are left, jutting from the water and crowned with seagulls like sentries guarding the way. The two women sit on opposite sides of the boat, silently rehearsing the conversation that doesn't happen.

The taxi reaches the edge of the city which looms out of the mist like a wall, and then

102

pushes inside down the first, narrow canal. Jess looks ahead, not wanting to recognise the buildings on either side. Without her noticing the taxi has turned onto the Grand Canal, heading east towards the palazzo. It could be yesterday that she was last here, stepping onto the private jetty outside Ca' Priuli.

The marble hall always smells of polish and there are fresh flowers in a vase—Jess doesn't know their name. The woman who takes her bag is young and new and averts her eyes.

'You should see him now,' says her mother.

Even if Jess didn't know where the room was, she would find it by the music. Some things never change. She recognises the Schumann cello concerto, first movement; she knows he was waiting until he heard them arrive before he put it on. She expects him to be in bed but he's wrapped in a blanket in a chair, looking out through the high narrow window across the canal to Santa Maria della Salute. He doesn't turn as she comes into the room but uses a remote control to turn down the volume.

He already looks dead; grey and fleshless. His face is stretched and there are dark hollows under the eyes but his hair is still thick, grey and square cut.

'Rostropovich . . . too cold for you, no doubt . . . But what a technician.' The voice shocks Jess most. Deep breaths between each word, and yet he speaks in no more than a hoarse

103

whisper. He hasn't taken his eyes from the window, new glass in the stone frame, but when he turns to look at her his whole body moves. 'I expect your mother told you that you look terrible? I wouldn't dare, of course.' His skin is matt and flaking around the temples but there are shiny channels from the corner of each eye. He looks used up, a discarded chrysalis that somehow manages to move.

'Sorry, that was ungracious of me . . . I should thank you for coming . . . although I hope you have another reason . . . than to gloat at an old man dying.' He pauses to catch his breath. 'You still blame me, don't you?'

'You believed him, not me,' says Jess. 'You called me a little tart.'

'Times were different then . . . Maybe I believed what was easier . . . for me to cope with.'

'That your daughter was a teenage whore?'

For the first time there's a fire in his eyes, or maybe it's just a reflection of light from the window.

'If it meant that whatever happened was your choice—yes! If it meant that you hadn't been frightened and hurt—yes!'

If Jess didn't know him better, she'd think he was crying.

'You still did business with him. You still spoke to him, even if you kept him out of the house. You knew the truth, but you made it my problem.'

The old man turns back to the window. 'You took my money . . . when you needed it.'

'Did you think that paid off your debt?' She's shouting now through her own tears. 'You have no idea of the adjustments I've had to make, just to get by. I lost my daughter, I lost my only child!'

And, she thinks, I forgot how to love.

A spasm of dry coughs leaves the old man gasping for breath. 'I can't . . . expect . . . forgiveness . . . and I don't. But I'm sorry, kitten . . . So, so sorry.'

The endearment surprises them both—she can't remember the last time he called her kitten, and the word rolls past her defences before she can stop it. But after all, this is why she came. The blame is all played out; maybe it happened when Gina stretched out her hand, a circle of forgiveness. Still, it hurts to let the hate go, something she's lived with for so long, like the comfort of a blind man's darkness when he finds that he can see again.

The music has stopped without her noticing. She kneels by the old man, presses her cheek against his like a child who hasn't learnt how to kiss, and they cling to each other, not sure who is doing the cradling.

This is a fragile peace, they both know that. When Jess asks, 'How long?' and he says, 'A week, a month, who can say?' she knows she has to leave, as any more words could destroy what took them so long to find.

Jess finds herself back on the jetty. The sun is hidden behind a haze, but somehow the dome of Santa Maria manages to glisten as if set with crystal. The young woman brings out her bags, never unpacked, and the boat takes her back to the airport where she catches the last flight to London, not quite as alone as she was on the way out.

*   *   *

It's been a long weekend. At first, Jess doesn't recognise the woman waiting in the screened-off reception area. Out of context she's a stranger until she pushes herself up from the faded orange chair. She smells of smoke even though the cigarette's missing, and her face glistens under the fluorescent tubes. There's no aggression now and she's small under the shapeless top and junk-food fat, little more than a child herself.

'It's Bryony, she didn't come home last night.' The harshness has left her voice, and she unconsciously kneads one hand with the other; an animal trapped in a cage.

Jess wonders why she feels no surprise, and realises that ever since she saw the girl at the school, clutching at her skirt to hide the bruises, she'd been expecting this news. As if that makes it any easier.

'Have you checked with her friends? And what have the police said?'

106

'She was round at Steffy's, as usual. Her best friend. And Marty's on lates so I went to bed. Bryony always sees to herself when she gets in, 'specially if I got a bad head or something.' She wipes her nose with her fingers. 'Marty said not to worry. He said kids are always acting up, staying out. He said she'd come back. He'd kill me if I called the police.'

Before she's finished speaking, Jess calls the FSU. That's why Carwen's here, she thinks, so that I can do what she's forbidden. Pav answers the duty phone, and Jess explains. Mentions the bruises, but not the picture; keeps her eyes on Carwen's face.

'I'll be round,' says Pav. 'Give me ten minutes. Keep her there.'

Jess feels like a jailer, standing outside in the car park with Carwen as she smokes. In the daylight the younger woman's clothes have become a network of stains and pulled threads and one of her trainers is split near the toe, its logo buried under a crust of grey mud. Twenty-two, twenty-three max. Fourteen years old when Bryony was born.

A BMW pulls up a few feet away, dwarfing the other cars. It has to be Pav. Heads turn as they weave through the office to the small interview room at the back, but when Jess turns to leave Carwen says, 'Stay, with me'.

Pav is wearing diamonds again.

She talks about Marty. You met him in a club? No family of his own? How do the girls

107

like him? Do they play together? She asks without looking up from the notebook, reading a script. From time to time both of them look over at Jess, Carwen like a supplicant, Pav like . . . an observer, thinks Jess. She's watching both of us.

They move on to Steffy, Bryony's best friend. How often do they meet, what are their games? Tell me about the family; where they live, what they do. Looking for connections, looking for patterns. Pav asks about Marty again, and Carwen begins to snivel. She looks like her daughter, thinks Jess, when I asked about the bruises on her legs.

Pav hands Carwen a card, tells her to call if she needs to, and they stand in unison. Jess sees them as if through a lens: the crying mother, stained and shrunken; the policewoman, an exotic stray from another world; and herself, all angles and spikes, pale as a corpse. She knows who she would choose to be.

Pav makes a call on her mobile as they walk out to the car park, then asks Jess if she's free to visit Steffy's house. 'We'll drive Carwen home,' she says, 'go on from there. If you have the time.'

It doesn't sound like a question.

The car is top of the range; cream leather and walnut and an engine like a sleeping cat. Carwen seems lost on the back seat, shrinking into herself like a threatened mollusc.

108

Jess runs her hand over the wooden dash.

'Police budgets must be up this year.'

'You should see my other car. Actually, I borrowed this from a friend—mine's in for a service today.'

Like, I hadn't worked that one out, thinks Jess. Beamer, diamonds and thousand-pound suits on a sergeant's pay? I don't think so.

When they get to Carwen's flat, Pav goes up to look around while Jess stays in the car. The interior has the smell they only get in the factory or after a valet. There's no trace of the owner, no empty Coke bottles rolling on the floor or crisp packets crumpled in the door pockets.

Inside the unlocked glove compartment there's a pair of soft brown gloves, lined with silk and too small for a man. Jess lifts one to her nose; under the smell of leather is another scent like vanilla, almost too faint to register. She tries it on, smoothes it along her fingers like a second skin. A perfect fit.

When Pav gets back they drive a few hundred yards around the corner to Steffy's house. There are no armchairs in the gardens of these maisonettes behind privet walls.

The man who answers the door has a tie pulled loose below his open collar, and the state of his suit says that he spends too long in a car. He studies Pav's warrant card before inviting them to sit around the kitchen table.

Jess wonders what game the sergeant's

playing, as she listens to Pav questioning the man as if she were still in CID, and not a family support officer.

'You're lucky to catch me,' the man says. 'My wife phoned after Carwen came round this morning, and I cancelled my other calls to come home and stay with Steffy. We kept her out of school today.' He talks quickly, without prompting. Pav leans forward and rests her hand on Jess's arm.

'Any chance you could have a word with Steffy while I speak to Mr Morgan?'

Jess finds her upstairs in a room that most of her clients would kill for: a computer with speakers playing a song she doesn't recognise, freshly ironed bedding, two pairs of new trainers lined up against the wall by a white fitted wardrobe. The girl in front of the monitor looks older than Bryony, an uncoordinated collection of limbs, with long fair hair scraped back from a bony face, piebald with freckles.

She seems happy enough to talk, chattering about school and her friends, but she barely mentions Bryony, as if the missing girl were no more than an acquaintance. Someone she saw in the playground, on the streets. Not someone who shared her secrets.

'She called you her best friend,' says Jess, 'came here every night to play?' She says it as a question and the grimace on the girl's face is more eloquent than any words; wherever

110

Bryony went after school, it wasn't here.

*   *   *

'Have you been to a mortuary?' says Pav. She's turned in the opposite direction to Jess's office. 'Sorry to hijack you, but it won't take long.' They park near the courthouse in Uskmouth, an anonymous municipal block of concrete. The windows are small slits in the rain-stained walls and there's no sign on the door.

'You don't need me to identify Perry,' says Jess.

'No. But I need you to look at something else.'

She doesn't want to be here. 'He's dead'— those are just words, abstract, they apply to other people. But seeing Perry's body will make it real and personal, her failure to save him.

The smell in the basement of the building reminds Jess of chemistry lessons. There's no sign of an operating table; she'd expected blood, and organs in basins but there's nothing except the giant filing cabinets in a room with no shadows, an archive of the dead. There are insects crawling over her body.

A technician pulls out one of the oversized drawers. Jess recognises the body at once, although it looks even smaller now than she remembers. His face is unmarked and

111

peaceful, with a sheen of candle wax, and Jess has to stop herself from reaching out to stroke the boy's cheek. The rest of the body is covered by a sheet which the attendant carefully folds back from both top and bottom until only the trunk is covered by a band of material. The marks on the arms have leaked and the skin covers flesh which has fallen into unfamiliar contours.

She no longer feels the need to touch.

'Look at his legs,' says Pav.

They have the same mottled patches as his arms, with scratches and deeper abrasions reaching up and under the sheet. But, clearly visible near the tops of his thighs, are two wide bands of faded bruises.

Jess feels nauseous. She nods, turns away and hears the drawer slide back as Pav takes her arm and leads her out of the basement, away from this sanitised death and into the cleaner fumes of the street.

'Sorry about that, but I needed to be sure that they were the same as the marks on Bryony,' says Pav. 'Are you OK?'

Jess doesn't want to say; I was expecting this, it's all part of a pattern. She's known since the first phone call about Perry that something was about to change.

*   *   *

Pav drops her back in the car park by the

offices. As the BMW pulls away, Jess locks herself in her own car. Talking to other people would be impossible; she needs to sluice the images in her mind, replace them with something familiar and kind. But when she turns the radio on the speakers are almost blown by the full-volume beat of a local dance station, music she never listens to. She turns it down, presses another button but gets only static. And again. The whole set has been retuned. She swears, switches to CD. At first there's more static and she thinks, fuck, the whole thing's screwed, but then a voice starts singing.

A woman's voice, singing 'Suffer'.

Her song.

Her voice.

She ejects the CD before listening any further. It's a home-made job, unlabelled, unrecognised. She thinks, maybe I recorded it, but she never listens to her own music once it's finished. Someone else has burned the disc and put it in her car.

And it must have been this morning; she was playing something else on the way in. There are goose-bumps on the back of her neck; she can almost feel someone behind her, breathing on her skin. She pulls the door handle but nothing moves and she bangs at the door with her shoulder until she remembers that she locked herself in.

She leans on the bonnet, trying to control

her breathing. There's no one around. She scans the other cars to see if anyone is sitting and watching, but they're as empty as hers. She checks the disc again, but there are no signs or labels, nothing to signify. Locking the car doors seems futile but she does it all the same, and tries not to run into the office.

Else is on the phone when Jess reaches her desk, but hangs up as soon as she sees her face.

'What happened? You had a fright, I think, no blood in your veins. Sit down, breathe slowly.' She brings a coffee and then goes to check the car after Jess tells her what happened.

'No damage, Jess. Maybe you left it unlocked? Maybe you should call the police.'

'And say what? "Hello—someone got into my car and left me a present. No, they didn't take anything. No, they didn't break anything." I have to work with these people, Else, I need to keep some credibility.'

'So talk to Ed—he's a friend.'

He answers on the first ring. 'Sounds like someone having a bit of fun at your expense. Is any client particularly annoyed with you?'

'Of course not—they all love me to pieces. As if.'

'You're lucky they didn't smash a window and rip the radio out.'

'I wish they had. This is more like a message.'

'Saying what?'

114

'I don't know. Something. And why that song?' She tells Ed about the website and the way the lyrics were changed.

'Hackers, Jess. There are thousands of them out there. The Met has a specialist unit but they only get involved if there's substantial financial loss. I could arrange for someone to come and take prints, but to be honest it won't get followed up. No resources, not for a case like this.'

'So what do I do? Sit and wait for something else to happen?' She hears Ed take a deep breath.

'Don't take this the wrong way, Jess, but sometimes people fit events into a pattern even where one doesn't exist. Especially if they're upset. If you think someone's out to get you, then you'll interpret even minor events that way.'

'So I'm overreacting? Ed, I'm holding the bloody CD in my hand. I'm not imagining it.'

'Doesn't mean it's part of a grand conspiracy. Look, why don't I come round your place later? I'll check out the security, put your mind at rest.'

He's right, she thinks, I'm overreacting to a stupid sick joke. Probably a client; the kids I work with are more than capable of burning CDs and hacking websites. Maybe Denny's systems aren't as foolproof as he thinks. Whoever it is will lose interest before long and leave me in peace.

All the same, she gives Ed directions to the farmhouse and agrees to meet him there after work.

*   *   *

She hasn't spoken to Denny since she was at Chana's and the virus trashed her computer. He answers almost immediately for a change.

'Den, is there any way you can see how often one of my songs has been downloaded?'

'Which one?'

' "Suffer"—the one we had the problem with.' As Denny checks his logs, Jess runs through the lyrics in her mind, looking for clues. But there's nothing she can find, nothing to tell her why someone would choose this song.

'Jess? I can't tell you how many people listened to it online, but it's been downloaded on eighty-three occasions. Popular.'

'When was the last time?'

'Looks like yesterday morning. Are you going to tell me what this is about?'

After she explains about the CD he laughs.

'Alzheimer's, Jess. Don't you remember; you weren't happy with some of the songs and I said you should listen to them outside the studio, the way someone else would hear them. I said, why don't you burn a couple of them onto CD, listen to them in the car.'

'But I didn't.'

116

'Who else would? Who's going to download one of your songs and then give it back to you? You're working too hard. You'll get home, find a box of blank CDs that match the one in your car and then you'll remember. Don't worry 'bout it. Put the CD back, play it to yourself on the way home and enjoy.'

Maybe Denny's right. Maybe her mind's playing up again, blanking things out at random. Maybe that's even more worrying.

*   *   *

When Jess gets back to the house at seven o'clock Ed's car is already there, and as she pulls up he appears from the bottom field.

'I was just looking round the outside. Lovely place you've got—bit isolated though. You can't exactly pop round the neighbours for a cup of sugar.' Jess lets him wander round the house like a potential buyer, listening to his footsteps upstairs move from studio to bathroom to her bedroom, and back down to the kitchen. It feels strange for him to be here, like an intersection of two different worlds. When Jess drives up the lane she leaves people behind; no colleagues, no clients. It's why she chose to live here, to be free of the need to interact.

Ed asks for the security code and checks her alarm system. 'Seems OK. But you should get it hooked up to a monitoring station. All that happens now is that it makes a noise. Might frighten off kids, but even if anyone else heard the alarm go off, who's going to do anything about it?'

'I take my chances.' And the whole point of leaving London was to come to somewhere safe.

'Your call.' They wander outside and look over the valley. 'When you see all this beauty,' says Ed, 'you just know that there's a God.'

'And then you see what we have to deal with every day,' says Jess, 'and you just know that there isn't. Sorry, Ed, you know I don't buy this religious crap. If it makes you happy, fine. I'll stick to reality.'

*   *   *

After he's gone, Jess takes a beer outside. The sun is beginning to dip over the opposite ridge and she props herself against the honey locust tree and closes her eyes. When she wakes the sky is a washed-out blue on the horizon but the sun has disappeared and the first pipistrelles of the night are skittering like tiny mechanical birds through the trees and over the terrace. Her skin feels damp and chill even though there's no breeze.

The CD is in the middle of the kitchen table. Jess takes it carefully by the edges, like something valuable, watching the gold of its surface split into rainbow segments as she

118

turns it under the light. She still hasn't played it again, hates listening to her own work except when she's writing or recording.

The CD player shows only one track on the disc. Jess sings along with the familiar tune, subconsciously adding a new harmony and barely listening. Then she realises that she's singing the wrong words and blushes, although no one's heard her. She skips back a few seconds and plays the section again, not singing this time.

It's her voice, her music, but the words are none that she's ever written. Instead, she hears herself singing the lyrics that were changed on her website, a paedophile fantasy turned into a love song.

She punches buttons at random on the CD player until the music stops and then runs up to the studio, remembering what Denny said earlier, but there's no box of blank discs.

The PC. She checks the folder where she keeps different versions of the tracks she records, but all the copies of 'Suffer' have the original lyrics, her lyrics. She calls Denny.

'Bring me the disc,' he says, 'I'm in the workshop, I'll sort this out.' This time he doesn't laugh.

It takes Jess less than fifteen minutes to drive into Abertrothy, and Den gives her a tentative hug when she walks in, as if trying not to break her. The shop smells of chips and vinegar, and Den clears some circuit boards off a chair for her.

'I've checked the version of the song on the website—it's fine. So if you didn't make the recording, someone else did.'

'You don't understand. I'm the one singing. It's my voice.'

'Let's check it out. I'll rip the track onto my hard disk so that I can break the song down into different wave forms, here on screen. We can see if someone's messed it about.'

He listens through headphones, clicking his fingers and swaying to the music, as a moving graph comes up on the screen with multiple curves in different colours. The lines rise and fall, but Jess can see by Denny's face when he reaches the changed lyrics; he becomes still and his expression sets. Jess wonders what he believes. Den turns back to the monitor and clicks away for a while, still wearing headphones.

'Whoever did this was bloody good.' Den's voice is too loud as he listens and watches, stopping the movement from time to time to check something on the screen. He looks excited when he turns back to Jess and takes off the headphones, still beating an unheard rhythm on the top of the desk.

'I think I know what happened. Whoever did this sampled your voice from the track on the website, and perhaps other songs he downloaded. Then he rebuilt a section of the song using the samples. Fucking ace. He re-quantised the section to smooth the timing so you can barely hear the difference, but on screen you can see where the patching's been done. This guy's a guru.' He sees the expression on Jess's face. 'And sick, really sick—but still a guru.'

'So this isn't something anyone could do? Kids are smart these days.'

'Not this smart. It must have taken hours of work to produce fifteen seconds of the song. The rest is unchanged, just two lines have been redone. Sorry I can't tell you any more.' As he hands the disc back his fingers brush against hers. 'If you're feeling spooked you can stay at my place tonight. Have a smoke, chill out. The room's a bit scummy but it's OK—I spend most of my time here. Come on, it would be really wicked.'

It would be an embarrassment, keeping him at bay. I'm cool, she says. No sweat. Things to do.

Her script.

She hears the shop door lock behind her, although the light from the window still brightens the pavement for a few yards. The roads are empty on the way back and she drives slowly, wrapped in a quiet, dark cocoon until she pulls up at the end of the lane. She left the lights on earlier and the house is bright and welcoming; Wagner is waiting on the gatepost, balanced like an escaped and hungry gargoyle.

121

The CD is still in her bag but the thought of having it in the house disgusts her. She wants to destroy it, stop it from existing. Whoever changed her song touched the disc and cells from his body are in her house and on her hands. She takes a small screwdriver from the kitchen drawer and attacks the disc, trying to obliterate the hidden words. When the surface is scoured and ridged she bends the mutilated object in half, in half again, and then cuts it into quarters. For a moment she contemplates burying the fragments in the fields, each in a different place to stop them recombining in the night, but that would be a step too far and she throws them in the bin outside.

Her hands are stained, her body corrupted. The images in her mind flick between Perry's damaged body and the blue-green striations on the golden CD. She turns the shower temperature up as high as she can bear and stands under the jet until the water begins to run cold and she begins to feel clean.

CHAPTER EIGHT

When Jess arrives at the office next morning, Joe is already waiting by her desk. He has the look of a man who dressed too quickly and forgot to change the blade in his razor. Else catches her eye and winks as Joe checks his watch ostentatiously.

'You're with me this morning; there's a meeting at County Hall,' he says. 'We should just about make it. Don't worry about your cases—I've asked Else to cover for you.'

The air is already hot and humid as they drive to Uskmouth in Joe's car, too old and basic for air con. The faint floral smell evaporating from his jacket is familiar and Jess hopes his wife wears the same perfume as Beth, or he'll have some explaining to do.

'It's the Stiffley case. The police have requested a conference, especially since the Pearce girl went missing.' Joe's words are clipped. 'You know, Jess, you really are screwing up. Why didn't you tell me about the girl yesterday, and why, for God's sake, did you go pratting around like a bloody detective? You know the police think we're interfering and useless, and you just keep giving them ammunition.'

If they weren't in the car she'd walk away.

She can smell sweat through the perfume on his clothes.

She tells him about Bryony, the painting hidden in the cupboard and the bruises hidden under her skirt.

She tells him about Carwen, shouting one day, crying the next.

She tells him about Steffy, the best friend who wasn't.

She tells him about the body in the

123

mortuary with its dissolving flesh, the bruises on its thighs, identical to Bryony's. And as she finishes telling him, she's shouting.

'If you hadn't made me close the case in the first place Perry might still be alive, so don't fuck with me. It's not my fault!'

But this time Joe doesn't answer and they drive the rest of the way in silence, the wind from the open window drying tears of anger on Jess's face.

*   *   *

The meeting is in the same building where Jess saw Pav a few days ago, but instead of an anonymous meeting room with plastic chairs and tables, Joe takes her to the conference suite on the same level as Beth's office. The carpet in the corridor smells thick and new, and the walls are hung with black and white photographs of Uskmouth in the nineteenth century.

This feels like a trial, thinks Jess, with Joe as her warder. The police—Pelham, Ed and Pav—are ranged like a tribunal on one side of the polished wooden table, with Beth Page at the head. The director looks tired, with deep shadows circling under her eyes, and nobody smiles as they take their seats.

Pelham looks different, and then Jess realises that he's peering at her over half-moon glasses; they give him an accessible, scholarly air at odds with her memory of him at the court. He doesn't wait for Beth but starts talking as soon as everyone is seated.

'We've got a murder—Perry Stiffley, and a disappearance—Bryony Pearce. Both children had similar bruising on the legs, so we're running a combined investigation. I'll be in charge, with DS Randhawa as principal liaison between CID, the Family Support Unit represented by DC Murchison, and Social Services.'

'Thank you, John. From our side Joe will be handling this, and I'll be briefed daily,' adds Beth. 'Miss Chadwick will be moving to other duties.'

Jess had seen this set-up coming. Compulsory disengagement, and then the scapegoating. So she's surprised when Pelham butts in.

'Crap,' says Pelham. 'Unacceptable crap. Jess knows the families, the kids, the history. And best of all, we rate her, unlike some of your muppets.' He's staring at Joe.

Beth starts to speak but Pelham holds up his hand. 'Humour me on this; we don't have time for politics. If Jess screws up I'll be the first one to kick her into touch.'

Why do you want me so badly? thinks Jess. Think I'll make you look good?

After a moment's hesitation, Beth nods. 'OK, OK. For now. It's your shout.' She almost sounds relieved. 'Now tell us how the investigation's going.'

'We questioned Perry's father,' says Pav, 'but there's nothing to link him to the murder. He was in the frame to begin with for the abuse case earlier this year, but nothing came of that either. As you know, the cause of death was a pulmonary embolism brought on by a mixture of heroin and alcohol, but Perry's father has no record of any involvement with drugs.'

Pelham looks at Jess. 'You saw a lot of him during the earlier case—what's your view?'

When she first met David Stiffley, so many months ago, the days were short but bright, and the first time she went to his workshop his carvings hidden in the trees glittered with frost that never seemed to thaw. When he came out to meet her he seemed like a figure drawn with a sharp pencil rather than charcoal, defined and contained. And he had the ability to focus all his attention on whoever he was speaking to. It came from the eyes; David would look directly into hers and when he blinked it was a measured concealment.

She doesn't tell them this, keeps it simple.

'Being an outsider doesn't make you a criminal,' she says. 'What's normal, these days?'

'What about the boy?' says Pelham. 'You thought he was lying.'

'No, I thought he was hiding something,' says Jess. 'I interviewed him in the video suite with Ed but he made no disclosures of any abuse, and without that all we had was the photo. But I know that something was happening to him, I know that he was the boy in the photos. I know we let him down.'

'We don't work on supposition and instinct, Jess, but on facts.'

'Don't knock instinct,' says Pelham. 'Best computer in the world, the human mind. Isn't that so, Sergeant?' Pav looks at him as if she wishes he were close enough to kick.

'We may get a lead through Bryony's disappearance,' she says. 'We caught up with Marty McKechnie yesterday evening. Carwen Pearce's partner. He moved down from Glasgow five years ago and seems to have multiple jobs; he's a part-time attendant at the public baths in Gwenstow, a security guard at a data storage facility on the road to Uskmouth, and from time to time he helps out at a small car-repair business on the Chellacote estate.' She smiles across at Jess. 'If it's any consolation, he likes the police even less than social workers.'

'What did he say about Bryony?' says Jess.

'He was on security yesterday, working a double shift from eight in the morning to midnight. When he patrols the site he has to enter a personal code at various electronic checkpoints—they place him at work from the time Bryony was last at home until after she went missing. He's a sullen bastard, but I can't see how he's involved.'

'One thing we do know,' says Ed. 'Bryony's been lying about where she goes every evening. This isn't a simple abduction. My guess is that she's got a hiding place somewhere. She's a loner, she likes to be by herself. This time she stayed out too late and got scared, but she'll be back.'

'And the bruises?' says Pav.

'Coincidence,' says Ed. 'With all respect to Jess, she's the only one who's seen the bruises on both Bryony and Perry. And as I said to her yesterday, sometimes we imagine patterns where they don't exist.'

Maybe he's right.

*   *   *

The conference has eaten into Jess's day, and this afternoon she's meeting Gina; she feels the mixture of freedom and anticipation a child has at the start of the holidays.

She was going to drive to London, but decides to take the train from Bristol instead, rather than risk traffic hold-ups on the M4. The station seems to have been rebuilt since she last used it and looks more like an airport terminal, a shopping mall with labyrinthine parking and trains as an optional extra.

Before leaving the car Jess swaps her trainers for sandals, and hopes that Gina won't be offended by a mother with toenails varnished green to match her cargo pants. At least she chose a top long enough to hide the navel stud. Whatever a mother feels like, she feels different.

The first section Jess tries has a puddle of liquid between the seats; it doesn't smell like coffee. She moves further down the carriage and finds an empty seat opposite a woman wearing a short checked skirt that holds her legs together, a tailored jacket and the sort of shoes that Jess stopped wearing as soon as she had only herself to please. The woman's make-up has faded with the day; there's a ladder in her tights and she struggles with a sullen laptop that's reluctant to perform. She swears sharply in a clipped South African accent and looks up for a moment before her eyes defocus as she filters Jess out of perception.

At Paddington Jess realises how far she's countrified since leaving London. The Tube smells more than she remembers; of burgers, damp bodies and subterranean grime. The carriage is full and the man next to her uses his briefcase like a shield, crushing Jess against the doors.

In another life Jess knew the stations by heart but now she needs to check the map above the seats. Five stops between her and Gina. She wanted to buy a present but didn't know what her daughter would like; in the end she chose a pair of earrings in acrylic and gold, a design she would have chosen for herself.

They already feel like a link between her and the girl she knows nothing about. Clothes size, the colour of her hair, the shape of her face, the openness of her smile. Jess thinks, I made her and she's a stranger, nothing more than a dream. For sixteen years she's been whatever I want her to be and now she's about to solidify, to set. She'll never be faceless at night again.

Her left eye starts to tic as if little bubbles are erupting. She tries pressing on the corner of her eyelids and realises that her face is covered by a sheen of sweat. Where she touches the skin a drop condenses and begins to roll down until she smears it away. She's suddenly conscious of her clothes. They feel the wrong shape, touching her in all the wrong places.

Gina suggested meeting at six under the clock by the platforms, but Jess is half an hour early. The cathedral space of the mainline station is a blessing after the narrow vaults of the underground, and she finds the nearest bar. In spite of a makeover in chrome and transparent plastic it has a shameful air, like betting shops and massage parlours; a place of solitary pleasures.

She planned to ask for a Grolsch but finds that she's ordered a double Scotch which she swallows straight. Her lipstick leaves a pale red barcode on the rim of the glass and she rubs it away, painting her finger with the grease. She checks her watch but there's still twenty minutes to go.

'Can I get you another?' He's older than Jess by about ten years, with a face tanned grey by fluorescent tubes and a suit that's wilted in the humid air. Before she can reply another glass is on the counter. 'One's never quite enough,' he says. Close to, the pallor of his face is highlighted by grey stubble, and he carries a faint scent of lavender. There's a brown leather briefcase at his feet; its stitched edges are burred and curling with use and age. He holds out a hand.

'Powell. Powell Unwin. In case you're worried I'm only offering a drink, not a marriage proposal.' His hand is hot and dry and Jess is aware that her whole body feels dank and chill in the heat as if she's sweating with a fever.

The first Scotch has reached her muscles and she realises how stiffly she's been holding herself. She still has fifteen minutes before Gina arrives.

'Jess Chadwick. Thanks for the drink.'

'I don't usually stop in here but I had time to kill before my train.' Powell empties his wineglass and signals for another. 'When's yours?'

'I'm just here to meet someone.'

'And he won't be pleased to see you sharing a drink with a stranger?'

'I'm meeting my daughter.' Why did she say that?

'How old?' He hasn't stopped smiling.

'Sixteen.'

'And she's four-Scotch scary? Cheers.'

Every fragment of knowledge Jess holds about Gina is like a jewel and she doesn't want to share them with a stranger in a bar. As she sips the second whisky, Powell takes a plastic container from his jacket pocket and works a small worm of cream into the skin of his hands. More lavender.

'What about you—any kids?' says Jess.

Powell tilts his head to one side as if considering whether or not to answer, and for a fraction of a second his smile disappears. 'A wife and a daughter. Except that they live with nice Uncle Elliot in Liverpool and I . . . I don't.'

Jess's glass is empty again, but she doesn't have the energy for this man; she has her own dispossession to cope with. If she stays any longer he'll want to show her photographs of his family, dog-eared from overuse like the rest of him.

'Sorry, Powell—gotta run. Thanks for the drink.' He says nothing and Jess wonders if he's still smiling as she walks out onto the concourse. She checks her watch for the hundredth time. Five to six. Gina could be here any minute now. She may already be waiting. Jess walks quickly towards the clock by the platforms and checks each motionless person standing in the archipelago of small isolations before she takes her place amongst them.

She doesn't know what to look for; a child, a woman? They're unequal; Jess's photograph is on her website, anyone could recognise her. Why didn't she ask Gina for a description? Will I recognise her immediately, thinks Jess, or will she look as alien as the people surrounding me? And then she thinks, I'm in competition with a woman she calls Mum. She wonders how she'll compare; younger, less elegant, less together.

Less than.

She can't think of herself as a mother; giving birth isn't sufficient. She feels like a fraud for telling Powell that she was meeting her daughter, as if she doesn't really have one.

A train pulls in behind Jess but barely anyone gets off. She tastes the whisky on her breath and feels in her bag for a mint, but all she finds is a stick of gum. She can't meet Gina while she's chewing. There's a kiosk about twenty feet away but she's grown roots. This is the only place she can stand; if she moves Gina won't see her. But perhaps she already has. Perhaps she's watching Jess from a distance, deciding whether she's worth talking to in person. The thought makes her nervous and she turns around, looking over to the walls and columns in case Gina is hiding somewhere.

It's six-fifteen. Jess pulls out her mobile but it's useless; they never swapped numbers. And even if they had, what would that have felt like? She needs to see Gina when she speaks to her for the first time.

'Not here yet?'

Jess pivots to face the voice so close behind her. Powell is still smiling as if a face-lift has stretched his mouth into a permanent grin. Jess finds an urge to push him away in case Gina thinks she's someone else and not waiting for her.

'She's been held up.'

'Kids, eh? Mine is just as bad. What does she look like?' He puts his bag between his feet and starts to scan the crowd, his chin in the air.

'Please, I'd rather wait by myself.'

'Nervous is she, your daughter? Won't approach if there's a stranger talking to Mum.' He stresses the last word. 'Don't blame her. I wouldn't come near me if I had a choice.'

'It's nothing to do with her. I'd like you to go now.'

'Go where? I thought you'd appreciate the company. Kids—whenever you're not with them it's like part of you is missing. Or maybe that's just me, maybe you feel differently.' Jess has turned away, but Powell moves round in front of her again. 'Why don't you let me buy dinner for you and your invisible daughter?'

'We have other plans.' She turns her back on him again and walks towards the ticket office. It's impossible to hear if he's following but she doesn't turn around until she reaches the edge of the concourse. When she looks back he's disappeared into the crowd.

*   *   *

Although Jess is conscious of other people on the nine-twenty back to Bristol, she doesn't hear them. The only sounds come from within her; the turgid movement of blood and slow beat of her breaths. Perhaps she failed the test, was too poor a match for Gina's expectations. How did the girl feel as she watched from a distance, evaluating and judging? And then the thought occurs that maybe judgement was passed long ago and tonight was simply part of her sentence.

Jess takes the earrings from their velvet box and hides them in her fists, the shafts pressing with a muffled sharpness into her palms. She exists in time of her own, a slow grey time where her body is hollow and alone.

CHAPTER NINE

The empty police van is out of place in the lay-by on the valley road. Jess pulls in next to another couple of cars; a line of people in shirt sleeves and fluorescent jackets are moving in a funeral procession along the field bordering the river, their gaze never leaving the ground. For all the sound they make, she could be alone; just the depleted river trickling around rocks and the whispering of the long grass brushing against the legs of the searchers. A little further down where the river deepens, a frogman surfaces empty-handed.

Bryony's only been gone a day, and they're looking for a body already. Jess follows a line of trampled grass out into the meadow to get a better view down the river. A couple of hundred yards away, Pelham is talking to a TV camera. His words are blown down the valley, away from Jess, but he looks ill at ease, his hands fidgeting by his sides as if searching for something to hold. The interview ends and Pelham walks slowly towards Jess while the camera team focuses on the diver as he wades back into the water.

Pelham lights a cigarette a few yards away. He's about to flick the match into the grass but then stops, looks at Jess and puts it back in the box.

There's a shout from one of the searchers; everyone freezes except Pelham and a couple of other officers who run clumsily through the waist-high grass to a line of scrub at the edge of the meadow. Jess hesitates for a second and then follows them, trying not to stumble on the uneven ground. Caught on the barbs of a hawthorn bush is a child's pair of pale blue tracksuit bottoms, ripped and crusted with dried mud. No one touches them. Jess crouches next to Pelham.

'What do you think?'

She shakes her head. 'Too small. And look at the state of them—they must have been here for weeks, months even.' On balance, she feels relieved.

'You sure?'

'These belonged to a four- or five-year-old; Bryony's nine. People picnic here at weekends, they probably got left behind.'

The line of officers begins to move again, and Pelham walks Jess towards the lay-by.

'Thanks for your support yesterday,' says Jess.

'You worked with Ed before, and Pav already seems to rate you.'

'I hardly know her.'

'You will, you will.'

Pelham leans against his car, lights another cigarette and takes the foil from the packet, creasing it into a series of folds.

'We had a press conference first thing. The usual crap from the press—we haven't mentioned the bruises yet. Beth did a good job of stalling, but they'll get your name before long, they always do. If a reporter catches up with you, just keep your mouth shut—even one word and they'll turn it against you.' He concentrates on the piece of paper in his hands. 'We started a house-to-house on the Chellacote estate yesterday, but nothing so far.

137

Not surprising.'

'You think she's hiding somewhere,' says Jess. 'You agree with Ed.'

'Sadly, no. Whoever murdered Perry Stiffley has taken Bryony. If we don't find her alive in the next twelve to eighteen hours, we won't find her alive at all.' He throws the piece of folded paper to the ground and looks up. 'You like Japanese food?'

'What?'

'Sashimi? Sushi? How about kabayaki—grilled eel?'

'What's this got to do with Bryony?'

Pelham half smiles and shrugs. 'Nothing—just wondered.' As he rejoins the line of police disappearing around the curve of the river, Jess reaches down into the grass at her feet and picks up the paper that Pelham had thrown away. Lying in the palm of her hand, the folds sharp as a knife, is a small but perfect model of a bearded man in a cloak, kneeling in prayer.

*　　　*　　　*

A Harrier jet from the nearby RAF base buzzes the treetops lining the road as Jess rolls the Jeep round the bends that follow the line of the river. At least my daughter's safe, she thinks. Gina may not want to see me, but that's OK.

She cuts off before Gwenstow and takes the

back road to Bryony's school. Melanie Happs is on playground duty but hands over to one of the other teachers and takes Jess through to the classroom.

'I knew this would happen.' Mel pulls Bryony's picture from the cupboard. 'And I don't know why you want to see this, now she's gone. All the time I sit here I can feel it behind me—I was going to tear it up.'

'Best not,' says Jess. 'The police will probably want to see it.'

'What, for identification?' They both smile at the poor joke. 'And what good is it going to do—only upset her mother if she knows.'

Jess opens the roll of paper; the lingering smell of the paint reminds her of childhood. She wonders why she's here. A phone call to Mel would have been enough, would have been easier. Maybe, she thinks, I need this connection with Bryony, to touch what she's touched. To feel what she felt.

The classroom door bursts open suddenly and a shirt-tail boy runs in, chased by another. Jess presses the painting to her chest until Mel has shooed the children away, then unfurls it again. It takes her a moment to register why it looks different and then she realises that the figure of Bryony has been scribbled over. No, more. Scratched out so violently with something sharp that the surface of the paper has flaked away.

She shows it to the teacher.

'It wasn't like this before.'

Mel checks the picture for herself. 'Little cow—she must have done it after your visit—I don't always keep the cupboard locked. I haven't thought to look at it since.'

She furls the picture into a roll, touching the paper with her fingertips like a librarian forced to handle some rare erotica.

'That girl's never run off of her own accord. Whoever gave her those bruises on her legs, whatever happened that made her paint that picture, that's where she is now. Better pray your friends find her soon.'

*   *   *

When she gets back that night the farmhouse has never seemed so welcoming. All day the thought of Gina has been infiltrating Jess's mind. All day she fantasised, scene after scene, the reasons why Gina didn't turn up at the station yesterday. Now she ignores Wagner batting her legs and checks her inbox for messages. Only one, and that's from Spider.

'hi chad, had a few problems with my website but i'll have it up soon—. not sure about moving to london now—don't think I'm ready. it'll please my mum—she likes me close—i guess all mothers feel like that. i want to know you get these messages—i share my life with you and get nothing back. perhaps you junk what I write. i

140

can be sending this to a black hole. if you want me to piss off just say so.'

What is it with me? she thinks. I didn't ask him to write but he blames me even when I do nothing.

He could be anywhere but Jess pictures him living in a bedsit in Bristol, cheap sheets and partition walls. Or he could be here, in the house, reduced and immobilised on one of the hundreds—no, thousands—of photographs she's taken on her safaris to the streets.

The thought reminds her of the prints from last week's expedition, still unexamined. Tonight can be for reflection, looking through the images for another song, another catharsis. She likes this part almost as much as the hunt; in another time, she thinks, I would have pinned butterflies to a board. She finds the photos and begins to classify; men, women, young, old. Groups and solitary figures, the happy and the angry. She writes a number on the back of each image, adds it to her lists and cross references. For the first time in days she lets herself relax, lost in her small bureaucracy, and it takes a few moments before she registers the sound of someone banging on the front door.

She feels annoyed at the interruption; apart from the postman no one ever comes up to the house—few people even know it exists. The only person she can think of is Ed but when

141

she opens the door it's Pav who hands her a bottle of wine.

'I was driving back from a late meeting and realised I was so near it would be impolite not to say hello. And I wanted to see your house for myself—Ed was knocked out by it.'

No beamer today. The low-slung Mercedes convertible looks fragile and exotic next to the dust-filmed Jeep. As Pav arranges herself at the kitchen table Jess feels invaded and pleased at the same time. Her visitor's lipstick is fresh, like the enticement of her perfume; almost an invitation.

The wine is well chilled and Jess wonders where Pav bought it. The off-licences nearby don't run to this quality; maybe the Merc has its own fridge.

Why is she here?

'I listened to Hacksaw's first album. Pelham lent it to me. It was good.'

'But not your style.'

Pav laughs. 'Right—but I know quality when I hear it. What made you throw it all up and become a social worker?'

'Rule number one—never talk about the old days. I am what I am, everything else just gets in the way.'

'You're too hard on yourself. We are what we've done, Jess. Maybe that's what people see in you, hidden depths.'

'Hidden depths my arse! I'm just a tired social worker who used to be someone else.'

The wine is relaxing her already. 'If we're talking about hidden depths, what about you?'

Pav's eyes seem darker than ever. 'What do you want to know?'

'You and Pelham, you're an item, right?'

Pav laughs again. 'He's not my style. Anyway, I know him too well. He's clever, but a bit too keen on the claret. And keen on you.'

'He hardly knows me.'

'He likes sassy women—you should have met his wife.'

'Is she still around?'

'She works for the Beeb—left John a couple of years ago. Working for CID is guaranteed to break up your relationship.'

'Is that why you got out?'

Pav waits a beat before replying. 'That sounds like code for—"Do you have a partner?".'

The bottle is empty, but Jess finds another at the back of the fridge.

'Sorry, this isn't up to your standard. And sorry, I didn't mean to pry.'

'Of course you did,' says Pav, 'and it's OK.' She pauses for a moment. 'We share an apartment next to the docks in Bristol. Her name's Annie—we've been together six years now.' She's watching Jess with a practised eye, as if looking for any small movements of rejection. 'It doesn't matter how liberal people are, they always treat you differently once they know. I'm not criticising, just observing.'

Jess feels the way she does on the streets with her camera, and hopes Pav hasn't noticed. 'People want to know if they're in the running or not. Anyway, I think you're lucky to have someone.'

'And you don't?'

They're both drinking quickly now.

'I've got my cat and my music—what else do I need?'

'Come on, Jess—you're not *that* tough. What about someone to tell your troubles to, someone to hold when you feel lonely? Someone to love?'

'Aah—love! You've got me there—how do you spell it?'

But she can't hold the smile.

'Sounds like someone got badly burnt,' says Pav.

'How do you know I didn't do the burning?' says Jess.

Pav waits for a few moments before replying, as if weighing the impact of her words. 'Because I'd say—or rather, the bottle of wine I've just drunk says—that somewhere inside you're a very different person from the one you show to the world. Someone fragile.'

'Whoa! I thought you were a policewoman, not a psychologist.'

'I'm still human.'

Jess pours more wine like a punctuation.

'Enough about me; tell me about Annie.'

'OK, I'll let you off for now. But I'll be back

. . .'

'Annie!'

'She's a consultant, works for one of the big accountancy firms. Earns more in a month than I do in a year. And from what she says, meets more crooks than I do.'

'What do the guys at the station think?'

'I don't talk about my private life, and they don't ask. I guess most of them know, but I don't fit their stereotype so I get away with it.'

'And Pelham?'

'He met Annie a few times. Made a pass at her once, the bastard, even when I was there. He has no shame, that man.'

'But you like him.'

Pav fingers the scar on her cheek. 'He's been there when I've needed him.' She checks her watch. 'It's later than I thought—I've got to get back.'

*   *   *

Jess goes upstairs, back to the photos, but the mood is broken and they've lost their potency.

She trembles again, more of a shiver now, wipes a bead of sweat from her forehead and goes back to the kitchen for a glass of water. She's about to clear the table and straighten the chairs, but stops herself and sits where Pav had been, wondering what the other woman saw as they faced each other earlier.

There's a mouthful of wine left in the glass

and Jess matches the marks on the rim to her own lips before sipping the dregs, slowly, reluctant to let the evening end.

CHAPTER TEN

The security light outside wakes Jess, and for a moment she's back in London, a street lamp illuminating the room. Nearly 3 a.m. The bed feels too cold and the sheets are soaked, her whole body damp with sweat.

She shuffles her body across to a drier patch and tries to reconnect with her dream, in consciousness no more than a memory of shapes, welcoming and warm.

*　　　*　　　*

For the first time in years she oversleeps. She calls the office but no one answers. Stupid— it's Saturday. She sinks back into the lethargy of her fever with relief. She tries to sleep again but fails, and lies in the damp bed listening to the scurrying sounds of small creatures in the roof space.

Staying in bed was a mistake. She hasn't heard a car but someone at the door is knocking the way police do, hard and loud, imperative. She knows what he is the moment she opens the door, with his quick eyes that look past her in a second, scanning the room behind. She hears invisible shutters click.

He flashes a card with his newspaper's name, a national tabloid.

'Wondered if I could ask a few questions about Bryony Pearce and Perry Stiffley.' It's not a question and he moves forward as he speaks, forcing Jess away from the door. He bounces as he walks, his head bobbing and turning from side to side like an overfed bird, and Jess can see down onto the beginning of a bald spot. The two wineglasses from last night are still on the table, one rimmed with lipstick.

'Haven't disturbed anything, have I? Was it a party last night?'

She'd forgotten the press conference yesterday; Beth and Pelham showing solidarity in the face of failure. The little man is looking her up and down as if she were for sale in a market, and she's conscious of her appearance; she feels undefined, as if her features have melted and blurred in the night.

How did he get her name?

'Come to think of it, you do look a bit peaky—must have been a shock when poor little Bryony went missing. Specially so soon after Perry's murder.' He pulls out a chair and takes her arm as she lowers herself like an old woman. She doesn't have the strength to pull away.

'I'll get you some water—don't worry, I'll find the glasses.'

He rinses the wineglasses and uses those, giving Jess the one Pav used with its red rim. She doesn't want to drink and they sit looking at each other while he sips slowly.

'You feeling better now, love?'

A headache has started suddenly, her balance changing even while she sits at the table and she barely makes it to the bathroom before vomiting a thin bile over the tiled floor, leaving the door open behind her.

Back downstairs, the reporter's looking at the single framed photo on the dresser.

'This you? Very nice—bet it was a few years ago though, no offence. I was in a band too— did all the local pubs. What about you—what sort of music do they like round here?'

Jess hasn't said a word since he's been in the house. She wants the invader to leave. She wants him not to have come at all.

He puts the photo down.

'So what about Perry? You were his social worker? My editor thinks he was let down by you people, thinks there's a story here. I'm not sure. Why don't you tell me what happened?' He's sitting back at the table, unthreatening, looking up with practised concern.

'People jump to conclusions. Your boss said there would be an internal enquiry. We all know what that means, Jess. Someone's going to be hung out to dry.'

Her head is pounding so hard he must be able to see it move. So hard that Jess steadies herself as the giddiness comes back like a whirlpool reaching down into her guts.

'I hear that his father was suspected of abusing him but you closed the case. I can't believe that. Not someone like you. Why did you do it, Jess? Orders? I've got to write something—help me here.'

He's scribbling in a notebook though she hasn't said a word. Even if she could, she wouldn't trust herself to speak. A draught blows down from the open front door, bringing the scent of roses from another world. If she goes outside perhaps he'll follow; she wants him out of her house.

At first he stays put, calling after her, but at last he comes out into the sun where she's sitting on the grass, propped against a low stone wall. He squats next to her, his suit bunching into new shapes around him, angles and shadows.

'Just tell me about Perry and I'll leave you alone. Your side of the story. Gotta stick up for yourself, Jess. You're lucky I found you first. Just talk to me and I'll keep the others away. No one wants second-hand news.'

Shutting her eyes helps. She can hear the sound of his voice but the words run into each other like buzzing insects.

She's alone when she wakes, slumped against the wall and cold now the sun has moved round. Her T-shirt feels damp and her left foot curls with sudden cramp. The fever has died away during her sleep and her head feels light but clear. There's nothing parked next to the Jeep, and all she can hear, apart from birdsong, is the sound of a pheasant barking from the next field. She checks the house to make sure he's really gone but there's no sign of any visitor, just two wineglasses empty on the table.

She picks up the photo of the band, wipes it with her sleeve and slips it into a drawer, then makes coffee and takes it back outside.

Gina. Sixteen years; nothing, and a lifetime. She rarely thinks of the time when she was pregnant. But that's OK; deal with it when you can, lock the memories away until then.

She's not sure that she's ready.

A buzzard is calling, a lonely sound that should be heard on a moor or fell, on an empty mountain.

The child was always small inside Jess, as if ashamed to show her presence. When she moved it was tentative; a slow turn, a flicker. She never told Jamie. When the child was born Jess didn't even hold her; told them to take her away. Her only memory is a glimpse of the creature in a nurse's arms, her body wrapped in shapeless white and a red face with too much skin and a thin cry that still seemed part of Jess's own self.

I never named my daughter, she thinks. I denied her before she was made.

A crow lands in the lower field, jabbing

down at a small corpse, one of Wagner's leavings. They like battlefields, she remembers, moving in after the slaughter, harvesting the eyes first.

She wonders if there's any news about Bryony and remembers the painting in the classroom, hidden from sight like an admission of guilt. She can't stay here any longer and dresses quickly, suddenly full of energy, then leaves the house, cutting across the top field to the track heading away from the valley, up towards the Dyke. Underfoot the smooth peaks of rocks are still half covered with mould from last autumn, and the one before that. The track has sunken over the generations and she walks through a roofless tunnel, banks of earth and roots and fragments of stone, striated with moss and ferns that never die. Around a corner a group of wild deer are browsing, pale spots showing through the grey-brown coats. They don't hear her at first and then they all freeze together, watching for a beat before they run up the track, some of them scrabbling to climb the banks which are almost too steep.

The ridge of the Dyke is ahead, no more than a dark block against the brightness of the sky. The track begins to flatten out and the banks shrink, as if in preparation for a last spurt to reach the top.

Jess had forgotten the shrine. Another corner, another frightened animal. Jess can't tell her age; maybe fourteen, maybe eighteen. Gaunt, a small face with sunken cheeks. Her waist-length hair is thick, uncombed bunches interspersed with thin plaits and ribbons, and her skirt looks like a collection of rags randomly sewn together, dull blues and reds, the hem skimming heavy boots crusted with mud.

The girl stands by the shrine, holding a posy of flowering grass with a single large feather, brown and white diagonal stripes against the golden stalks. She stares at Jess for a second, her face unreadable, then she bobs quickly to place the offering and runs off down the track, holding her skirt up from the mud.

There should be petticoats.

Jess has never seen her before, but guesses that she comes from the commune behind the ridge. They don't work the land or keep animals, just a few small plots of vegetables and some horses grazing. For the summer solstice one of their fields was filled with small tents and camper vans, and in the middle a tepee that was visible from the village a couple of miles away. For all of the signs of occupation she rarely saw any people, and one day they were gone and the horses were back.

She searches around for an offering of her own, although she doesn't know to whom. She doesn't even know what is acceptable; maybe there are rules and prohibitions, heresies. She snaps a spike from one of the stands of wild foxgloves that surround the shrine and wraps three of the bells in a small fern leaf, purple and green, tied with a long stalk of grass. When she's satisfied with her gift she props it below the girl's posy, next to a straw doll that's been there since she first found this place, and walks slowly back down the track towards the house.

*   *   *

She still can't settle, her mind racing as if she's dropped some speed. Maybe she could earth some of the energy by joining one of the lines of people moving across the fields as they search for a sign of the missing girl, but she knows that's not her job, just her need. As a compromise she calls Ed to find out what's happening.

'We had a strategy discussion this morning,' he says. 'Joe said not to bother you on a Saturday. There were concerns about Rhiannon, Bryony's sister, but we decided to leave her with her mother, for now.' He's speaking quickly, to stop Jess from interrupting. 'As Beth said, we don't work on hunches. Sorry.'

She doesn't have the strength to argue. 'What about Bryony—any news?'

'Nothing so far. There are three Schedule One offenders on the Chellacote estate but none of their patterns fit this, just the usual

153

family stuff. And they've all got alibis for Monday night.'

*   *   *

She almost wishes that it were a weekday so that she could escape to the office, but instead she drives into Abertrothy. Denny's hunched over the guts of a computer, swearing softly as she enters the workshop.

'Hold on, Jess—nearly done.' He hasn't looked up from the metal skeleton on the bench.

'I could have come to steal all your stock. How did you know it was me?'

'I don't know. I just did. Must be your aura.' Something small falls to the floor and he swears again. His stubble looks patchy, as if he's tried to shave in the dark with a blunt penknife. 'I didn't expect to see you today. You haven't finished another song already?'

'You *are* joking. I was in town and I thought I'd see how you were.' Now that the fever has gone she's hungry for company. Even Denny. She recognises the look he gives her sometimes, a blend of awe and desire, and she half smiles as she looks at the boy hunched over the machine. No, she thinks, you wouldn't know what to do with me.

Denny straightens up. 'I haven't checked the website this morning—we can do it now if you like.' He leads her over to a large monitor

154

on a table at the back of the workshop. The last time she was here, Denny was checking out the CD from her car; she's almost forgotten that.

She expects to see the familiar first page of her site, but the screen is covered with names and dates.

'This is a record of activity—it shows any changes to files so I can see if someone's been messing around. Should be OK though, no one can get through the new firewall.' A few more clicks and he stiffens.

'Shit—look. There's been a change on another file, last night.'

'What is it?'

'Someone's altered one of the links.' He touch types so quickly that one screen barely appears before it's replaced by another. And then the procession stops and the picture fills the monitor, one Jess hasn't seen before. But she recognises the subject immediately, a photo of Bryony's painting, the one from the classroom.

'Doesn't look like one of yours,' says Den. And then, 'There's more—an audio file.'

From the computer speakers comes the sound of a young girl's voice; she falters over some of the words, but there's no doubt as Jess hears her trying to sing the warped words to 'Suffer'.

Denny turns it off. 'Fuck's sake—you know who that is?'

Jess feels faint, as if all her blood had drained away through her feet.

'It's that girl, isn't it?' says Denny. 'The one that's missing.'

Jess nods, not trusting herself to talk for a moment. Now there's no mistake. Someone knows her, knows where she works. Knows about Bryony.

She watches Denny's hands race across the keyboard. 'I've deleted it from the website and from my server and I checked; no one accessed it since yesterday, thank God.' Denny takes a CD from the drive. 'I thought I'd better copy it onto this . . . but do we have to tell the police? I could be done for having child porn.'

'Sorry, Den—I have to make the call.'

'If you must.' He pauses. 'Shit—it's on last night's backup. I'll have to wipe that as well.'

Jess has never seen him panic before. He's always so laconic, always nearly stoned. She watches as he does what he has to, exorcising his machines.

'I think someone doesn't like you,' he says when he's finished.

*　　　*　　　*

Jess waits at the back of the workshop until Ed arrives half an hour later. Denny locks the front door behind him and pulls down the blind.

'This picture and the song—they're nothing

to do with me, right? I don't want to be done for pornography or something.'

'Just show me.' Ed sounds tired and looks diminished in his Saturday clothes, ill at ease in a pressed polo shirt and chinos. His eyes are hidden behind the reflection of fluorescent tubes in his glasses.

This time it isn't so bad; Jess knows what to expect. Ed shows no reaction, as if he's listening to a nursery rhyme.

'Are you sure this is Bryony's voice?'

'Who else is it going to be? For God's sake—some bastard's made her sing this . . . this sick crap!'

'And the picture?'

'Bryony painted it at school—her teacher was keeping it.' Jess checks the image again. 'This photo was taken after I saw it the first time, the day we got the referral in from her teacher about the bruises. See how that figure's been scratched out? That was done after my first visit.'

Without asking, Ed ejects the CD from the computer. 'I need this. And I'll need to impound all the computers here until they've been checked out.'

Den looks as though he's about to collapse.

'Jesus, man, you can't do that! This is my business. Most of these machines aren't even mine, they're in for servicing.'

'This is nothing to do with Denny,' says Jess. 'Whoever did this was getting at me. Come on, give him a break.'

Ed walks up and down the workshop for a couple of minutes.

'OK, for now. Just as a favour to Jess. But make damned sure there are no other copies of this file on any of your machines. I mean it.' She's never heard Ed swear before, even so innocuously.

'What will you do now?' asks Jess

'Have our people look at this.'

'What about Carwen?' says Jess.

'She doesn't need to hear the song, if you can call it that.' He looks at Jess as if she's to blame.

'At least Bryony's still alive.'

'Unless she recorded it on one of her mysterious evening outings.'

When Ed leaves the hum of computers is the only sound for a while, until Denny breaks the silence.

'I've got a backup of your website, I'll put it up on a different server.'

'No, I want you to shut it down for now.'

But she knows it's useless; whoever photographed Bryony's painting and recorded her voice is the same person that changed her song and broke into her car.

And whoever it is will find her again. Today has been a hallucination, a bad trip, and she wonders if there's any way down.

CHAPTER ELEVEN

News travels fast. Pelham calls on her mobile as she walks back to the car, wanting to talk about the picture of Bryony. He offers to come up to the house but Jess has had enough invasions for one day and they settle for a pub in Abertrothy, large enough to be anonymous, and better than a room in the police station.

Neutral territory.

She expected a note-taker—Ed or Pav—but Pelham's alone, filling a corner table and peering down at a newspaper through his half-moons. The bottle of red on the table is already almost empty. He's made no concession to the weekend, his suit the only one in the half-empty bar; Jess wonders how much sleep he's had since Perry was found on the Dyke.

'Looks like you need this.' He fills a glass and pushes it towards her, but at the first sip she breaks into a sweat as if the wine has woken the dormant fever. 'We saw Carwen Pearce this afternoon, told her as much as she needed to know, but she still wanted to see the picture.'

'And?'

'At first she didn't react at all. Then she locked herself in the bathroom; she was still crying when I left—a female officer stayed with her.'

'What about her partner, Marty?'

'The arsehole with the tattoo? He's down at the station for questioning. We took his computer and a digital camera, but I don't think we'll find much else.'

'From what Den said, whoever's been messing with the website is an expert. I wouldn't have thought Marty was that good.'

'Come on, Jess! A seven-year-old can get pictures onto a PC.'

He knows even less about computers than she does. Jess tells him about the other changes to her site; the pornographic lyrics, the CD in her car.

'How long have you known Denny?' he asks.

'Six months, maybe seven. Just after I moved down from London.'

'See him socially?'

'He just helps with the website, and he set up my studio at home. I don't see him often, usually phone or email.'

'What about relationships? Denny, that is.'

'He's only interested in computers,' she says. 'He wouldn't know what to do with a real woman.'

'So he's into—what? Internet porn?'

'How would I know? It's just that I've never seen him with anyone. And for the record, until today he didn't know I had any connection to either of the children.'

Pelham leans forward to pour her another

glass and she catches the sharp smell of aftershave, although his face hasn't seen a razor for hours.

In spite of the location and the easiness of the wine, this feels to Jess like an interrogation. The bar has filled and they're leaning across the table to hear each other.

'Not exactly squeaky clean, your Denny,' says Pelham. 'Not his real name, by the way. He was implicated in a bank fraud a couple of years ago, using computers to make dodgy transfers. Don't ask me the details. But the bank didn't press charges—they never do. He changed his name, moved away from the Smoke and set up down here. Funny old life.'

All the time he's been talking, Pelham's been folding an old petrol receipt into the squared-off shape of a husky dog which he balances on its tiny legs next to his empty wineglass.

'This place is pissing me off. Let's walk.' He's halfway to the door before Jess is out of her seat.

They make their way down to the path by the river that runs through concrete banks ten feet or more below the level of the road. The water is tinged with red from the evening sky and lies motionless as they walk beside it.

'If we cut out computer boy,' says Pelham, 'who else could be involved? Ex-boyfriend of yours? Dodgy clients?'

Jess shrugs. 'There's no ex-boyfriend, and I

161

get bollocked by clients all the time. It goes with the job.'

'Maybe. All the same, we need a list of all your cases since you moved here. I'll clear it with your boss—Parvati will be in on Monday for the details, first thing.'

The riverside path disappears into playing fields and they climb a flight of concrete steps back to the road.

'I was going to find somewhere to eat,' says Pelham. 'Join me?'

The wine has left her hungry, but she can't face another room full of people and tells him, sorry, no, another time, maybe.

*   *   *

The post must have come late today. The handwriting on the yellow envelope is unfamiliar, written with the precision of a child, but it's not Jess's birthday and Christmas is three months away. The surface of the envelope is greasy, as if it had been handled by someone eating buttered toast, and the postmark is a smear of dark ink.

The card inside looks homemade, the edges not quite square, the picture a snapshot, digitised and printed.

The teenage girl is standing in sunlight, posed, half turned away from the camera. She looks model-thin, in a short denim skirt and white crop top. Her long blonde hair flows in

162

folds over her bare shoulders, and maybe it's the way the shadows fall but her cheeks look sunken, accentuating the planes under her eyes. She's halfway between a smile and a laugh, and Jess wonders who held the camera, told the joke.

Jess studies the face for resemblances, the body for familiar shapes, but she knows who the sender is even before she reads the careful words on the back of the card.

'Sorry about Wednesday. Something came up, too difficult to explain.
I'll be in touch soon, promise.
Love
Gina'

It's turned to summer again as Jess holds the card that her daughter sent.

Gina wrote this, Gina touched this.

She studies the picture again as if it hides another image, and then at the words as if they're in a code that she can't decipher. I'm analysing my daughter, she thinks. I'm reducing her into parts, to make this bearable.

She lifts the card to her face and breathes in, imagining that she catches a relic of her daughter's perfume. For the past three days she's wondered why Gina never turned up, wondered if there would even be another contact, and now this . . . this gift. She forces herself to breathe deeply, works the muscles in her shoulder and wishes she knew how to let go, the girl looks so young and beautiful.

*   *   *

Jess expects the office to be deserted when she arrives on Sunday lunchtime but Beth is sitting at her desk, working through a pile of folders.

'The police want a list of your cases and I didn't want to bother you on Sunday. But now you're here . . .'

They sit in silence, reading and summarising other people's lives. Some of the cases are so familiar that Jess could write the notes without the files. Others were dealt with so quickly that she can barely picture the families, the children's faces merging into one all-purpose archetype. In spite of this she's slower than Beth, wondering if she's writing down the name of a killer or a kidnapper.

Somehow it feels comforting that Gina is watching from the card, propped by her phone.

After a couple of hours Beth makes them both a coffee.

'John Pelham told me about the picture of Bryony, and I thought what a shock it must have been. With everything that's going on I wondered if you need some time off. A break, away from the office.'

Here we go again, thinks Jess. I knew you'd find some excuse to get rid of me. But before she can say anything Beth continues.

'Do you remember the Liddells? The son was autistic, parents couldn't cope any more.'

'Wasn't the son called Thomas? We found him a place in a residential unit.'

'Bledworth Hall, the other side of Bury St Edmunds. I don't like out-of-county placements but it was the only unit with a vacancy. There's a review fixed for tomorrow. I know you've got a load on your plate, but a few hours away from this place won't hurt. Go up tomorrow morning and stay over, come back here for Tuesday afternoon. Not much of a break, I know, but . . .'

Not so much a rejection as a reprieve; Wagner can cope without her for one night. But for now Jess carries on summarising lives, looking for the clues to a missing nine-year-old girl and a murdered boy.

*   *   *

Jess knows that Pav is waiting even before she enters the office; the heavy scent hangs in the air like an invisible thread. She pauses before going through the main doors and wishes she carried a mirror in her bag.

Pav is talking to Else, but turns and smiles as she hears Jess approach.

'I heard you were ill on Saturday—hope it wasn't the wine. You should be used to it—all that sex and drugs and rock 'n' roll.'

'I'm reformed.' Jess hands Pav the case summaries. 'How did it go with Marty? Pelham said he was being interviewed on Saturday.'

'Nothing so far. I saw him with Ed, but apart from some inventive descriptions of my mother he couldn't tell us anything. We can't arrest someone for being a bastard, unfortunately. I don't think he had anything to do with Bryony's disappearance, not that he seems to care much about her.'

'Didn't you take his computer—and a camera?'

'There was nothing obvious—the lab will do a detailed investigation when they get in today, see whether he's tried to delete some files, but I don't hold out any hope.'

Pav's almost out of the far door when she turns and walks quickly back.

'I forgot. Annie was given some invites to a private view at a gallery in Bristol on Wednesday evening. One of her corporate beanos.' She pauses for a second. 'We wondered if you'd like to join us? Meet Annie and then go on for dinner afterwards. I don't know about you, but I'm going to need some light relief by then.'

What does this woman want with me, thinks Jess. What can I possibly offer? But what else would I do—play guitar, try to write a song, watch TV, go hunting. Put another brick in the wall. Wither a little more.

'I'd be delighted,' she says.

The drive to Bledworth Hall takes nearly four hours and Jess gets there with minutes to spare before the meeting starts. Even the light seems flatter here, on the other side of England. She realises how quickly she's become accustomed to hills and valleys, a region of turnings and hidden places.

The Hall is a large Victorian house set in its own grounds. Built of dark red brick with pointed gables and thin windows, the whole building seems to have been stretched vertically like a tall ascetic monk; Narziss in a garden. On either side of the half-mile drive are stands of dark evergreens and isolated oaks.

The woman who comes out as Jess pulls up in front of the main door looks as though she should be in a farmhouse kitchen with flour up to her elbows. She introduces herself as the manager of Bledworth and leads Jess through the house to the meeting in what must once have been a morning room at the back of the house, with large French windows leading onto a stone patio. There are two children on the grass further out, a boy and girl, with two adults standing nearby. Although they are near each other the children seem separate, the boy lining up objects on the ground, stones and twigs; the girl standing quite still, seeming to listen with her head cocked to one side.

Tom's parents both stand as Jess is introduced. The father is a small round man made out of circles and spheres. What's left of his hair encircles his head like a fine black diadem and his eyes are like dark pennies, barely blinking. His wife has something of the Celt about her; pale skin and fair hair of no certain colour, bobbed neatly to offset the length of her face. They smile at Jess in unison, uncertainly, as if she's about to withdraw their privileges and send them home with the son who lives to his own tempo.

Next to the mother is a man who seems almost familiar, like hearing a phrase from Bach through a rapper's beat. He's Jess's age or maybe younger, none of his features sharp enough to register; a man who stands by walls at parties. The manager introduces him as Anton, Tom's teacher; his hello is tinged with an accent she can't quite place.

Today she's the observer, listening to reports of progress, watching the parents as they listen to strangers telling them about their son's life. They seem relieved that his disruptions fall within the boundaries of what constitutes normality here. Jess sees it in their eyes; the knowledge that they can leave soon, just the two of them, justifying their abandonment to each other on the long drive home.

She listens to the reports of the staff; the

carer describing Tom's small triumphs of control, the nurse confirming his state of health. Anton surprises the parents by describing Tom's musical ability, how he sits for hours at a piano, picking out remembered melodies, constructing chords even though he's never touched an instrument before.

'Tom communicates in different ways from you or me. It's as if he's found his own language in music and numbers. And he loves arithmetic lessons. He plays with figures the way he plays with notes on the piano, looking at how to combine them to create harmonies. He's really very talented.'

Jess watches the parents as they listen to Anton's enthusiasm. No one's said that about their son before, and they blush with pride.

The meeting breaks up just before five. Jess can be home in four hours, and she regrets booking the room a few miles down the road. Standing on the steps outside the front door she's about to phone and cancel when Anton joins her and lights a cigarette. He offers her the pack.

'No thanks—I'm reformed.'

He slips the pack into the top pocket of his shirt.

'Are you going back tonight?'

'I was going to stay over—I booked a room in a B&B just outside Bury.'

'Was?'

'I think I'll go home after all. My cat will

appreciate the gesture.'

'Perhaps he's got something else planned, invited a few friends round to do a bit of cream and catnip. You could be cramping his style.'

He holds the cigarette as though he's never smoked before, as something delicate and precious that could be damaged by rough handling. There are braided strands of dark leather around his neck and wrist, and when he flicks back his dark hair Jess can see that he's wearing a gold stud with a deep blue stone.

'There's a new Thai restaurant opened in Bury, supposed to be good. I know that sounds incongruous, but I've been meaning to try it; maybe we could check it out together. Compare and contrast a selection of dishes, that sort of thing?' Before Jess can say anything he continues. 'The rush hour round Birmingham can be appalling. You could be stuck in a jam for hours if you leave now.'

And it's so easy to say yes.

*   *   *

Jess is the only guest in the B&B and takes her time in the shower, clouds of steam hiding every detail in the small room. She has two hours before Anton will pick her up. Back in her bedroom she turns off the mobile and feels safe; hidden and unreachable. She feels tired.

The light by the mirror is stronger than at

home and she studies her face. It's like looking at a stranger. She's lost weight; her eyes appear sunken and bruised, her face is pale and there are the beginnings of lines running down from the corners of her mouth like the droop of a sad clown. She rarely bothers with make-up but tonight she takes the time, hiding the shadows, smoothing away the troughs. She'd forgotten how comforting a mask can be.

Anton turns up in a car that looks as though it's driven off the set of a 1950s film; dark green body with an open top, and ribbed leather seats burnished to an indiscriminate colour between red and black.

'If you were about to be impressed, don't. Noisy, dirty, uncomfortable, and not ecologically sound. Say hello to my girl, Maisie.'

He doesn't drive fast along the lanes but still needs to shout above the throb of the engine. 'She was my grandfather's—I think Maisie was his first girlfriend. When I was a kid my treat was to sit behind the wheel and pretend to drive. Car was in the garage, of course.'

'When did you get it?'

'He left her to me in his will—my other car's a bicycle.'

Jess so wants to be impressed. She wants to appreciate the boy's performance, to take part in his show, but even as the wind flicks at her hair she can't help but feel his difference, and it doesn't take much to know which of them is the outsider.

*   *   *

The restaurant hides in a side street that curves as if to follow the contours of some long buried structure of the town. The low buildings lean against each other for support, with the dark exposed beams of their skeletons set at odd angles into the walls of pastel pinks and yellows. Inside it could be any new restaurant in London; chrome and pale wood, acid-etched green glass tables. The place is already half full, and everyone seems the same age as them, mostly couples leaning towards each other and smiling, cradling their drinks.

Jess feels more comfortable than she expected but wants Anton to talk first; she'll feel safer when he's categorised.

'My father was Austrian,' he says. 'Came over in the sixties to make his fortune as a photographer. All very David Bailey.'

'Did he—make his fortune?'

'He did OK. Got himself onto the circuit; parties with the Stones, claimed to have slept with Marianne Faithfull. If he did he was probably too blasted to do anything. He met my mum in a club, a disco. She used to be a dancer in a cage hanging from the ceiling.' He laughs, as if at a memory. 'There's a photo of her somewhere; I can see why he fancied her.'

'Do you still see them?'

He shrugs. 'My mum's living in Manchester with some guy I've never met. My dad went back to Vienna for a while but couldn't hack it. The last I heard he was in Manila, trying to run a hotel, though knowing him it's probably a brothel.'

He finishes his beer.

'He did a lot of acid in the sixties and seventies, lost it completely over the past few years. I'm surprised mum stayed as long as she did.'

He tells it like a well-rehearsed story, but his eyes are focused outside the room.

'You sound as though you miss them both.'

'Dad brought me up to believe that we should respect the choices people make about their lives. He didn't believe in predestination; he was more of a "God is dead" man, and all that German shit. Maybe he didn't live up to his own standards.'

Jess wonders whether Anton would respect her choice, giving her daughter away before she had any say in the matter, but she doesn't want to find out yet.

'What about you?' he asks. 'Why social work—it must be the most masochistic profession around?'

'If I knew the answer to that I'd leave and get a proper job.' She's already decided not to talk about Gina, or the music, or her cases. She doesn't want a therapist.

Anton's younger than she thought, or perhaps she just feels old tonight. She's never been good at the dating game, never needed to be, and it's as if she's forgotten the rules.

'You'll probably hit me for this, but you remind me of the kids at the school,' he says.

'Now that is the most original chat-up line I've ever heard.'

'They always seem to know more than the rest of us, like they can see into another world and they get frustrated at how limited we are.'

'And I remind you of them?'

'Maybe not the frustration. But I get the feeling I'm only seeing part of you, like an iceberg.'

'So first I'm autistic, now I'm an iceberg. How long's it been since you had a girlfriend?'

His eyes are sparkling with embarrassment.

'Seven months.'

'And what did you compare her with? A monkey? Dead twigs? Bacteria?'

'Probably all of them. I give in, Jess. I was trying to say that you have an air of mystery that I find very attractive.'

'See, that wasn't so difficult.'

'Maybe not from where you're sitting.'

'It did sound a bit pompous, though,' she says.

'I don't know why, but I feel like I'm failing an audition.'

Jess tries not to smile. 'And do I take it that if I didn't have an air of mystery, you wouldn't find me attractive?'

'You don't give in easily.'

And if she did, would that be a blessing or a curse?

*   *   *

Anton's cottage is the other side of Bledworth Hall, on the edge of a small village. Under the low ceilings, the walls are covered with woven hangings and the alcoves are crowded with brass statues, like a shadowed bazaar in Nepal. There's a familiar scent in the air; it takes Jess a few moments before she realises that it's the incense Nic used, in another life. For a second she feels disoriented but then Anton starts showing her his books and Buddhas, describing his travels, and she feels the past evaporating.

She feels comfortable even with Anton watching her checking out the titles on the shelves, the CDs stacked and scattered on the floor. Kerouac and Cohen, Hesse and Van Morrison. At random she opens a slim book, *The Spice Box of Earth*. The pages are frayed and curled with use, and the notes against some of the poems are written in a careful, round hand.

They sit in the garden with a bottle of red, two glasses and a joint. It's been a while since Jess smoked and the hit comes instantly, like a release. They swap fragments of poems and songs with misremembered words as they watch the sky pale and darken, and the high walls around his garden soften into shadow. Time out, no need to rush. He's waiting for me, Jess realises. He knows I'm not sure. And as if this small revelation is enough, when the air chills, she stands first before they go upstairs.

His hands are gentle and the skin over his back is soft, and she closes her eyes, the better to ignore the hidden burn from his face as it brushes hers while they kiss; and she tries so hard not to feel someone else's teeth, like small white daggers, leaving a pattern from her neck to her breasts as the haze of incense becomes the spice of perfume.

She so wants this tenderness to be enough. And all the while they slide in the heat of the night until she brings it to an end; and as Anton sleeps she watches the moon grow shadows up the walls, like ivy.

1986—3

It's only the third time Jax has flown into JFK, and she still feels a childish thrill as they leave behind the lakes of the north and head down towards Manhattan, circling the indented coast and the buildings that stand like hands reaching out to heaven, like a promise. The first couple of times she was with her father; but even now she doesn't feel alone.

Her scalp is beginning to itch under the hairpiece she borrowed from her mother but she daren't take it off; maybe the hat would have been a better idea. The engine note changes, and five rows down across the cabin, she watches Chad reach across to Jamie and pinch him awake.

'Wha' the . . . ?'

'We're landing.'

Jamie turns his back to her for a moment, then kicks off his blanket like a child in a pram and pushes himself up in the seat, rubbing his eyes with the heels of his hands. Across the aisle, their agent's seat is empty, blanket neatly folded on the floor, but he returns as the seat-belt light flashes on. The scent of cologne trails after him.

Chad calls across. 'Hey Freddie—how ya doing?' She knows how much he hates the dirtiness of travel.

'I still don't understand why you want to do a charity recording. And why couldn't it be done in London, or even at bloody Stonefield?'

'You're a mean bastard, Freddie. You were pleased enough when we were asked.'

'But right in the middle of an album? We're all mad.' He sits upright in his seat like a headmistress, fidgeting with his jacket.

*   *   *

Jax makes sure that she leaves the plane before them, clears immigration and on to the arrivals hall. Hand luggage only; she probably has half an hour while the others wait for their baggage. Even in this sterile space she can begin to smell the city, or maybe it's just her memory—vanilla and cinnamon, the signature of the streets.

It's easy to find the right man, holding up a piece of cardboard. Jax had worried that the booking would be in an unfamiliar name, but nobody else would have reserved a limo in the name of Hacksaw. She feels her heart speed up and her skin become so tight that her nerve endings are like needle tips sampling the air. Antsy, that's what they call it here. She feels antsy, wants to get out into the open. The man's smile fades as Jax explains that his customers have, regrettably, taken a later flight and will not be requiring his services. I'm such a fool, she says to him. They changed the reservations so many times I can't remember which hotel they ended up with—where were you taking them?

The Coke tastes different here, sweeter; she remembers it from last time. Sweeter and thinner, and really cold. She checks her watch again, shifts the holdall on the floor between her legs, pulls at the unfamiliar long hair brushing her cheek. She wants to take the Labrador tin from her bag, open it in public, but as she reaches down the first trolleys push through from the customs hall and she recognises faces from her flight.

At one point she thinks Chad has recognised her in spite of the wig and the lack of make-up, but then Freddie returns from his search for the driver, raking back the fringe that flops across his left eye. Jax can't get close enough to hear the words, but even from their appearance Chad and Jamie look too chilled. They should be angry, what's the point if they don't get angry? You go to all this trouble, and they barely notice. But, there's still the hotel.

Jax takes care not to turn around in the taxi line; the others are no more than a couple of places behind her; too close. The storm breaks as the cab reaches the hotel, overlooking the southern edge of Central Park. Within seconds it is as dark as dusk and all but the nearest buildings are hidden by the bead curtain of rain. The street temperature feels ten degrees lower than the car, and the hotel lobby is like a chiller cabinet. Jax finds the nearest washroom, swaps the wig for a beanie hat and folds the coat over her holdall.

Jamie sees her as she returns to the reception area but there is no recognition in his eyes, and Jax feels her nerves tingling again. Better than sex. This time she stands close enough to hear their conversation at the desk.

'This is getting to be a habit,' says Jamie. 'First the limo, then the rooms. Are you losing it, ma man? You're gonna tell me now they don't have any space for us.'

'How did you guess?' says Freddie. Close to he looks older, forty or more. Rain and sweat have flattened his hair and the patches of scalp showing through are the pink of a newly healed scar.

'We're in New York,' says Chad. 'There must be a thousand hotels we could go to.'

'That's no problem, ma'am,' says the receptionist. 'When she phoned, your assistant told me that you have a new reservation at the Novotel.' She says the word slowly, syllable by syllable. 'I'm sure you will find it more economical.'

'My assistant, as you call him, is a young gentleman,' says Freddie. 'There's no way he would have changed the reservation.'

The receptionist shrugs.

'I can't be arsed with all this,' says Jamie.

'Just find us a bed somewhere while I have me a wee ciggy.'

*   *   *

Jax leans against a parked car on the opposite side of the road and counts the windows of the hotel until she finds Chad's. She smiles as she imagines the air conditioning fan clattering like a machine gun, the unwatched TV in the corner flickering from frame to grainy frame, the drone of Broadway like a mosquito that won't go away.

Superstar in a Novotel—got to be worth a laugh.

CHAPTER TWELVE

Jess has only been away for twenty-four hours but it feels like a week. At midday she's barely back in the office when Denny calls her mobile, the whine of his voice like an accusation.

'Where were you?' he asks. It sounds like— who were you with?

She tells him about the trip, but not about Anton. And not about the dreams that she still hasn't deciphered.

'Do you know what happened yesterday?' Denny asks. 'Do you know what your friends have done to me? Didn't you tell them?'

'Slow down,' says Jess, 'I just got back.'

'Yesterday morning, first thing, I'm invaded by these fascists in white overalls, like a terrorist or something. Every machine in the place was taken; mine, customers', everything. They really fucked me over.' He stops to catch his breath. 'They had me in the *police station*. I thought they were going to arrest me. That guy who was here, that friend of yours, he thinks I did it.'

'Who, Ed?'

'I don't know his fucking name! The bastard you called on Saturday, thinks he's in the Gestapo. They had me in this fucking little room with tape recorders! Took them three hours before they let me go, but they kept all the computers. I'm really fucked, Jess.'

His voice is so loud that Else has heard it; she brings Jess a coffee and hovers.

Jess asks, 'Could they find anything? No, don't shout. They can't touch you for the normal porn, everyone has it, you think they don't look at it too?'

She holds the phone in mid-air and waits until the noise subsides. Why is he reacting so badly; Denny's no fool, he knew what would happen after they found the picture. Then she remembers what Pelham said about Denny's past. Maybe he has other secrets, other lives. She wants to say—remake yourself any way you like, who am I to judge?—but all she does

182

is listen until the shouting's stopped and the only sound is Denny breathing like a frightened animal. She tries to calm him.

'What about the computers you're servicing for customers?'

'I don't check what's on their disks. You people are the thought police, not me.' He sounds wounded. 'I could lose my business. A place like this, I could get bricks through my window if they think I had anything to do with kids. You know what it's like, the trouble is you don't care. You don't give a flying fuck for me, do you?' Before Jess can say anything there's a click and the line goes dead.

'Your music friend?' Else sounds concerned.

'There was a . . . problem . . . over the weekend.'

'I heard—the little girl's voice . . .'

At least, thinks Jess, I managed to forget for a few hours.

She checks her voicemails; the usual litany of referrals and complaints. But the last is from Carwen Pearce; can she meet Jess today, this afternoon, not at the flat.

When Jess calls back, her voice is almost a whisper as if she's too frightened to talk.

'Come to the Mall,' she says, 'outside Uskmouth. Five o'clock.'

*   *   *

Jess tries to concentrate on paperwork in the

afternoon but has the attention span of a two-year-old. She can almost hear them all, whispering at the edge of hearing: Anton, Ed, Pav, Pelham, Denny—like wraiths circling her, waiting for their share.

'You OK, Jess? You still got that fever maybe.'

'Tell you what, Else, let's swap. I'll retire next year and you can have my job. How about it?'

'You go mad if you leave. This place needs you, just like you need the kids. Today, this week, this month, is all bad. Next month is better. Trust me, I seen it in the stars.'

'Right! If your stars are so clever, why don't you tell me where Bryony Pearce is?'

'I wish, Jess, I wish.' She pats Jess's hand, a tentative movement that reminds the younger woman of how few people she touches. She still doesn't know whether Anton was an aberration, a beginning or an end.

*   *   *

The Mall is getting its second wind of the day as offices empty. The place feels alien, the way Jess imagines a domed city would be on Mars, everything filtered and protected. The central atrium is shadowed by improbable trees, and the water from the fountain has the green of a lagoon, but smells of chlorine. Carwen is nowhere in sight, and Jess watches a little girl trying to reach coins thrown into the shallow pool, until her mother pulls her away from the edge and slaps her legs, making her cry.

'Miss Chadwick?'

Jess turns to the voice behind her and sees a deflated creature, her face no longer swollen. Her eyes are rimmed with dark smudges from make-up she's slept in, and the cigarette must have been lit just before she arrived. She doesn't want to sit in one of the cafés on the ground floor so they find a corner upstairs in the anonymous echoes of the Food Hall.

Now they're together Carwen seems uneasy, shifting in her seat and looking around with jerky, birdlike movements. They sip coffee and watch the crowds, waiting until Carwen is ready.

'I left Rhiannon with Steffy's mum,' she says finally, after she stubs out the next cigarette. 'Didn't want her to see this—kids talk. Some of them.'

See what? thinks Jess, but before she can say anything Carwen continues.

'They took Marty in, asked about his computer. Didn't find nothing. They got no idea.'

She reaches into her bag, as dilapidated as the rest of her, and hands Jess something heavy, wrapped in a child's red T-shirt that's about the right size for Bryony.

'Marty don't think I see nothing,' she says. 'I knew where he put this, though. He'd go mental if he knew I found it.'

Jess unpeels the fabric to reveal a dark translucent plastic bag, and inside that a metal box, a little smaller than a paperback. On one of the short edges are a couple of sets of prongs, like thin plugs set into the casing. It looks unfinished, as if it were never meant to be seen, but somehow Jess knows that Den would recognise it immediately.

'The day Bryony went missing he locked himself in the bedroom—he does that when he uses the computer. I heard him fiddling with something, like he was taking it to bits, things falling on the floor and him swearing. When he finished he took stuff out to the rubbish bins in the front.'

'This is what he threw away?'

'I found it after he went out. He put it in with some old takeaway cartons—I cleaned it up best I could.' She pushes the metal box and its wrappings across to Jess. 'He'd batter me if he knew where I was. I gotta go. He should be at work but . . .'

Jess waits until she's out of sight before calling Pav to explain what has happened. There's excitement in the detective's voice as she says, 'Come to the station, don't touch the box; come now.'

*   *   *

The rush hour traffic holds her up and it's

nearly an hour before she reaches the station near the centre of Lydford. Pav takes her through to Pelham's borrowed office, a small room with a framed print on the wall—Chinese or Japanese, two small figures on a mountain path.

Jess opens her bag but Pav stops her, puts on a pair of thin gloves that remind Jess of David Stiffley, and then takes the bundle of wrappings, places it in the centre of the desk and carefully unfolds the red cloth before taking the metal casing from its bag.

In spite of the faint smell of curry, Pelham's grinning as if he's just found the Holy Grail. 'Gotcha!'

'Do you know what this is?' says Pav. Jess shrugs.

'It's a hard disk drive from a PC. When we checked Marty's computer it was clean—a few basic programs, but nothing else. You expect to see all sorts—cached files, music, pictures, Web pages. But nothing. It hadn't been erased, it was like new.'

'And this is why,' says Pelham. 'The bastard swapped disk drives. Let's get it dusted, and then check it out.' Pav disappears down the corridor with the naked metal box and its wrappings and Pelham takes a bottle of Scotch and two glasses from the drawer of his desk. It's the first time Jess has seen him since Saturday night, the day they found the photo of Bryony on her website.

'I should apologise for the other night,' she says. 'It was a bad day and I was less than . . . gracious.'

Pelham salutes her with his glass. 'Accepted. But don't expect me to ask you again in a hurry. All I wanted was something to eat, and you acted as though I was about to jump you.'

The picture this brings up is so ludicrous that Jess can't stop herself laughing, and Pelham joins in. Through the heavy flesh on his face she can see what he must have looked like once, before fat blurred his features and the capillaries ruptured and he gave up.

He would have made a good subject then. Even better now.

Pav comes back into the office, out of breath, with the drive in a new plastic evidence bag.

'We can match the prints later. And I got hold of IT—a tech will be up any minute with a spare machine, he'll fit the disk here.'

'Time for a leak then.'

Pav waits till her boss has gone, then asks, 'How was the trip?'

Jess feels the temptation to talk but it would be an imperfect confession, almost like an excuse for being unfaithful. And how could she explain whose face she saw, each time she closed her eyes?

'OK,' she says. 'Tiring—the drive.' And she tries to ignore Pav's half smile as if the woman already knows.

Pelham gets back at the same time as someone pushing an old computer loaded onto a trolley: he looks like a young Denny, with skin the colour of cement. Pav hands him Marty's disk, the metal casing dulled by a film of powder which the boy wipes off on his sleeve.

'Crap drives these,' he says. 'Not surprised he chucked it. And it's old, only twenty gig—barely worth having.'

'Just fit the fucking thing,' says Pelham. 'And then clear off out of here—I don't want to be accused of corrupting the young.'

The boy works quickly and checks that everything is OK before Pelham shoos him out. Pav moves to the chair in front of the screen.

'I'll search for any JPEGs, GIFs or bitmaps. That's pictures or photographs to you, John. Of course, if Marty was really trying he'll have renamed anything dodgy or hidden them in some other way . . . yep, nothing there.' She stares at the screen for a moment before leaning forward and trying again.

'OK—I'll look for any file over a certain size—see if anything unusual comes up.' A list of filenames scrolls up the screen, hundreds of them, moving so fast that the names are unreadable. 'Here we go—there's a whole bunch with unusual extensions. Someone's renamed them but it's not very sophisticated.'

She works the keyboard as quickly as

189

Denny, then points at the screen. 'They're in a set of folders that have been set as private—wouldn't have been accessible by anyone who didn't know what they were looking for. Of course,' she turns to look at them, 'it could be nothing more than bored housewives or a bit of S&M—no use to us.'

She clicks on one of the files and a picture appears almost instantly. 'No, I think we just hit pay dirt.' And then, 'Oh shit . . .'

Jess turns away, but not until she's made sure that it isn't Bryony on the photograph.

'There are hundreds here,' says Pav. 'Someone's been spending a lot of money downloading these.'

'Maybe,' says Pelham, 'he took them himself.'

'I don't think so. The pictures are all of different children.'

Pelham is already making calls, organising teams to hit all the places Marty might be, and Jess is thankful to be in the background this time. But there's something important, something at the edge of her memory, and then she remembers.

'Rhiannon!'

'Who?'

'Carwen's other daughter. She was left with a neighbour when Carwen met me at the Mall—we need to get her out, now.'

'Fuck—that's all we need,' says Pelham. 'We'll have to do it under a police protection order. Jess, best if you come with us to the flat to look after Rhiannon. Lucky you're here.'

'What about Ed?' says Pav.

'On leave today—doesn't that man ever work? We'll handle this without him.'

*   *   *

Pav drives the pool car with Pelham beside her and Jess in the back. The journey seems endless and no one talks. Jess wonders if Carwen knew what was on the disk, if she'd ever sat with Marty and looked at those images. But even if not, she knew enough to give the disk to Jess.

Who else is on there? she thinks. Faces that I recognise, more children that I've failed?

They arrive outside the flat at the same time as the uniformed backup, and Pelham tells Jess to stay at the bottom of the stairs while he and the others go up to the red front door. She hears the banging, Pelham shouting to be let in, and then a loud crack as the door is broken down.

It's too much—she can't wait at the bottom like an afterthought.

As she runs up the concrete stairs there's silence from above; no further shouting, nothing. The door is hanging off one hinge but Pav holds her back in the doorway to the living room. The flat still smells of stale tobacco smoke but it is overlaid now with a sharper,

191

metallic scent. The chair where Carwen sat on their first meeting has tipped onto its side, and the television screen in the corner is smashed, shards of glass scattered across the carpet from the small explosion. On the wall opposite the door are dark smeared marks at head height, as if a rag had been dipped in brown paint and dragged across the surface. Pelham is crouching beside Carwen's body, crumpled on the floor below the marks. She looks unreal, a badly made Guy Fawkes, but her eyes are shut and her hair is washed with blood and one of her arms is at an odd angle as if it's been stuck on the wrong way round. Jess can't see if she's breathing but she doesn't need to; Carwen has a stillness about her, a new heaviness. This must be what people mean when they say they go numb at a distressing sight; there's no sensation in her skin, as if the nerves have pulled away from the surface, afraid of what they might feel.

'There's no pulse. Body's still warm but in this temperature . . .' Pelham stands up slowly.

'What about Rhiannon?' says Jess.

One of the uniformed officers answers. 'There's no one else here, just her.' He nods towards Carwen's body. 'We've checked everywhere—it's a small flat.'

Jess almost falls down the stairs, pushing through the crowd that's already gathered outside. Pav catches up with her as she turns the corner towards Steffy's house. They're evenly matched but Pav gets there just ahead, banging on the door until Steffy's father opens it.

'You're too late,' he says. 'Marty picked her up about an hour ago. Funny, they only live round the corner but he was in a car. Never knew he had one. Sorry—didn't see what type. No, he didn't say where they were going.'

He calls after them, asking what's happened, but neither of them answers as Pav races ahead on the run back to the flat. An ambulance has already arrived by the time Jess arrives, panting, and Pelham breaks away from talking to the paramedics to join her.

'The Scene of Crime Officer's in there now and the pathologist is on his way. But Carwen must have been killed within the last couple of hours, given the time of your meeting at the Mall. If we'd got here even a few minutes earlier . . .'

'I called you as soon as I could, as soon as Carwen had gone. She was nervous enough.' There's a stitch in her side and she tries to catch her breath.

'You've no idea where Marty might have taken the girl?'

'How should I know? The guy's a complete flake. But I bet my life he's not doing this alone.'

'Because?'

'You met him—you think he's got the skill to hack into my website?'

'It may not be connected,' says Pelham. 'He may not have meant to kill Carwen. Maybe it was an argument that got out of hand, an accident.' But he sounds unconvinced.

From the moment Jess had walked into his office earlier that evening she knew that there was another story, something he shared with Pav.

And it feels uncomfortable. That's why you have your own secrets, so that you can be an insider at last.

The crowd has been pushed back now, behind a line of blue and white tape. Like an audience in a theatre everyone is quiet, even the kids. This isn't the scene Jess expected when she drove here earlier—this time there is no show, no struggle, no screams as children are taken from their mother, and what wouldn't she give to have that drama rather than this deathly quiet now that no one is left to cry.

It's after nine, and the daylight has faded without her noticing. Four hours ago she was drinking coffee with a woman whose dead body is being photographed upstairs in her living room, and Jess feels contaminated, as if death is catching. She wonders how far she contributed to Carwen's death. Did Marty know that Carwen saw her today? Maybe he followed her, maybe they argued, maybe she should have stayed with Carwen and taken her to the police station. But instead there was another betrayal and now she's standing alone, like an intruder on the wrong side of the tape. There's nothing she can do here. She would pray, if she thought there was anyone to hear. She would pray for Rhiannon's safety. She would pray for Marty to leave the girl alone, set her free, but she doesn't know who would hear or how her prayers would be answered.

The movements of people have slowed, the sense of urgency drained away. Police radios crackle in the still air; sudden bursts of noise that feel like a disturbance, like someone speaking in a church. The crowd is waiting, and a low whisper rolls through it as the paramedics come out from the stairwell with a covered stretcher, slide it into the ambulance and drive away without fuss, slowly and quietly. The crowd parts to let them through, and then disperses; within seconds the street is empty.

CHAPTER THIRTEEN

First thing next morning Jess tries to get news on Bryony and Rhiannon but the only person she can raise is Ed, and he cuts off the conversation almost before it starts. He's never done that before.

'You want to tell me about it?' Else breaks into her swearing.

'That was Ed Murchison—bastard's clammed up on me, won't say how the investigation's going.'

'You want to be on their team, go join the police. Let them do their job, you do yours.'

'They think I'm involved. They're cutting me loose, I can feel it.'

'Bullshit. You think too much, that's your trouble. I keep telling you—get a man in your life. Take your mind off yourself, spend your time hating the bastard. Works for me.'

But not for me, thinks Jess. She takes the digital camera from her bag and checks the battery and the memory, cleans the lens. She needs to be ready, she needs to get her balance back.

*   *   *

It's a surprise when Pelham calls at lunchtime to ask Jess to a meeting at Lydford police station. She imagines an interview in a bare room with tape recorders but Pelham reassures her—why would we do that? It's just a briefing, he says, I thought you might like to be there. No pressure, we start at three.

The traffic holds her up, and she arrives after the meeting has begun, in a briefing room a floor down from Pelham's office. She knows about half the people there; officers from FSU and CID, and a few uniforms. Someone passes her a chair and she squashes herself between a filing cabinet and a bulky sergeant she doesn't know. The blinds are closed against the sun, the air feels used up and someone in the room forgot to use deodorant this morning.

Pelham is backlit by a projection of Marty McKechnie. It's an overblown snapshot, grainy and blurred; the man looks younger than Jess remembers, with a glass in his hand, longer hair and a suit that once belonged to someone else, as if he'd dressed up for the wedding of someone he didn't really care about.

'Sorry about the lack of air conditioning,' says Pelham. 'I'll make this as quick as possible. You'll have gathered that McKechnie's car was abandoned in Worcester—blood all over the shop. There's no analysis yet, so it could be anybody's.' He clicks a remote and the picture of McKechnie is replaced by the interior of a car, with blood stains covering the passenger seat and splashed across the windscreen as if someone had thrown a can of paint through the open door.

There's no reaction in the room, and Jess realises that they've seen all this before. The man beside her whispers, 'You OK?' and she nods, trying to ignore the taste of bile, looking away from the screen until Pav's voice breaks the silence.

'Maybe Carwen injured McKechnie in the fight?'

'But hers was the only blood in the flat. No—someone who was alive at the time has been sliced up in that car.'

'There's something not right here,' says Pav. 'Think of McKechnie for the moment. His behaviour is typical of a paedophile; he finds a single woman with children and starts a relationship so that he has easy access to feed his addiction. It's clear that Bryony was being abused and McKechnie's in the frame for that, especially after what happened yesterday; but—he had an alibi for the night Bryony went missing. And most abusers like to farm their stock. They milk them, not hunt them to death.

'And then there's Perry. There's no evidence of any link between McKechnie and the boy. Maybe the incidents *are* unconnected and the bruising on the legs is no more than a coincidence.'

'Perry was murdered,' says Pelham, 'and it wasn't an accident; he didn't die because of rough sex, though God knows I've seen that before. So why was he killed? To keep him quiet? Maybe he was about to tell someone what was happening to him.' He turns to Jess. 'And then there's the stuff on your website.' The sound of Bryony's voice falters from a hidden speaker, and for the first time there's a reaction, an undercurrent of people swearing softly.

Another click, and the shot of Marty

reappears as a number of people in the room turn to look at Jess.

She feels herself blush. 'Den, the guy who runs my website, he says it was an expert job, especially the changed song on the CD. Even hacking into the site would be difficult—that's what he says.'

'So the bad news is that more than one person is involved,' says Pelham. 'Paedophiles are bad enough, murdering paedophiles are worse but a conspiracy of the bastards . . .'

Jess sees him exchange a glance with Pav.

'I still don't understand why Marty killed Carwen,' she says.

'I think it was an accident,' says Pav. 'Either McKechnie found out that she'd found the hard disk, or she confronted him. Maybe she suspected something going on between him and her daughters.'

'Or maybe she was complicit,' says Jess. 'Turned a blind eye for an easy life. We've all seen it happen; they fool themselves into thinking that nothing is wrong.' She feels more comfortable on her home ground.

'Whatever. They ended up fighting and she died when her head was smashed against the wall,' says Pav.

'Repeatedly smashed against the wall,' says Pelham. 'Some accident.'

'But then why take Rhiannon?' says Jess. 'She'll hold him up and be more noticeable.'

'Why take Bryony?' says Pav. 'We looked at

more of the images on the hard disk Carwen gave you. These weren't for the "I love children" brigade. The people who pay for these pictures like to be in control. They use kids to destruction. If McKechnie was into that then maybe he just couldn't hold back any longer with Bryony.' She pauses. 'Some of the children in the pictures we found must have been badly injured as a result of what was done to them. Some of them may have died.' Her voice catches and for the first time she looks vulnerable.

'And now they've got Rhiannon as well,' says Jess.

'Every police force has their descriptions,' says Pelham. 'There are teams checking all the small hotels and rooming houses around where the car was abandoned, and we'll also be keeping our eyes open in Glasgow in case McKechnie goes back to his old haunts.' He pauses. 'And the last search is along their presumed route from Carwen's flat to Worcester, in case he dumped the body along the way.'

The screen blanks, the blinds are opened and for the first time Jess notices Ed, pressed into a corner at the back of the room. He looks like someone who never made it home after closing time.

'If there are no other leads in the next few hours,' says Pelham, 'we'll break this to the press and get the public involved. Maybe there's been a sighting of McKechnie, or maybe he's taken Rhiannon to join her sister, wherever she is.'

As the meeting breaks up Ed pushes his way to the front and leaves without speaking to anyone.

'Major row with his wife, apparently,' says Pav. 'That's why he's been taking so much leave. It looks like they're about to split up.'

'But they're a perfect couple!'

'No such thing, Jess—you should know that.' They stop by the main doors. 'I gotta tell you, I could do with a night out tonight. Are you still on for the private view? Annie's really looking forward to meeting you, and maybe we can spend a few hours pretending this crap doesn't exist.'

How could she have forgotten?

'With all this going on?' says Jess. 'I thought you'd be working twenty-four hours a day, camping out in the station.'

'I take the breaks when I can. If you can't make it, I understand—the last couple of days have been really difficult.' But her voice says— Come.

As if Jess could say no. It's like taking a drug, she thinks. The preparation, the anticipation that make the rush all the bigger when it comes. The camera can wait for another day.

*　　*　　*

Jess hasn't been to Bristol for some time and all the roads have changed, funnelling her into one-way systems that refuse to take her in the right direction. Eventually she finds the car parks on the docks, next to the Arnolfini gallery. The cool breeze blowing off the water promises autumn, and Jess wishes she'd worn something warmer; vanity won over function tonight. She recognises the BMW parked in the next row, its engine ticking as it cools.

The gallery is on a side street a few hundred metres away from the waterside. These buildings were all warehouses originally, but now they've been scrubbed and stained, partitioned and glass-fronted into retail units for designer labels; places to be seen. The pavement outside is littered with people holding glasses of wine. Herds again; the men in loose cord trousers, the women in shapeless dresses hanging from their shoulders and scarves that follow their movements when they turn. Pav is waiting just inside the doorway, as if to waylay her.

'Jess, I swear I didn't know, not until we got here. I didn't look at the invitations or I would have seen. We can leave now if you want.'

For a moment Jess doesn't understand. The expanse of the long room is uniformly white and brightly lit. Although some of the walls are hung with paintings, most of the space is taken up with sculptures, fragments of Gormenghast.

Dead, bleached wood forming turrets of spikes, or twisted bodies stretched out of proportion, like giant Giacomettis; racked, drained and dry. The one nearest the door is displayed on a black pedestal, a desiccated foetus, curled and bony as a fish with oversized eye sockets hidden in shadow. The last time Jess saw a figure like this was in the forest by the Dyke, peering blindly at her from the trees.

Near a table set out as a bar, halfway down the room, David Stiffley is talking to an elderly woman with grey hair tied back in a turquoise scarf. In this crowd Jess sees how tall he is as he stoops over the woman, shaping the air with his hands as he explains something important.

'Jess? Do you want to go?' Pav's voice pulls her back.

'I thought he wasn't a suspect.' The room is a temple, to leave now would be sacrilege. Out of the forest the sculptures seem even more potent in this enclosed and sterile space, and she wonders what it would be like to live with one of these creatures, to know the texture of the grain, the shape of every curve.

She looks up as a woman comes towards her and knows at once that this is Annie, expensively dressed in cream and gold. Silk shirt, chinos, Ferragamo loafers, a slim shoulder bag that costs more than Jess makes in a month. Her hair is a short, dark chestnut that matches the colour of her eyes, her 'hello' is warm and pitched low and she shakes Jess's hand with an unexpected formality.

'I hope this isn't too embarrassing—Pav explained about David Stiffley. We don't usually talk about her cases so when I was given the invitations the name didn't register.'

They make their way across to the wine and David excuses himself from the turquoise woman as he notices Jess.

'Miss Chadwick! This is most unexpected. I didn't realise that you appreciated my work.'

'I came with some friends. To be honest, I didn't know it was your exhibition.'

'Ah, that explains it.' He looks expectantly at Pav and Annie, butterflies to Jess's moth, and holds out his hand. 'Unless I'm mistaken you pursue different professions from Miss Chadwick.'

'Management consultancy,' says Pav quickly. 'Not very exciting.'

'The excitement is all mine, believe me. I'm mercenary enough to be delighted when I meet people who can afford my work. Modesty and reticence are wasted assets for an artist.'

Jess can't believe how calm he looks, how he can drink and laugh with strangers while his son's body lies alone in the mortuary.

As if he could read her mind, David explains, 'This exhibition took nearly a year to prepare. To cancel would have let down too many people—and how would it help Perry?'

A few metres away a screen is showing projections of flickering images. David follows her glance.

'Some of the works here are collaborations with a colleague. Our current project is to video changes, month by month, as one of my little friends decays in the woods near my home.' He talks quickly, using his hands.

A few feet to one side is a sculpture of driftwood like bones, waist high on a low plinth, a Brueghel demon that has been skinned and gutted and captured mid-scream. Pav wrinkles her nose as if the thing had just risen, dripping, from a pit of ordure.

'Your art's already dynamic enough. But do you have to make everything so disturbing?'

'I wasn't aware that I had to produce . . . peaceful . . . works, although I'm sure a psychologist would find a correlation between my sculptures and the state of my mind. But do you label Hirst a psychopath for slicing up cows and exhibiting them? Maybe we need to be shocked to see the world in new ways. I simply give shape to the objects that usually stay in our dreams.' He smiles like someone who knows what's behind a locked door. 'Perhaps I face up to my fears.'

'Don't misunderstand me,' says Pav. 'I like your work, sort of. It makes me think of mortality, that there's an inevitability in our lives.'

'I knew you'd understand,' says David. 'My creatures are the whisperers in the ear of the king.'

Annie has moved away to look at one of the paintings, and Jess can't trust herself to join in the conversation. She's about to ask if David would mind her taking some photographs when a slight man comes towards them. He looks like a scaled-down version of the sculptor, with identical hair and underlip beard, exquisitely detailed like an Indian miniature. He rests his hand on David's arm and Jess sees him stroke with small, surreptitious movements.

'Dee, you *must* come and talk to Evan. He's looking very opulent tonight.'

David looks directly at Jess. 'Now you see, Miss Chadwick. Perhaps I conform more than I like to think. And if my memory serves me well, you have an artistic past. I'm sure you appreciate my sensibilities.' He leans towards her so that Pav can't hear. 'As you see, my tastes are less juvenile than you supposed. I hope that you aren't disappointed.'

He moves away into the crowd, and the room seems emptier.

'A powerful man with a very weird mind,' says Pav. 'And damned cool for someone whose son was murdered a week ago. I wonder what he's like when he loses control.'

*   *   *

Annie has booked a table at a nearby restaurant and the wine she orders makes the

206

drinks at the gallery seem like vinegar.

'The clients expect this sort of quality and I've got used to it,' she says, 'but it could be Ribena for all they know. Philistines. I don't know what happens to men when they go out to play. In the office—fine. Out for lunch—fine. But get them on an awayday with champagne aperitifs and their higher brain functions all seem to shut down. The more they drink, the more I feel myself metamorphosing from an intelligent business person into some kind of high-class tart. I'm just another part of the entertainment package.'

'You love it—you flirt outrageously,' says Pav, with a smile.

'Yeah—right. Some day I'll take a photo of one of these guys when we're at an event. Sweating, balding, belly hanging over his belt and fake Ralph Lauren shirt with the stain that his wife just *cannot* get out. Then I'll show him the photo when he's sober and say—do you really think I'd spend more than a second in your company if I wasn't paid to?'

'So you *are* a tart,' says Pav. 'You just don't go all the way. Anyway, if you want the real thing come and work for the police. They'll show you what misogyny really means.'

'You mean someone like Pelham?' says Jess.

'He's a teddy bear by comparison with some of them. And you should see him when Annie's around. Got a little pash for you, dear, hasn't he?' says Pav.

'That's because I abuse him. The man's a secret masochist—I bet he's got an account with Miss Whiplash. Perhaps he lets her use his handcuffs.'

'Or perhaps he wears her undies—the DI in black lace,' says Pav. 'Trouble is, Annie, you've got a rival. Jess has a sort of funky austerity that is just up Pelham's street—I think he's ripe for a bit of rock chick, and you're just corporate chic. So nineties, so passé.'

'I give in,' says Annie. 'He's all yours, Jess, with my blessing.'

Jess makes the mistake of telling them about Pelham's invitation to dinner.

'Jess, that is so excellent! You have to go out with him, it's imperative. Then you can report back—I can't wait.' Annie almost knocks over a glass of wine in her excitement. 'And don't worry, you don't have to go all the way on the first date unless you really want to.'

'You must be mad,' says Jess. 'It would feel like being serviced by a hippo. Thanks for the offer, but I'll stick to my own matchmaking.'

While the plates are removed Jess looks at the two women on the other side of the table. They look like nothing more than friends enjoying a night out, but her mind is full of snapshots of them behind a locked door, the patterns their bodies draw as they touch, surface to surface.

Pav refills the glasses and smiles at Jess, her

mouth slightly parted to show the tips of her teeth, and for an instant Jess can feel them bite gently into her lips. She looks away, dropping her gaze in case Pav sees the scene reflected in her eyes; too many dreams.

'I'm sorry, girls, I have to go. The last couple of days haven't been easy.' She holds herself stiffly as they air-kiss goodbye, taking care not to let them touch her skin.

On her way back from the restaurant Jess passes the gallery, taking the opposite side of the street. The pavement outside is empty now that darkness has fallen but the interior is still crowded, with David standing near the open door. He looks over to where she's standing and lifts his glass in a salute before turning back to his companion.

Next to the Arnolfini Jess props herself against one of the mooring posts by the edge of the dock. The breeze has dropped and the water is almost still, studded with amber reflections of lights that wink out and reappear as ripples hide them. There are few people around and the only sounds are water slapping the stone dockside and echoes of dislocated voices and laughter, rising and dying quickly back to silence.

*　　　*　　　*

Jess drives back carefully, checking her speed every few minutes. She should have taken a cab but the roads are quiet and she reaches home without any problem.

Time to re-establish a routine. She hasn't checked her emails since Saturday; there hasn't seemed much point. While the modem connects Jess looks at the card that Gina sent. Such an ephemeral image; Jess looks for signs in her eyes, the way that she laughs, anything to show that this is her daughter but it's so hard to tell. She tries another image; Jamie. Maybe that's him in the tilt of the head, the twist of the lips; enough to make the connection.

An icon flashes to show that she has a new message. Just one, but since Saturday only someone with her private address can get through. Maybe Spider sent this before the website went down; how long do emails take?

'hi chad. i know i said i wouldnt write again, but i had to say sorry. i bet so many people write to you its impossible to reply to everyone. i was feeling bad that day, you know, everything screwing up. the thing i like best is writing to you, you dont tell me to fuck off. i know you wont write to me but would you do one thing. i asked for a read receipt to this message. all you do is press the button on screen to say you read this message and i get to know. ill know you don't junk me. you don't have to write anything, just press the button so i know you're there. Please Chad, it won't take a second. hope youre writing

some good stuff i want to hear it soon. spider.'

There's a window on her screen asking if she wants to send the receipt. Such a small thing to do to please someone. She's not really making contact, breaking her rule. It's no more than an act of politeness. The arrow on her screen hovers over the Send button, and her finger twitches involuntarily on the mouse.

Done.

The cat flap rattles as Wagner comes in, chirping to tell her that he's brought an offering. He crouches on the floor near the range, his catch between his front paws, but as Jess gets closer she sees a flash of something yellow, almost the colour of a primrose. She pries the object away from him; a small yellow sock, just big enough for a child of maybe a year old. She recognises the pattern, identical to one of the unsent birthday gifts she bought for Gina all those years ago, folded and stored in the long box upstairs.

Suddenly she can hear every sound throughout the house and her skin feels flayed.

The sock is bulky, as if it's been filled with something heavy but soft. She finds some rubber gloves and peels back the grass-stained wool; how it got there she doesn't know, but wrapped inside is a small shrew, its eyes open, still shiny and moist, and the body is soft and flexible as if freshly killed. She takes the corpse outside and throws it over the stone wall into the lower field for the crows to find tomorrow.

Back inside she locks the door behind her and checks the yellow woollen scrap again, rinsing it under the kitchen tap. Identical. She leaves it in the sink and runs upstairs to the spare room. The box is where it should be, under the bed, but her fingers are clumsy as she pulls it out and opens the lid. Everything seems in place. She lifts out each year's present until she gets to the bottom layer, the first clothes she bought for Gina. A matching set; dress, tights, hat, and a top and trousers with matching socks, all in yellow and white bands. She takes out each piece carefully, but only one of the socks is there. She goes through the gifts for every other year, in case she misplaced it, but after ten minutes of searching through everything in the box she can find just one. The other is downstairs, stained and wringing wet after being used as a shroud for a dead animal.

She forces herself to put everything back neatly, checking as she goes to make sure nothing else is missing. She remembers the last time she looked in here, a few days ago after one of the emails from Gina. Maybe one of the socks fell out then, maybe Wagner found it and took it into the fields, maybe the shrew crawled inside to hide or nest.

Maybe she'll turn on the alarm tonight.

CHAPTER FOURTEEN

Thursday morning. She'd forgotten last night until she saw the small yellow sock on the draining board, still damp.

Beth suggested she take a break; maybe now's the right time. Everyone would understand. Pack a bag, drive down to London and crash with Chana for a while. Disappear.

And then there's the seductive thought of leaving for good. Who'd care, apart from the cat? She could swallow her pride, fly out to Venice, ask her father for more money. But even as she lets the thoughts run through her mind, she knows she can't break the links to Bryony and Rhiannon and Perry, even though they aren't of her making.

Pav had promised to let her know immediately if she heard anything about the girls or Marty, but when Jess checks there are no messages on her mobile. And as Else said, finding the children isn't her job.

*   *   *

On the way back from a meeting with foster parents near Abertrothy Jess calls in on Den, a chance to mend fences. She hasn't seen him since they found the photo of Bryony on her website, hasn't spoken to him since he hung up on her a couple of days ago.

The workshop seems back to normal, with computers on benches, cables on the floor and a drooping pizza box balanced on top of the screen, but Denny looks drained, like everyone she knows, and she wonders where the life-force goes. It seems that no one is immune except Pav and Annie, recharging each other.

He stares at her for a moment as if she were a stranger, and then relents and smiles. 'Sorry, Jess, I was wired the other day. Friends?' She lets him kiss her cheek; he smells of onions.

'When did you get your stuff back?' she asks.

'Yesterday morning. I lost three days' work, I've got customers bollocking me because I promised to get their machines back—and your friends held on to the Web server, said I wouldn't get it back until today. I'm still checking the rest—fuck knows what they got up to.'

As if on cue the shop door bangs open; Pav follows a man carrying a computer which he brings round the back and puts on the floor. The policewoman turns to Jess as if she were expecting to see her.

'Recovered from last night? I felt awful about letting you drive home—maybe you should have stayed with us.'

Denny interrupts. 'Hey guys—whenever you're ready . . .'

Pav smiles at him. 'Sorry. We brought the

Web server back, and we want you to put Jess's site up again, but with a few changes. We reckon we can use software traps to detect any hacking and send an immediate alert through to our technical people.'

'Software what? You've lost me,' says Jess.

'Way out of my league,' says Denny.

'But, as they say, we have the technology,' says Pav. 'It means we can track whoever's doing this through the Internet. This guy knows what he's doing. He can spoof host names and IP addresses to cover his tracks. He'll use a hundred different names, a hundred different handles. He'll be anonymous. Remember, he could be anywhere in the world. Even if he's doing this from next door he could be working through servers in the States or Asia, anywhere.'

Pav lost her a few sentences back.

'Just accept that it's difficult, Jess.'

And it's going to take too long for a couple of missing children. Somewhere there's a connection that she should be making, something that links her and Perry and the girls, but she can't find it and feels as if she's losing at some game where she's the only player who doesn't know the rules. Somehow she knows that whatever they do with the computers isn't going to help find Bryony or Rhiannon.

Pav is explaining something to Denny, and Jess realises with surprise that the policewoman knows what she's talking about. It's like listening to two people speaking a version of her language where the words sound the same but all the meanings are different; she's about to ask them to explain when a call comes through on Pav's mobile, and she walks outside to take it.

Denny looks as though he's just won the lottery.

'Where did you find her? She's, like, an expert. She's a major guru.'

Pav comes back in, looking excited. 'There's been a possible sighting—a girl matching Rhiannon's description with a man, except that he doesn't sound much like Marty. A couple of birdwatchers were walking in the Beacons yesterday and saw the girl being carried from a car into a converted barn. Sounds very isolated. They thought it looked strange, but didn't contact us until they saw the news this morning, after our press release about the abduction.' Her phone buzzes again. 'They were texting me the details—this should be it. Sorry, Jess, gotta go.'

Jess follows her outside. 'I'll come with you; we can take the Jeep. I know the Beacons; some of the roads around there are crap.' She doesn't wait for Pav to argue. 'There's an Ordnance Survey map in the side pocket; show me where we're going.'

She could have guessed it would be off the main tourist routes. 'According to the map the only access by road comes in from the west, but if you look here there's a track across from the next valley. If we take this it could cut nearly an hour off the journey; you map read.'

They take the main road as far as Brecon, still crowded with tourists in new boots and backpacks, and then head north through ever narrower lanes. Each time Jess backs up to let someone pass on the single tracks she can feel Pav's impatience. The main horseshoe of the Beacons is behind them but they climb steadily, Pav making quick decisions about which small turning to take. How many talents does this woman have? thinks Jess.

Eventually they come to the end of the road, by the field gate where the birdwatchers had parked. A track carries on, but now it's unmetalled and deeply rutted. Jess puts the Jeep into four-wheel drive and moves off slowly, trying to let the car find its own course. After ten minutes the track flattens out to cross a fast-moving stream running down from the peaks; Jess picks up speed but brakes sharply as soon as they are across. The track has narrowed suddenly with a steep drop on one side, maybe a couple of hundred feet. They've been climbing all the while and are surrounded by a mountain landscape of low scrubby bushes and scree slopes. The track is barely wider than the car.

'We should have taken the main road,' says Pav.

'No way—it would have added an hour, even at this speed.'

And then they've reached the crest, and the track is dipping down into the next valley. The converted barn is still half a mile away, the only building in sight. The track winds down through a small copse and Jess pulls up before they leave the cover of the trees. The building looks peaceful and deserted; no parked cars, all the windows shut.

'You want me to get closer?'

'Best not—anyone in there would hear the car approaching.' Pav takes off her seat-belt and settles back.

'So what now? You're not just going to sit here?'

'We have to—procedures.'

'There's no one else around, and the girls might be in there. We could get them out now—someone could come back at any moment, before your mates get here.'

She feels afraid. Not of being hurt, but of what she might find in this desolate building that makes her farmhouse feel like the centre of civilisation. No one would choose to live here; it's a place to hide in.

Or a prison. The girls could be alive in there, frightened, praying that someone will find them. She thinks of Marty, undressing them, posing them in front of the camera. She can't wait.

Pav tries to stop her as she opens her door.

'Jess, get back. This isn't the bloody television—you shouldn't even be here.'

'How are you going to stop me?' They're both talking in aggravated whispers as if someone in the barn could hear them, even from this distance. 'I don't work for you. And do you think I haven't been threatened before? I've been alone with people who I know have killed their own children. I've been threatened with knives, guns. It's just a matter of degree.' She pulls away and walks quickly down the track towards the building, but before she's gone more than a few yards Pav joins her.

There's no cover, anyone waiting in the barn would be able to see them if they looked out. Jess tries not to think about what happened to Carwen.

Close to, the building looks even more deserted, all the doors and windows closed even though the day is hot. Buttercups and ragwort have pushed up between the paving slabs of the small patio outside the front door, bright yellow against the buckled stone, and desiccated grass covers the sloping fields that surround them. One of the gutters is broken and hangs from the eaves, the stone wall below it stained dark. Someone once tried to make a garden but it hasn't been tended for some years, and from a distance Jess hears a couple of deep booms and realises that they must be close to the Army firing range in the next valley.

There's no other sound, and Jess peers through the first window. She can tell immediately that this is a place to stay for a while, not to live. There's little inside; a side table with two mugs, a couple of kitchen chairs, a newspaper on the floor. The front door has no Yale lock and she tries the handle, surprised when it opens. She looks at Pav as if for permission, but the other woman merely shrugs.

The inside of the building is cool and shadowed. There's no movement, no presence, and she knows without looking any further that the place is devoid of life. A sudden noise behind makes her jump, but it's just the fridge motor cutting in and sounding too loud in the silence.

The whole ground floor is one open space, with a kitchen area at one end. The two women make their way to a staircase halfway along the back wall, leading up to a gallery, and climb slowly. Though the place seems deserted they pause after each creak of the stair tread as if expecting someone to rush out.

The bathroom looks as though it's never been cleaned. There's no seat on the toilet bowl which is stained yellow and brown, and there are hairs caught in the cracks on the soap. Even the air feels sticky, and Jess wishes she had a pair of David Stiffley's gloves. In the silence she can hear her heart.

The first bedroom could be in a hotel somewhere, anonymous and impersonal. The double bed has been slept in but not made, a crumpled grey sheet the only covering. There's no other furniture, no clothing. Whoever slept here takes their world around with them.

By Jess's reckoning the last room must be over the kitchen area, and stretches the width of the building with windows at both sides, covered with blinds. The light is filtered as if it comes from nowhere, attenuated. As soon as Jess opens the door the smell surrounds them like something palpable and familiar. She takes a few seconds to locate it in her memory; the smell of houses from which they take children away as soon as they go in, houses which are never cleaned, where children and animals shit and piss wherever they want until the floors are thick and you can't touch anything and no amount of washing gets you clean.

But this is on a different scale. This isn't neglect, this filth is part of a plan; she can almost hear the echo of screams.

'Jesus wept.' Pav lays her hand on Jess's arm. 'Whatever you do, don't touch anything. SOCO will want to take a look at this.'

'Don't worry—I've done this before.' But she hasn't, not like this.

There's no bed, just two chairs and a table with leather straps lying on the floor around the legs. She doesn't want to think what has caused the stains on the chairs. The rack over the table is like the one Jess has in the farmhouse for drying clothes, with a waxed rope running through an eyelet set into the ceiling and down one wall, so that the whole apparatus can be raised and lowered. One of the wooden slats is cracked as if something too heavy has hung from it, and another has been replaced with a length of dull metal.

Along the end wall is what looks like shelving for a music centre, and marks in the dust show where something has been moved. There are cables on the floor, power leads and others she doesn't recognise; something to do with computers? In the corner is a high metal rack. Jess remembers seeing something like it in Den's workshop, but this one is empty, the smoked-glass door half open showing multiple power sockets inside.

A car draws up and they hear Pelham's voice.

'I hope you're ready for this,' says Pav.

Pelham bursts into the room like a star turn coming on stage, followed by three officers in white one-piece suits. Without any instructions they go to work, lifting and turning and checking, using their fingertips as if whatever they touched was as fragile as something from an ancient tomb, ready to turn to dust. A photographer precedes them; the constant flash makes Jess nauseous but she can't stop herself looking at every shot he takes, as if she were the camera.

'What the fuck is this smell? And what the fuck is she doing here?' He points at Jess. 'Get her out, now!'

But before she can move, one of the officers calls out. He's kneeling by a cupboard under the shelf where the music centre might have been. The photographer pushes forward and flashes off a number of shots before the crouching man stands with an object cupped in both palms. All the activity in the room has stopped as they cluster around; at first Jess thinks it's a doll, and then she gets closer and sees the ragged flesh and white bone of a human hand, severed at the wrist; the blood seems barely congealed. Around three of the fingers a few strands of long blonde hair have been knotted, like ponies' tails. For a second she's reminded of one of the offerings left at the shrine below the Dyke.

A gift, a sacrifice.

The hand could be a model if it weren't for the dullness of the flesh, and Jess turns away as if it were bad form to look, like catching sight of a stranger, naked.

She looks at her own fingers, as if comparing. Who lost this relic? she thinks. A man, a woman, a child? No, not a child; it's too large and rough. But then again, it's so hard to judge, seeing it in isolation without a body to give it context. The room is silent; no one says anything until Pelham moves his bulk to cover

223

the sight and then there's a sigh as if everyone has been holding their breath.

At that moment Ed comes into the room. He looks even worse than yesterday, wearing the same suit and talking to the floor, barely audible. 'It's clear downstairs, but there's fresh milk on the side. Looks like we just missed them.'

'And you look like shit, man. Go home and sort yourself out, talk some sense to Liz or whatever it takes. Go on, bugger off,' says Pelham. As soon as Ed's out of earshot he says to Jess, as if it's her fault, 'There should be a law against marriages breaking up in the middle of investigations. Bloody bad timing.'

There's nothing she can do here and she needs fresh air. Outside, in the sunlight and away from the stench of the room, she waits by one of the police cars until Pav and Pelham join her. Pelham points at a satellite dish mounted on the end wall. It looks out of place, too large for the building.

'They don't use that for Sky—what the hell is it?'

'Broadband,' says Pav. 'High-speed Internet. In remote locations like this you have to use satellite to get the connectivity. Gives you the same sort of download speeds you get in an office. Expensive though, not the sort of thing your average punter would have unless they're running a business from home.'

'And the missing stuff upstairs?'

'Racked equipment, but there's no way we can tell what it was. From the look of the empty cabinet I guess they had servers, mass storage, raid arrays, routers; who knows. Whatever it was they've taken it with them.'

'Technology—might as well be voodoo,' says Pelham.

A man joins them; Jess recognises him as the pathologist from Carwen's flat. Inside the evidence bag he's holding the decorated hand is visible, muted by the plastic.

'The amputation was done some time ago—don't know when, not yet. My guess is that they kept this in a fridge until they needed it. Someone knew what they were doing, but the marks on the bone are very strange—I'd love to know what tool he used. It's almost certainly male, and before you ask—no—not from a child. I can't say any more until I've had a chance to check it out at the lab. But from the evidence of the bleeding he was alive when it was removed.'

'For Christ's sake, man, show some emotion!'

'Not a luxury I can afford, Inspector, not in my job.'

'What about the tassels of hair?'

'I'm a pathologist, not a psychologist. I shouldn't think the hair came from the same person as the finger, but as to what it means, your guess is as good as mine.'

The other three move off leaving Jess alone.

That's when the trembling starts, deep inside. She feels as if she could come apart, all the connections in her body broken, and she forces herself to walk up the track to her car.

The exertion calms her. When she looks back towards the barn no one is calling after her, no one's missed her, and she drives back the way she came, not caring if she gets lost.

*   *   *

It's a relief to be writing up a court report that evening, for an adoption case. Something positive. She works at the kitchen table and bribes Wagner to stay close with rationed titbits of chocolate. And then a car crunches on the gravel; Jess looks out, sees Pav at the wheel of her Mercedes and goes out to meet her.

'Sorry I ran off earlier,' says Jess. 'I felt like I'd abandoned you. I just . . .' If she says any more she'll lose it again.

Time could have stopped. Less than an arm's-length between them, and a quiet waiting. One movement, the thinnest sliver of an inch forward and they'll be in each other's arms. Jess sees Pav's eyes widen and darken, as if to pull her forward, but she leans away, breaks the moment; breathes again.

'It's OK,' says Pav, as if nothing had happened. 'Pelham gave me a lift back.' A beat. 'I should never have let you come in the

226

first place.'

'I didn't give you much choice.'

'Maybe not. Maybe "fragile" isn't the best word to describe you.'

'No—just stupid.'

The danger's passed for now. They go inside and Pav scans the papers spread across the table.

'I didn't mean to interrupt—just wanted to make sure you were OK.' She points at Jess's half-empty glass. 'Though I wouldn't mind a drop of whatever you're drinking.'

She looks tired, Jess notices. Plain gold studs instead of diamonds and shadows under her eyes. Although it's the reason for her being here there's no more mention of the barn, the upstairs room, the severed hand.

'I never thanked you for the other evening,' says Jess. 'The gallery. Weird, but OK. And the meal was great—Annie's a lot of fun.' She tries to sound sincere.

Pav's eyes flicker away before she answers. 'She'll be having fun somewhere new before too long. Off to New York—a couple of weeks to start with, but looks like she'll be staying.'

'Staying? For how long?'

'Three years. An opportunity she just can't pass up—that's what she said, anyway.'

It's the first time Jess has heard Pav sound bitter about anything.

'When did you find out?'

'She phoned while I was still at the barn.

Couldn't say it to my face.'

'But what about you—would you go out as well?'

Pav almost chokes on her wine. 'What, join the NYPD? Come on, Jess—do I look like a wet rabbit? And even if I wanted to go—which I don't—Annie made it clear that I'm not part of the package.'

'I'm really sorry—I thought you two were so together.'

'Did you?' says Pav. 'We put on a good show, but we live in different worlds. And I think there's someone else—the guy who will be her new boss.'

For a moment Jess is confused. 'A man? But I thought . . .'

'She changed the rules and I can't compete. And to be honest, I don't want to, not any more. It's time to move on.'

That's why you're here, thinks Jess. You're on the pull, and I'm in your sights.

She could enjoy this.

'I checked out some of your songs,' says Pav. 'I thought they'd be like your old Hacksaw stuff, but they're so . . .'

'Sad? Suicidal?'

'Sad, but brilliant. And all the time I listened I kept thinking that the words were just a disguise, that I was missing the real meaning?' She says it as a question.

'I'm not that clever. A song's just a song. Different people find different meanings—

that's fine. All I do is write.'

'Far too modest,' says Pav, but she's interrupted by the phone. Jess answers, then passes over the handset.

'It's someone for you—wouldn't give his name. Says your mobile's off.'

And while Pav takes the phone outside, Jess wonders how her colleague knew where to call.

When Pav comes back inside her smile has gone. 'There's been another problem with your website.'

Back to reality.

'Remember earlier, when we brought the kit back to Denny's workshop?'

It feels like a year ago but it was only this morning.

'Someone hacked in this afternoon—a new image this time. A photo.' Her skin has turned to the colour of stone.

'What was it? Come on, Pav, tell me. Bryony? Rhiannon?'

Pav shakes her head slowly. 'A hand, a severed hand. The image was put on to your site almost to the minute that we found it at the barn.' She grabs her bag from the chair by the door. 'You keep the place alarmed?'

'Ed checked the system for me after I found the CD. I always turn it on when I go out.'

'Use it at night,' says Pav. 'And if you can, lock your bedroom door.'

CHAPTER FIFTEEN

She barely slept last night, keeping herself awake so as not to dream. Every animal noise was an intruder scuffling at the door, every owl call the secret signal to start the attack. As soon as the windows begin to lighten she dresses, goes outside and checks all around the house to be sure that no one has forced a way in and is waiting for her, silently, in another room.

She can't stop thinking about the hand, how it was removed, what it would feel like to wake to such a loss. And what sort of creature could do that to another human being; how it would be possible to look at someone's face as the work was done.

She leaves a message on Joe's voicemail; it's impossible to work today. Everything feels forbidden. She could walk to the shrine on the Dyke but the offerings would only remind her of the tassels of hair. She doesn't even want to start the computer in case, just by touching it, she releases something inside that is waiting to escape.

Most of all she doesn't want to be alone, and without any feeling of guilt she wishes that Pav had stayed, for comfort if not for anything else. She's still not sure what the agenda is.

Maybe she can use today to get a

perspective. There's at least one person out there whose life must be hell right now. At first she thought David Stiffley was unfeeling for holding his show at the gallery so soon after Perry was murdered, but maybe that's too harsh.

What do I want from him? she thinks. Tears? Hysteria? Total collapse? Shouldn't I appreciate someone who knows how to control his emotions? His mask. And whether it's her fault or not, maybe it would help to say sorry; for what happened to Perry, for her suspicions. For not trying harder.

*   *   *

The carvings hidden away in the trees have lost their menace as she approaches the workshop, and the pitch of some machine is rising and falling in a regular rhythm as it cuts and rests, cuts and rests.

The open double doors have released a mixed smell of animal skin, wood and polish, and a shaft of sunlight glitters with dust spiralling up to escape.

Jess stops in the doorway, letting her eyes adjust to the shadowed light, taking in the walls lined with stacks of bleached driftwood and the roof beams hung with sheets of skin like sails, halfway to leather.

The sounds of the machine come from a workbench where David Stiffley is bent, carving patterns into a piece of wood with a small electric instrument that reminds Jess of a dentist's drill. His eyes are invisible behind Perspex goggles.

There's no music playing today.

The man seems so absorbed that Jess is content to watch and wait until he finishes and notices her as he stretches his back. Jess wonders how he'll react as he lifts the goggles and turns towards her.

'Excuse me not shaking hands,' he says. 'The dust—gets everywhere.' His smile disappears as quickly as it came. 'Has something happened? Have they found something?'

'Sorry—no—I don't know . . .' Maybe this was a mistake. 'We barely talked at your show—I wanted to say how sorry I was.'

Or maybe I just wanted to make myself feel better.

David streaks the dust on his face as he wipes the sweat from around his eyes. 'It's only just sinking in, after all these days. Denial, isn't that what it's called?' He leads Jess outside into the sun. 'I could smell autumn this morning. Last year I swore that I'd put decent heating in the workshop but I still haven't got round to it.'

They sit next to each other on a low stone wall, looking across the clearing to the line of trees.

'Perry was two—just over—when his mother

left. Up till then he'd been a real chatterbox, but the day after she went he stopped talking. Didn't say a word for months.'

'Why did she leave?'

'Because of me. Because she knew that what I wanted, really wanted, wasn't her. And I tried so hard.' When he looks at Jess, she wonders what he's asking. 'When I saw that photograph, the one they said was Perry with that man . . .' His voice breaks. There's no sound in the clearing, as if even the birds are listening. 'And then all the questions—you, the police.'

Jess tries to speak but he interrupts her.

'You were just doing your job. I realise that now, but at the time I thought there was some conspiracy against me.' His voice drops to a whisper. 'I thought Perry was to blame.'

And maybe Perry would have agreed, thinks Jess. The biggest sin of all—she's never yet found a child who didn't feel guilty about being abused.

She hesitates for a moment, then lays her hand on his arm. It's as if she's breached a wall. David covers her hand with his, to stop Jess from moving away, and begins to sob, a silent shaking that seems as if it will never end; and it's only when he's left her for his carvings and she's walking back through the woods that she lets her own tears come.

*   *   *

233

It seems unfair, but her crying has buried the memories of the sleepless night. Jess goes through the house, opening doors and windows, and feels strong enough to check emails. Gina could have changed her mind again; that would be a gift worth having. Instead, the only message is from Spider.

'Chad, you are awesome! now it feels like i'm really talking to you. like you're here with me. i never meant that stuff about seeing other girls i got photos of you on my walls. i look at you when i'm in bed. you look like you're up for it. you could sing for me, i want to hear you sing out. and then you'd respect me. we got so much to talk about. be seeing you.'

What a fuck up! Why did she ever send that reply? Why did she even read his pathetic emails? Now there's a grubby teenager somewhere fantasising over her. She'll need to ask Den how to junk any more emails from Spider—she doesn't ever want to hear from him again.

*   *   *

Next morning she's in the studio, working on a new song, when Anton calls. They haven't spoken since she left his cottage on Tuesday morning; five days that feel like a year.

'I'm in Birmingham,' he says. 'A cancelled meeting—don't ask—only an hour from you. I could pick up a toothbrush on the way . . .' But he's hesitant, probing, as if he knows that this is not straightforward.

Jess is about to say no. And then she remembers the noises in the night and relents; having him to stay might be an exorcism.

*   *   *

He calls again from halfway up the lane, with Maisie defeated by the hill. Jess backs the Jeep for half a mile down the single track until she sees sunlight flashing from chrome and Anton sitting on a fallen tree by the side of the lane, chewing at a long stalk of yellow grass. They kiss like friends before he moves his bags into her car and they drive back to the farmhouse.

It's hard to believe they made love. As they drink beer in the garden, looking at the Welsh hills in the distance, the blue stud in his ear catches the sun. It looks like a fragment of sky, Jess thinks, distilled and captured in a crystal. He's young and attractive, as close to normal as you could want. He's almost a stranger.

'The sheep over there, they're being moved to another field.' Anton points across the valley. 'Those two black dots must be the dogs rounding them up.'

They watch the flecks of white merge into one mass funnelling towards the single point

235

through which they flow, disappearing from sight behind the trees. They reappear further down the slope, the whole movement taking place in reverse as the point becomes a line which separates into blobs of white spreading across the new field.

'Transhumance in miniature,' says Anton. 'English version—very orderly.'

'Wales, actually. You're looking across the border.'

'I know. I just wanted to hear you put me right.' He ducks out of the way just in time as Jess aims a slap at his face.

Anton still knows nothing about her. He mapped her body, not her memory. Even as they laugh she knows how unfair this is; she stayed with him because she was lonely, because he wasn't a threat. Because he was there.

'You want to climb a hill?' She wants to move, not to think.

'A hill? What hill?'

'Skirrid—the Holy Mountain. More like a lump actually. Come on.'

They park in a lay-by near the start of the track, half an hour's drive away, and pace each other through the woods on the steep slopes until the path breaks out into the open moorland and Anton follows Jess up the straight path to the ridge.

'Not quite the Tyrol,' says Anton, 'but not bad for a start. Still, if I'd known I'd have

236

brought walking boots.'

Jess takes the lead, walking quickly along the track until they reach some stone ruins at the end, where the ridge tumbles down the steep escarpment. And all the way along, across the outcrops of rock and around the grassy depressions, she listens to Anton's nonsense; stories of his car and his childhood in Austria and the woman he didn't have an affair with in Hanoi.

She knows she's testing—herself, not Anton—and for the flicker of a moment she wishes she could be the woman he wants. But it doesn't work that way. When he turns to kiss her as they sit by the foundations of an old chapel, she can't stop herself stiffening, even though she wants to please him.

He pulls away, deflated. 'I knew it would be a mistake, me coming here.'

'My mistake, not yours. I'm sorry.'

'Do you want to tell me?' he asks. 'Is there another guy?'

He's so beautiful; in another life, Jess thinks, it would have been so much easier.

'Another guy,' she echoes. 'If only.'

Anton reaches for a late buttercup and hands it to Jess. 'You remind me of a poem by Heine,' he says. 'One my Oma taught me in Austria. *Du bist wie eine Blume, so hold und schön und rein; Ich schau' dich an, und Wehmut schleicht mir ins Herz hinein.*"'

'I don't speak German.'

'You're lovely as a flower, So pure and fair to see; I look at you, and sadness Comes stealing over me.'

On the way back they stop at a pub, all flagstones and blackened beams.

'So tell me about her,' says Anton. 'What's her name? What does she look like? What's her job? Does she know how you feel?'

'Did I say it was a woman?'

'Didn't have to. Let's be honest—no man can compete with me so it has to be a woman.'

'OK, ten out of ten, you arrogant bastard.'

Anton toasts her with his beer. 'So, you going to tell me or not?'

'I'm not sure if I should be offended,' says Jess. 'I thought you'd be more upset.'

'We had a great night together—it was like a gift. Maybe that's my real question—why did you stay with me?'

'And why do you ask so many questions?'

This time he laughs. 'Jess—you are remarkably good at this. The best.'

'Good at what?'

'Not talking about yourself. If you hadn't noticed, I quite like you. And I still like you even if you don't fancy me. It's called being friends—and rule number one is to share. I tell you about my life, you tell me about yours. Doesn't have to be your darkest secrets. You don't want to talk about this woman—fine. How about where you go for your holidays, or your favourite band, or your fantasy netball team?'

Until he stops talking to mop away the tears on her cheek, Jess hadn't realised she was crying.

'Don't like netball.'

'Me neither. How about tennis? Navratilova—twenty-five years ago of course—versus Serena Williams—what do you reckon?'

'Navratilova, every time.'

'See how easy it is? Friends—a very good word.'

*   *   *

Three hours later, after they've picked up his bag from the farmhouse, Jess watches him back Maisie down the lane from where he abandoned her this morning.

A gift, that was the word he used, and that's what today feels like. They'd talked about Perry and the missing girls, about Pav. About Gina.

OK, she tells herself, not everything but a good start.

Before he left, Anton had said, 'You can't solve them all—no one expects you to. Pick your target—let yourself win for a change.'

*   *   *

She sleeps late the next morning, and if there

were dreams they evaporated in the daylight.

'This confession lark seems to work,' she tells Wagner as she puts his bowl down. 'What do you say—shall we start going to church? No? Maybe you're right—not my style.'

But she feels stronger than she has for weeks, months; strong enough to call Pav and say—are you around—can I come over—now?

'Give me an hour,' says Pav. 'No, ninety minutes.' She must be working; the voice in the background sounds like Pelham.

Jess chooses her clothes with care, as if this were a first date. By the time she's decided on the least appalling of all the options it's time to leave. She can picture the address Pav gave her; walking distance from the gallery where David had his show, but this time Jess takes the road along the side of the estuary, past the pipes and gantries of the chemical plants and smelting works that edge the city.

She's about to park near the marina and find the apartment on foot when a silver Mercedes passes. Jess follows the car for another couple of streets, half expecting it to disappear into one of the gated car parks, but it stops outside one of the new developments facing across the water.

Pav must have noticed her, and waits by the car until Jess arrives. One look at her smile and Jess knows she's made the right choice.

'Perfect timing,' says Pav. 'I would have been back sooner but we thought we had a lead on the last image on your website.'

'The photo of the hand?'

'It was a dead end again, but we'll get there, promise.'

She leads the way inside and they take the lift four floors up. The apartment is just as Jess had imagined; she'd bet that Annie's office looks much the same. Sharp lines and brushed steel, white leather furniture and a couple of formula abstracts to match the colour scheme, costed by the foot.

Apart from them there's no other sound in the apartment.

'Annie not home yet?'

Pav busies herself with blinds, covering the room-height glass doors out to the balcony.

'She often works on Sundays. Sometimes she takes a hotel room for the weekend, especially if she's entertaining clients. I've stopped asking questions.' She pours them both a glass of white. 'But luckily, Annie never questions the wine bills.'

She laughs suddenly. 'Look at the two of us—I'm power dressed to keep up with the boys and you look like you just got back from Iraq. What the hell are you doing here?'

She toasts Jess, holding her gaze without blinking.

If I reached out now and touched her skin, thinks Jess, we'd melt into each other. I wouldn't know where one ended and the other began.

But before she can move there's a sound at the front door and Annie crashes into the room with a bunch of flowers.

'Sorry, Pav—thought you'd be out. I came back to pick up my bags—my flight's been brought forward to tomorrow morning, so I decided to spend the night in London and go to the airport from there. I thought it might be easier.' She hands over flowers. 'I got these for you yesterday—I was going to leave them . . .' She disappears into the bedroom in a flurry of coats and bags.

Pav looks at the flowers with an unreadable expression, then lays them carefully on the low glass table.

'I think it's best if I go, if you're OK,' says Jess. 'Things to do, hungry cat—you know the sort of thing.'

'I guess this isn't a good time,' says Pav. 'Sorry.'

It's been a long drive for a small result, but Jess sings to herself all the way home.

*   *   *

She's surprised to see Ed's car outside her house when she gets back from Bristol, but it's his wife that gets out as Jess parks the Jeep.

'Hiya Liz.' She peers into the car but there's no one else inside. 'Isn't Ed with you?'

'I thought he might be here.' Liz has tried to repair her make-up but there are still smudges of mascara under her eyes.

'My God, Liz—what happened? Come inside—I'll get you a drink.'

Liz doesn't move. 'I thought you and Ed . . .'

It takes a few moments for Jess to register the accusation. 'Ed and me? No way, Liz. I haven't seen him since . . .' She counts the days back to the scene at the barn. ' . . . Not since Thursday. It was to do with the missing girls.' She remembers Ed, looking defeated, being dismissed by Pelham. 'When did *you* last talk to him?'

'Thursday morning.' Liz's voice is little more than a whisper. 'He hasn't been home since and his phone is switched off. I didn't know what to think.'

'It's been a hard couple of weeks. Maybe he needed some space, went to stay with a friend.'

'We don't have many friends, not like that.'

'Family?'

'I tried his cousin in Gloucester—we see quite a lot of them. But Leslie was out, and his wife said they hadn't seen Ed for a couple of weeks.'

'I don't know what to say, Liz. Have you tried Inspector Pelham—maybe Ed's doing something for him?'

'Maybe.' But she doesn't sound convinced. 'Sorry to disturb you. Stupid of me. Should have known better.'

She drives too fast down the track, scattering stones and dust, then skids around the far corner and guns the engine as she disappears down the lane.

At first he thinks it's Chad standing by the door of his apartment but then realises she's too thin, a touch shorter, the hair a different shade of blonde. And the hungry eyes.

'Hiya babe—it's Jax, right? How'd you find me here?'

She's wearing a short leather jacket over a dark singlet, jeans and new trainers, and a large plastic tote bag.

'It said in NME that you were doing some work on the new album at the Church Studios. I followed you from there a few days ago.'

'Right little Miss Marple.'

She hasn't blinked in all the time she's been standing there, her eyes so dark that the pupil and iris merge.

'Are you alone?' she asks. 'I mean, is Chad here?'

'Aye, I'm alone; no, Chad's got her own place. She doesn't own me.'

Jamie takes her through to the main room, gets them both a beer and moves a guitar to make space for her on the sofa. She holds her bag in her lap, her shoulders hunched and hollow.

'It's smaller than I thought—the flat,' she says, and thinks—Alice's quarters are probably bigger than this.

'But you should see how the wee men in suits live. Bastards.'

'So you don't stay in, like, really posh hotels when you travel?'

'Fuckin' aye—some of the places we play don't even have hotels. Doss houses, more like.'

'What about New York—NME said you were there a couple of weeks ago?'

'You practising to be a travel agent, or what?' He finishes his beer, closing his eyes as he swallows. Jax holds her bottle with both hands, untasted. 'I was gonnae order pizza— you want some?'

He makes the call, watching as Jax absorbs his room.

'What were you doing before I got here?'

'Working on a new song—I cannae write during the day.'

'How many guitars have you got?'

'There's the Rickenbacker I use on stage mostly; a Gibson—won that off some tosser in a game of brag. And then this acoustic for when I'm writing, as well as the old joanna.'

She reaches for the guitar but stops before she touches it, and turns to Jamie.

'May I?'

He smiles at the unfamiliar politeness and moves across with his arms ready to cage around her.

'I'll show you how it goes . . .' but she's already forming the chords, finger picking a melody, looking at him while she plays something he's never heard before.

'Way to go!'

She plays with her eyes closed for a couple of minutes, then lays the guitar down carefully and pulls a folder from her bag.

'I write songs myself—would you look at one?'

Jamie expects words scribbled on a scrap of paper, but she hands him a few leaves of manuscript, the notes neatly marked in pencil with words underneath. In A, Chad's key.

'You did this?'

'I've played piano since I was six, and guitar for the last three years. And I have singing lessons.'

Rich kid.

'How old did you say you were?'

'Sixteen.' She holds out her hand for the manuscript. 'You want me to play this?'

She goes to the piano, an upright pushed against the wall, starts to sing. Her voice is lighter than Chad's, a semitone higher, and she transposes automatically as she plays. Jamie taps the beat on his thigh, already hearing the bass line and the harmony.

Jax sings unselfconsciously, within her limits.

'Again,' says Jamie. He takes the guitar and improvises over her melody, and when they finish she turns to him, triumphant. She looks older now.

'That was fucking great!' He means it.

'I wrote it for Chad . . . and you. I'd love to hear her sing it.'

'She'd go fucking ape if she knew you were here—the woman's got a wee temper on her when she's riled.'

'Say you wrote it. I don't mind, just as long as you play it.'

*   *   *

Jax finishes her pizza before Jamie's halfway through, then asks for the bathroom. While she's away, Jamie examines the manuscript. The notes are clear, but the words are almost impossible to read, slanting so far to the right that they're almost horizontal. He can barely believe she wrote something so subtle, with progressions he would never have thought of.

When she comes back they sit together, share another beer and a joint. She says, remember I'm sixteen, legal. As if it mattered. She's wearing the same scent as Chad.

When he goes to the bathroom he realises why she took so long; the piece of barely digested pizza dough under the seat, the sharp smell of bile not quite hidden by her perfume spray.

In the bedroom he looks at Jax, her thin, naked body displayed on top of the covers. He feels guilty and finds a condom but she stops him—it's OK, it's safe. I want to feel you come inside me.

Her fingers feel soft on the skin of his prick, stroking from root to tip so lightly that he can feel only a sensation on the border of pain. She takes control, pushes him on his back and sinks down onto him. Her breasts are barely large enough to cup in his hands as she rides him slowly, never making a sound, moving just enough to bring him to the edge and then her muscles close around him with unexpected strength, squeezing until he cries for her to stop.

She doesn't stay.

CHAPTER SIXTEEN

Jess counts off the hours during the night and falls asleep only after the windows begin to lighten. Twice she reaches for the phone to call Pav and twice sits in the dark looking at the luminous keys, wondering what to say that wouldn't be an interference.

Even though most of the weekend had been an unlooked-for win, today is one of her precarious days, when she feels as if she's reached a boundary and doesn't have a map.

In spite of the shop's apparent emptiness there is already a queue at the one open checkout, but Jess doesn't notice the person behind her until she feels the heat from his body as he leans forward, his face hidden but his breath humid as he speaks into her ear.

'Did she turn up in the end?'

He's standing so near that Jess can't help brushing against the fabric of his clothes as she spins around. None of her clients could afford a suit like this, the only creases there by design. At first all she can smell is his lavender cologne but this close there is another odour about him, the sour musk of a teenage boy's bedroom. Under the supermarket lights his skin is almost translucent, his beard already waiting to sprout as the day wears away.

They're standing as close as lovers but he doesn't move and Jess backs away from his grin.

'Your daughter—did she meet up with you? Such a shame that she kept you waiting there, alone.'

Now she places him, the man from the bar at King's Cross, the day she didn't meet Gina. Drinking wine, getting in the way, acting like a prick. She wonders if he grins in his sleep. He reaches into the wire basket that Jess holds in front of her like an old woman's handbag, studying each item.

'Thought you'd be a single-malt girl—and only a half? The speed you drink, that wouldn't even see you through an evening.'

He drops the bottle back into the basket with a flourish.

'Some people say there's no such thing as

coincidence, but what do they know? Or is it fate? Kismet? Always sounds faintly oscular, don't you think?'

Jess doesn't want to speak to him, to create any connection.

'Jess, isn't it? Powell Unwin—you remember me, from the station? Bought you a drink. Kept you company.'

'Why are you here?' She doesn't mean her voice to be this shrill. 'I thought you lived somewhere near London.'

'Work, my dear, work.' He holds up the briefcase, a talisman. 'One of my little patients has moved to this charming neighbourhood and for reasons which escape me I agreed to hold a session at Uskmouth General. I am a mere slave to these children.' A vaudeville shrug.

'You're a doctor?'

'Psychologist. But I like to think of myself as a favourite uncle they tell their troubles to. Of course, all Tiffany can do is talk about those missing girls. What were their names—Bryony and Rhiannon? Welsh, were they? Sisters? I shouldn't say it but kids, they're like flies. Noisy, dirty, move too quickly. Now if people treated spiders with more respect, there wouldn't be so many flies.'

His grinning face is an insult. Under the expensive jacket his shirt is crumpled and the breast pocket is torn, peeling away with threads of cotton like tiny worms erupting at

251

the seams. Jess wonders why she's letting him stand next to her, as if acquiescing in a relationship.

The checkout girl is saying, 'Good morning, madam,' for the second time. All the while that Jess has her back to the man behind her she expects to feel him touch her, on the shoulder, in the middle of her back, her hair.

She expects a commentary as she packs and pays for her new possessions.

She keeps thinking, *oscular.*

She leaves without looking at his eyes, away from her car, into the first clothes shop she sees. With a single movement she takes a handful of hangers into a changing room. She sits with her feet up beside her on the narrow bench along the back of the cubicle, waiting until a girl with a badge asks if she's OK.

*   *   *

It's half past nine when Jess gets to the office. Joe is waiting for her, one buttock propped on the corner of Else's desk.

'How good of you to grace us with your presence, Miss Chadwick. Will you be staying, or is this just a courtesy visit?'

'Not now, Joe, this is not a good time.'

'I try to make allowances, Jess, but you're getting close, let me tell you, very close indeed.'

'Close to what? I have absolutely no idea

what you're talking about.'

'You've become completely unreliable, Jess. And you're impertinent.'

'You're talking shit, Joe. I had a bad night, I had a bad morning. Now shut up and stop pissing me off.'

OK, she shouldn't have said that. But it's hard to be tolerant of this man with hair sticking out of his nose and stains under his arms and limbs that seem to belong to somebody else.

'The Inspectorate have called for all the Stiffley papers—they went over on Friday. No doubt they'll want to interview you at some point this week, always assuming that it doesn't interfere with your detective duties.' He limps back to his office without waiting for a response.

Else looks up. 'Joe is worried. Not just the Stiffley case—those poor little girls.'

'It's been too long,' says Jess. 'One week since Rhiannon was taken by Marty, two since Bryony went missing.' They both know the score; the police will just be looking for bodies now, whatever they pretend to the family.

And then she remembers that there is no family.

The air settles around Jess. She tries to write, drinks water, crashes her computer. A bead of sweat crawls between her breasts. She can smell her own body.

Whenever she looks down, Jess hears

whispers; she can't face this office with its ghosts of schoolchildren playing around the desks.

'If Joe wants me, tell him I'm working from home. And tell him not to call.'

Jess lets the case files spill over the passenger seat. The car has been in full sun all morning and the air inside has a tropical sweetness. Damn, she thinks, something in the shopping has gone off. It'll have to wait until she gets home and she drives fast with the windows open, letting the autumn air wash her clean.

*   *   *

Back at the house there's just one thin envelope caught in the letterbox. It's expensive, woven cream with an embossed logo and a return address to a firm of solicitors in London. At first she doesn't register the name on the front.

'Dear Madam

We are informed that you are responsible for an Internet website purporting to represent the songs of Ms Jessica Chadwick. We act on behalf of Ms Chadwick, previously a member of the musical group "Hacksaw" who claims that you are acting without her consent and in violation of her copyright.

You are therefore required to immediately

remove access to this website, destroy all material held electronically or in any other form . . .'

There are three pages, closely typed, paragraph after paragraph . . . warnings . . . civil action . . . need for a written apology . . . disclaimer of any rights to the material.

She doesn't understand; she's missed something. She reads it again, to the end, more slowly. She shakes the envelope to see if there's a covering note.

Nothing.

The pages of the letter fall to the ground like sycamore seeds.

There's something inside her body; moving, stretching.

The house is silent and Jess starts talking out loud, to fill the space. It's just some sick bastard, she says. Someone trying to scare me. Someone trying to make me part of his pathetic life.

Just like stalkers in the music business, following bands around. Trying to borrow other people's lives—no, not borrow, steal. Someone trying to steal my life.

She gathers the pages from the floor, and looks at them again. The trouble is, these are concrete. These exist. Thoughts mean nothing.

She needs to look at her birth certificate. She walks towards the study as if towards an executioner's block, and finds the file where she keeps her personal papers, tipping the contents on the floor and scrabbling through the pile without any order to the search, while Wagner watches from the doorway.

Bank statements, phone bills—all have her name, but they're not enough. She knows what she's looking for but it's not here. She closes her eyes to see it better, the old brown envelope where she keeps special papers. Her birth certificate, Gina's adoption papers. Gina—of course.

She finds it in the long brown box in the spare room, under the clothes she bought for her baby. The envelope is sealed with Sellotape that has become brittle and yellowed with age, but Jess forces herself to run her finger carefully under the flap, not wanting to tear the precious documents inside. The red and cream certificate smells official, as if she'd sealed dust and the air from a third of a century ago in with the paper. She strokes the thick parchment between her thumb and fingers and begins to breathe more slowly.

She reads the certificate, checks it against the letter.

Counts her breaths.

Reads the name again.

Jennifer Chatterton.

And again and again.

Jennifer Chatterton.

It's like picking at a scab.

The copperplate handwriting in violet ink is all too plain, written in the days before computer errors. Jess checks the father's name and there it is again, *Chatterton.*

Someone else.

She speaks the names out loud. Chatterton, Chatterton, Jennifer Chatterton. All she can think is that it sounds like a train.

Jess reaches into the box and finds a miniature shoe. She wants to feel something hard, with edges. She sits slumped against the bed frame. The walls are receding and the ceiling is too tall—all the surfaces of the room are mobile as if she has smoked some bad skunk.

She looks back into the envelope and pulls out Gina's adoption papers. They look unfamiliar and innocuous. Pieces of paper. Did they make people sign their own death warrants? Jess wonders. The signature looks like her writing but childishly rounded, written slowly and carefully.

Jessica Chadwick.

Too many names, too many labels; it's hard to know what they all mean. She leaves the papers scattered beside the brown box and walks downstairs slowly, holding onto the banister. Without looking at the words she takes the solicitor's letter and crumples it into balls, starting with the envelope and then each page, screwed up and thrown across the floor.

In the mirror by the front door her reflection seems wrong, as if she were looking at an impersonator; almost, but not quite, perfect. She runs her fingers through her spiked blonde hair to see if the reflected image matches her actions.

She needs an anchor, something to tie her to reality. She scans the room, looking for something personal, but all she sees are a couple of framed prints, an African mask, some earthenware jugs that she can't recall buying.

There used to be a photograph but it seems to have disappeared; was it stolen or did she hide it? Not that it matters.

She forces herself to count breaths, slowing her heartbeat, but just as she's beginning to feel calm she remembers Denny. He hosts the website, the solicitors will have tracked him, will have written to him too.

He answers the phone with her name said carefully—Hi Jess—and she knows that he knows. He sounds like someone she's never met.

'I already took the site down,' he says. 'I'm in enough trouble already over that recording of the girl. I can't afford any more.'

'You know it isn't true.' She tries not to plead. 'It's just some bastard bullshitting me. I'll sort it.'

'Sorry, Jess, but I got enough to worry about. Best leave it for the time being. When you've sorted things out we can start again, maybe.'

A click and he's gone. Scurrying away, Jess

thinks, as if he could catch something from me over the phone. A few days ago he thought I suspected him of abuse, now he thinks I'm a liar.

I've become the stranger.

On her way to the fridge she kicks aside one of the letter balls, and breaks stride to flatten another with her foot.

No beer.

She tries the cupboard, less than a capful of Scotch, less than useless. Her eyes start to prick with tears at this final cut and then she remembers the shopping in the car. The path outside is wet; while she was looking through the papers there must have been a shower. The sky is already clearing and the air is soft and comforting. She stops for a moment, forcing herself to concentrate on what's around her. The smell of damp earth and wet stone, moving shadows on the slopes across the river, the sound of sheep that she watched with Anton. The thought of his generosity grounds her, and she manages to smile as she remembers his lecture on transhumance and wishes she had his friendship; here, now.

*   *   *

The Jeep is patterned with raindrops as she opens the tailgate and the smell rolls out, thick and sweet. One carrier bag falls to the ground and tins disappear under the car, the others are crammed in the spaces around something hidden under an old tartan blanket that she doesn't recognise. It isn't hers. It wasn't there this morning when she put the shopping in.

The bumps and contours give no hint of its shape under the cover, and she takes hold of the blanket between her thumb and fingertips, but stops before she pulls. This is another moment of change from which she can never return and she's frozen, not wanting to leave behind . . . what? The past is as uncertain as the future, all that she has is this.

Jess lets the blanket slip back between her fingers, mindful of the rough, soapy texture of new wool, the edges knotted into tassels. She removes the carrier bags one by one, placing them carefully next to the rear wheel, but they hide too much and she empties each bag, arranging the tins and boxes in patterns on the ground.

Leaving the biggest present to last.

The last bag sounds as she moves it; a muffled bell, another reason to delay. The half bottle of Scotch is made to drink from, a poor man's hip flask, and Jess pulls on it so hard that she breathes at the same time and the liquid burns as she snorts it through her nose and chokes.

For a moment she is blind, fluid leaking from her eyes and nose and mouth. She can feel the shape of her lungs. She coughs and spits and stamps a dance around the gravel, swearing as her voice returns.

For the moment she can smell nothing but the acridity of alcohol. She positions herself equidistant from the sides, takes the edge of the blanket with both hands and pulls it away with a flourish, a conjuror.

Jess had known from the moment she opened the tailgate what was under the cover, and the stubble and ginger hair almost come as a relief. He's wearing a singlet that was white, and the tattoo on his arm is still visible although the skin around it has a greenish pallor, covering a deeper mottling like rough marble.

Marty.

Death has shrunk him and he's been folded into a foetal position with his face hidden under one arm, like a sleeping bird, but Jess's movements have disturbed the arrangement and the arm flops down suddenly, hanging over the edge of the tailgate, ending in a stump where the hand used to be.

Exposing the face.

Even through the whisky she can smell him now. His eyes are shut but there seems to be a movement under the lids, a slow undulation, and then she sees his mouth, twice as wide as it should be, slashed into a clown's grin. She wants to turn away but can't, as if someone were forcing her to watch. The spell is broken only when something detaches itself from the grey flesh at the wrist and falls onto the gravel, continuing to writhe with a life of its own. A maggot.

Jess manages a couple of steps back towards the house before she vomits Scotch over the gravel.

*   *   *

Stay inside, says Pav's voice on the phone. Touch nothing. Move nothing.

See nothing.

Don't lock the door.

Speak to no one.

The house is still silent, but Jess wants a crowd. She wants voices. She wants confirmation.

She does nothing, except drink.

*   *   *

Jess can think of no reason why she should lift her head from the table. The wood under her cheek is slippery and cold. If it were my mother's, she thinks, it would be warm and smell of wax polish but this is hard and smells of nothing.

When Jess opens her eyes again Pav is kneeling beside her, wiping her tears or stroking her face, touching her anyway, her bare hand soft and dry against Jess's skin.

Jess stills the hand against her face, pushing against it.

A voice is calling—Jess, Jess, look at me Jess.

Pav's skin smells of frankincense and myrrh, not of whisky or maggots, and with the thought Jess feels them crawling up from her throat and their soft mouth parts sucking at her flesh and if she doesn't open her mouth they'll split and hatch and she thinks she'll throw up again; and there are voices by the door and when she opens her eyes she's lying on the sofa.

Pelham flicks ash into the saucer balanced on the edge of Wagner's chair.

'There's a mug of coffee on the floor—don't knock it over.'

Jess focuses on the saucer and swings her legs to the floor, slowly, slowly. It's easier with eyes open.

The inside of her mouth is etched with acid and she lets her fingers trace the shape of her lips.

The coffee has no taste, only heat and sweetness. Enough.

'It's your own fault. Why the fuck didn't you call us?'

'You'd have looked . . .' Her throat feels like she's smoked a packet of Gauloises.

'I had to assign someone from uniform to puke duty, cleaning up after you.'

'Whoop-di-do.'

'I was going to call a doctor, but there was more Scotch on the ground than inside you. Good thing you missed the body or you'd have

263

really buggered up the evidence.' But his voice is tender with a concern she's not heard before.

The front door must be open. A current of air feels cool against Jess's cheek, and Pav's voice is outside, calling someone. Not her.

Pelham stubs out his cigarette and puts the saucer on the floor. Jess wonders what's happened to her cat.

'You know the next bit, Jess. We need to find out how Marty's body got into your car.' His gaze moves from her eyes to her lips, and back again. 'Tell me where you've been today. Where you parked, who you saw.'

'No,' says Jess, 'I didn't look in the back of the car before I left here. I went shopping. I shopped in Uskmouth. Because it isn't where I live. I parked in the multi-storey. As usual.

'I was late for work,' she says, 'trying to avoid this idiot from London.'

'Tell me about him,' says Pelham, as if asking her to describe the checkout girl.

Jess is back at King's Cross, waiting for Gina in the bar, drinking with a man she's never met, going home alone with her daughter's earrings piercing the flesh of her palms.

She tells this to the policeman in her armchair. She tells Pelham about Gina. What she looks like, how she smiles. She tells him about the emails, about the relationship that was nothing more than phosphorescent dots, perceived but never touched. She shows him the card.

Pelham takes a pair of glasses from a soft case, the half-moons, rimless. He looks more like a teacher than a policeman. She didn't expect him to take his own notes.

He stops writing a few moments after Jess stops talking.

'Why didn't you say all this before?'

'Why should you be interested in my mistakes?'

'You're public domain.' He lights another cigarette, holding it like a prisoner.

There's a sound of machinery from outside, the rhythm of a heavy engine. Pelham levers himself from the armchair and goes to the front window.

'They're taking your car away for examination,' he says. 'Let me know if there's anything in there you need, and I'll get it back to you as soon as possible.'

A uniformed constable walks over and says something to the inspector. The two men block the daylight, their backs no more than fabric-covered slabs. Jess had forgotten how much space some men take up.

Pelham returns to the armchair, screws the cigarette into the saucer. Jess counts the stubs. Four, all half smoked, tobacco spilling from the broken paper.

'And then?' The notebook and pencil are waiting.

Is this what confession is like? thinks Jess. Have I sinned and not noticed?

She doesn't tell him about the letter, starts by desciibing what happened when she went out to the car, but Pelham stops her.

'No post? Always the first thing I do when I get home.'

Public domain.

'Who is Jennifer Chatterton? Friend of yours?'

He isn't writing.

'We found the birth certificate, and the adoption papers.'

His voice is a quiet caress.

'We'll need to take them with us. Just for a while.'

Take whatever you want, thinks Jess. Take everything—it doesn't belong to me.

'Have you heard the name before?' he asks. 'Is it familiar?'

How can she answer? Over every thought, every spoken word, she's heard that incessant rattle.

Chatterton, Chatterton, Jennifer Chatterton.

It already belongs to her.

*   *   *

Pav is sitting in the gloom, little more than another shadow.

'John told you about your car? Not that you'll be driving anywhere tonight, but if it's any help you can borrow Annie's; her company haven't repossessed it yet. You won't get the Jeep back for a while.'

'What happens now?'

'I'll stay with you. The others have already gone.'

The voices and engines have stopped, and Jess feels glad that she's not alone.

'It may be the last thing you want, but you should eat. You wait there, I'll sort something.'

The coffee mug on the floor is cold. Jess pushes herself into the cushions, wishes that she had a blanket to stop her trembling and wonders where the tartan cover came from, that couldn't keep Marty warm. The shivering just gets worse.

CHAPTER SEVENTEEN

Jess awakes to the unfamiliar perfume of a new body in her bed. She listens to Pav breathing, feels the touch of breasts against her back.

Last night Pav came to the bedroom to say goodnight.

Stay, said Jess.

I will, said Pav, I'll be in the next room.

No, said Jess. Stay here. With me.

The warmth of Pav's body stilled Jess as it penetrated her shivering, and she fell asleep enveloped in Pav's arms and the scent of her skin.

When they woke Jess forgot and said, 'What about Annie?' but Pav said nothing, and only smiled as she let Jess trace the curve of her scar. Jess fell asleep again, trying to remember the word for the colour of Pav's eyes.

And now she's gone. Jess waits until all of the night's warmth has left the bed, then finds the phone to tell Joe that she won't be at work today, tomorrow, who knows when.

When she gets downstairs, Jess looks for the letter but it's disappeared, along with the certificates and the old brown envelope. She remembers Pelham taking them. Forgeries, are they? he'd said. Bloody good—could almost be the real thing.

Wagner's bowl is full and Pav has left cereal, a jug of milk, two aspirin and a note, with a promise to drive Annie's car round this evening.

She can't come too soon.

*   *   *

Jess opens the front door and watches the curtain of rain disappear in a layer of spray a couple of inches above the flagstones. Even the nearest trees are hidden.

She has no car.

She hoovers up the ash that missed Pelham's saucer.

She can't find bleach for the sink.

She stacks the dishwasher with every plate that she owns, but doesn't turn it on.

She opens the front door, and listens to the rain.

She turns on the heating for the first time since spring and listens to the air in the pipes.

Her clothes feel loose this morning. She forgot to shower. The flowers need changing.

She wonders if it would help to cry. 'Another Tear Falls'—her mother used to play that track on their stereogram, singing along with the Walker Brothers.

She watches the phone, but it doesn't ring.

*   *   *

Jess is stretched on the sofa when a banging on the front door wakens her. At first she's still in her inchoate dream where the rain sounds like waves on shingle, and then the banging again. Not a knock, but a demand.

This is when she wishes there were a chain on the door. Stupid, stupid. She stands flat against the wall, feeling ridiculous, and looks through the window to the man outside. His clothes are monochrome in the grey light, sculpted by the rain into dripping static folds. He looks familiar but she can see only a half profile and his hair is moulded to the shape of his skull.

'Jess—I know you're there. Open the bloody

door.'

Ed swearing?

He doesn't look at Jess as he falls through the doorway, wiping his glasses ineffectually between his finger and thumb. He's shrunk in the rain, like a cat caught without shelter so that another shape shows through the usual disguise of hairstyle and clothing, thinner and naked.

Jess finds him a towel, makes tea and wonders if she should offer food. She can almost feel his hunger.

She wants to leave a space around him.

All this time he says nothing, looks at the table, gives her no signs. Only when he finishes the buttered toast does he raise his eyes.

'Where have you been?' says Jess, all she can think of. She wants to shout—what the fuck are you doing? What about Liz? Why are you here? You're scaring me.

But all she asks is—where have you been?

He doesn't know how to answer her. Jess can see from the way he looks at the ceiling, silently inventing. He hasn't planned this well.

'I spoke to Liz—she was worried,' says Jess, as if he needs coaxing.

'I've been on assignment, for Pelham. Special duties, you know, undercover. To do with the missing girls.'

Jess wonders why he bothers; they both know the words are rehearsed.

'I stayed with my cousin.'

Does he have a gun, she wonders? A knife? The way he looks, she reckons that she'd beat him in a fight.

'You can do better than that,' she says. 'Why didn't you tell Liz? Why are you telling me? Better, why didn't Pelham say anything?'

'I'm sorry you had to find Marty.'

'Maybe I should call Pelham, get a car to take you home.'

'I don't want you to be hurt.'

'Who wants to hurt me?'

He shakes his head impatiently, as if she had asked something stupid.

'Don't care about you, Jess. Not Pelham, not Pav. They'll use you like bait if you let them. Go away, now. Go to your new boyfriend, or back to London. Don't stay here.'

So he doesn't know everything.

Before Jess can reply he gets up and opens the front door. For a moment he stands framed against the unfocused backdrop of rain, opens his mouth but says nothing. He never got dry, thinks Jess.

If it weren't for the crumbs on his plate, she could believe that he'd never turned up.

*   *   *

Pav sounds pleased to hear Jess, until she mentions Ed's visit.

'What did he mean, about me being bait?'

271

asks Jess.

Pav is silent for a moment. So many people preparing what they say.

'There are things we should explain. Stay where you are, I'll be there as soon as I can this evening. I'll bring John.' It's the tone of voice you use to a child, slow and concealing. How can she do that, thinks Jess. Hold me in the night, then talk to me like a stranger.

*   *   *

Is this what it feels like, to be circled by wolves? Carefully, like probing the raw flesh of a wound, Jess lets herself think about yesterday. Not Marty's body, but the letter.

Jennifer Chatterton.

Why does she hear the name in Nic's voice? She lets herself listen to the memory, picking, picking. Always Jennifer, never Jenny. Formal and polite, professional, like Pav on the phone this morning.

But she never felt Nic's hands on her body in the darkness, never heard him sigh 'Jess, oh Jess', never let him kiss her back to sleep.

Stress, she thinks. Stress makes you forget, makes you confused. They'll find the girls and whoever killed Marty, then all this nonsense will stop and my life can restart.

I've been caught in someone else's game, she thinks. Not everyone needs a motive. I'm incidental, all I have to do is stay calm and

272

rational.

I can do that.

*   *   *

Jess runs a hot bath peppered with geranium oil, and shuts the window so that steam fills the room. She slips down into the water until her head is submerged and all her senses are diminished. She can hear nothing but her body, she is all there is in the world.

Then a sound that is not a sound, just a noiseless vibration through the water. The front door being closed, slammed.

She's up and out of the water in one motion, eyes stinging as she fumbles for a towel. There's movement downstairs, and a voice.

'Jess? It's Pav—are you upstairs?'

*   *   *

She chooses clothes without care, a motley collection. Yesterday's make-up has bruised her eyes and become indelible.

They are here too early.

The warm lethargy of her bath has drained away. Jess tries to read something into Pav's smile of hello but it is too brief, erased as they shuffle into their places, ignoring the chairs and standing too close, like strangers at a party.

'This is confidential,' says Pelham. 'We are

273

not here.'

This is not about her.

'DS Randhawa has persuaded me that you are neither complicit nor expendable. She works, by the way, for the National Hi-Tech Crime Unit. Bit of a boffin. I lead a team in the National Crime Squad. These facts are currently unknown to members of the local constabulary and shall remain so until I decide otherwise.'

'A large-scale operation—we're working undercover,' says Pav.

'Undercover?' They seem surprised to hear her voice, and Jess wonders if she should have asked for permission to speak.

'Have you heard of BestFrendz?' says Pav. She spells out the name, watching Jess's eyes.

'Right up your street,' says Pelham. 'But a bit secretive. Like us.'

'They're a paedophile network, the best we've come across,' says Pav. 'Webmasters, chat rooms, system monitors, security systems. Their technical experts are as good as ours— that's why my unit is involved.'

'Why are you telling me?' says Jess.

'You are an anomaly,' says Pelham.

Anomaly.

'You don't fit the pattern. Our predictions don't work around you.'

'We need to know where you fit,' says Pav.

'They operate across Europe,' says Pelham. 'Membership strictly by recommendation. No

274

one knows more than two other members—all communications are through the Internet.'

Anomaly.

'Once you're in, you can't get out. The membership fee is fresh, unpublished images that meet their criteria,' says Pav.

'What pattern?' says Jess.

'These guys go the extra mile and then some,' says Pelham. 'Their speciality is violence—you saw the equipment in the barn.'

'Remember Marty's mouth?' says Pav. 'They reserve that for Fallen Angels, members who do something wrong. We think it's meant to be a smile.'

'We don't know that,' says Pelham.

'But it's part of a pattern. The hand, though—that was something new.'

Jess realises that they've stopped talking, waiting for her. She hadn't heard a question.

'Anything you want to ask?' says Pelham.

She wonders if everyone she knows wears a mask.

'They have an unusually high number of female members. Procurers,' says Pav. 'Often the mothers. Maybe they've been threatened, maybe they think they'll protect their own children from the worst parts.'

The image on Marty's hard drive. The girl was being held by a woman's hands.

Pelham is walking around the room, examining the window sills and mantelpieces, peering at the small collection of ornaments. A ceramic angel from one of Jess's clients, an old birthday card from Chana. He has his back to the others and Jess wills him to turn, wanting to see his lips when he speaks.

'They're very upmarket. Professionals. Lawyers, vicars, police,' he says. 'Social workers.'

'They get in everywhere,' says Pav. It sounds like an apology.

'Local plod were underperforming,' says Pelham. 'Leads not followed up, evidence going missing.'

'Cases were closed when they should have stayed open,' says Pav.

'No photographs?' asks Pelham. He's holding the angel.

'What?'

'You know, memories of those special days. Ice cream by the seaside, happy families, cat.'

Jess still can't see his face. Whatever Pelham looks at, he touches, leaving an invisible mark.

'Tell us about Ed,' he says. 'Tell us how he looked, what he said. Everything.'

'He was wet,' says Jess.

'Wet?'

'He was walking in the rain. He called me bait. You called me an anomaly.'

'Why did he come here?' says Pelham. 'What did he ask you? What did you ask him?'

'He was hungry—I made him some toast. I think he was frightened.'

'And you?'

'I was frightened. I didn't recognise him.'

'The man in the supermarket, the one from London,' says Pav. 'Did he ever give you a name?'

'Powell. Powell Unwin.'

'Would you recognise him—in a photograph? It won't take long.'

The room has become small. Jess walks into the garden, waiting for one of them to stop her. The rain has paused, but the air is dull and flat and filled with moisture. Her clothes ignore the light breeze, clinging to her body as if it were charged to overflowing with static electricity. She walks across to the two cars parked in her drive and uses her fingertip to join beads of rain on the bonnet of the BMW. Pelham's car is colourless, the raindrops merged into a thin slick across the surface.

Jess wonders why her car is not here. Perhaps she has returned to the wrong home, a discarded address. Something that people do when the boundaries of memory become relative.

*   *   *

They travel in Pelham's car; he drives slowly, unused to the potholes. The interior smells of pine, sterile and empty like something borrowed. Jess uses her elbow to clear a patch on the misted window.

277

The lane looks wider than usual and the perspectives have changed. There are trees she doesn't recognise. There are buildings across the valley that she's never seen before.

'Tell me more about BestFrendz,' she says.

'There are maybe a hundred people in the organisation,' says Pav. 'We've been following them for a year or so. One of their new members in Birmingham made a mistake and sent some of his latest snaps to the wrong email address. The woman who got them was scared shitless and got in touch; it was the break we needed.'

Jess doesn't ask who was in the photos.

'If they're into kids why have they targeted me?'

'That's what we need to find out. Maybe you just got in the way.'

*   *   *

Last time she was one of them. This time they sit her in a small bare room with the table, two chairs and a laptop. The screen is a film strip of faces, one morphing into the next, anonymous men made special by the context. There is no other pattern.

It takes thirty minutes and five hundred faces before Jess achieves recognition. His face is mobile, eyes focused behind her, a still image captured from a film. Smiling, the way he had on the platform.

278

Jess takes her hands from the keyboard. She let this man buy her a drink. She told him about Gina.

He has another name, they say. A record. Suspicious activities. We have a watching brief. We'd like to meet him. We have nothing else. What did he say his job was?

Jess can't remember; what he said, what she said.

She tells them that she needs the bathroom and washes her hands, holding them under the hot tap for as long as she can bear. She fills the waste bin with sodden wads of paper towels.

Under the fluorescent lights her face in the mirror has the same pallor as Powell's. Her cheeks are as shadowed as her eyes. She forgot to brush her hair and it frames her face like a jagged blonde halo.

Jess looks for signs of recognition, a mole, a familiar skin blemish, but the light has airbrushed them away.

They're waiting for her outside the door, one on each side.

*   *   *

Pelham drives back a different way, dodging through the estates, always turning just in time before they meet a line of stationary traffic. Jess is lost within minutes.

Back at the house, Pav hands Jess the keys to Annie's car.

279

'Go and stay with Anton,' she says, and Jess wonders what she said while Pav held her in the night. 'Stay for a few days. Just have the car back by the end of the week. Oh—and Jess?'

'Pav?'

'If Ed contacts you again call one of us immediately. And if he turns up here, don't let him in.'

As Jess watches them lurch down the lane in Pelham's car, she feels Wagner rubbing against her leg and thinks—My cat, what about my cat? Maybe Den could feed him if I go away. And then she thinks—What about Den? I never asked about him. Is he safe? Is he clear? Is he clean? When they raided his shop, how real was his anger?

Collusion. Ed and Denny. More patterns.

Jess is walking around the room, picking up each object that Pelham touched, wiping it on the edge of her T-shirt. Sometimes she mists the object with her breath, as if it had a magical quality to dissolve and cleanse. She remembers, that's how my mother used to clean pairs of spectacles.

In her circuit of the room she reaches the phone. She weighs it in her hand, studying the buttons, but she can't remember Anton's number. This time the address book falls open at the right page. If she has to go away, she wants the company of a friend, with no complications.

The phone rings and rings in his cottage on the flat side of the country; she listens until the handset becomes heavy in her hand, then polishes it on her T-shirt before replacing it in the charger.

*   *   *

Holidays in Florida. Why is it always holidays in Florida? If Den were here he would show Jess how to junk this spam. If I don't read it, she thinks, it doesn't exist. When I click delete it evaporates into oblivion. No residue. True creation and annihilation, from nothing to something to nothing again.

She leaves the screen, pours herself the dregs of the Scotch, but her stomach heaves at the fumes and she leaves the glass on the table in the kitchen.

Time was, only a week ago, that she couldn't wait to get home, log in, look for a message from Gina. A few days of unlooked-for hope. A tease. Now, when she sees Gina's address on one of the new messages halfway down the screen, it doesn't register.

And then it does.

From: Gina

Subject: blank

Date sent: today. This morning.

This morning, Gina sat at her computer, wrote an email. Somewhere.

The cursor is excited, skittering over the

281

messages either side of Gina's. Jess clicks at the wrong point in its erratic swing across the screen and wastes a couple of moments trying to understand why her daughter is offering her cheap Viagra.

She takes her hand off the mouse, flexes her fingers, breathes slowly, tries again.

She would never have believed how nothing could have a physical effect. How blankness is like a punch to the stomach. How an empty screen could say so much.

Not even an attachment.

Jess stares at the screen, waiting for the message to appear. Maybe it's some electronic equivalent of writing with lemon juice or milk; maybe the phosphorescent dots need time to warm up, to deliver their payload.

But there's nothing, as if the empty email was a tease, an unfulfilled promise. She stares at the screen a moment longer and then starts shouting.

'You bitch, you mean little bitch . . .'

The mug of cold, stale coffee explodes against the wall above the screen, spraying into Jess's eyes. Shards of crockery cover the keyboard, their broken edges pale and clean.

*　　　*　　　*

This time she lets the phone ring until Anton answers. They dance around the reason for her call, neither asking nor telling. Jess worries that Anton will find business elsewhere, but all he says he is, 'Come tonight, come now, drive safely, phone me.'

Jess wraps a spare key in a plastic bag and buries it next to a rosemary bush. If Den is compromised, Pav will feed the cat.

The backpack is mostly empty. Underwear, a couple of tops, a spare pair of jeans, make-up and a toothbrush. Travel light, Jess says to herself. Travel light, with a light heart.

It's already dark. The moon is almost full, flickering through the remnants of clouds herded by a fast wind that doesn't reach to the ground. Jess looks back at the house which seems drained of colour by the moonlight. Inside, the computer is still on with coffee soaking through the keys, but the building looks empty. She forgot to set the alarm, but it doesn't seem to matter now.

Jess drops her backpack on the gravel, where Marty's arm had fallen from the Jeep's tailgate, but snatches it up before it has a chance to settle and bangs it against the rear tyre of Annie's car, as if some maggots had been hiding amongst the stones and started to burrow through the canvas.

There are too many controls in unfamiliar places. The dash lights up like a cockpit; she could read by the amber glow. The headlamps create a tunnel of white light and she drives slowly, but even so the soft suspension grounds in the ridges and potholes every few yards.

Where the lane joins the main road, a few
yards from the bank of the river, Jess stops for
a moment. Although the road is clear in both
directions, she sits with her foot on the brake
as if waiting for something to happen. Even in
the moonlight the waters seem black, lapping
high up the banks.

'Motorway or forest?' She lets the car move
forward, beginning to turn south towards
the motorway, but almost immediately pulls
the wheel round to the right and heads in the
opposite direction towards the small roads
through the forest.

The road climbs steeply in a series of sharp
bends that take it up and over the Dyke, past
man-made lakes half hidden among the trees.
She remembers reading how these are the last
remnants of all the forest industries, mining
and quarrying and charcoal burning, and God
knows what else. A place that's been left
behind.

There's a sudden buzzing from her bag on
the seat beside her, and she scrabbles through
it with one hand to find her mobile. In the
darkness the small screen is bright.

Ed.

The backlight dims but Jess continues to
stare at the phone until she realises that she is
veering across the road into the path of some

oncoming headlights, and brakes hard before pulling onto the verge.

She flips the phone's cover.

'Jess? Don't hang up. I know you saw Pelham—you've got to believe me, things aren't what they seem.'

The words come out in staccato rhythm, as if Ed is trying to catch his breath.

'Are you there, Jess?'

'I have to tell Pelham you phoned,' says Jess, looking for the door locks.

'Listen to me first.' He's silent for a few moments, but Jess can hear him breathing in the background. 'I think I know where Rhiannon is, but I need your help.'

'Call the police, Ed. It's nothing to do with me now.'

'Please, Jess.' He pauses and she can hear a dry coughing away from the phone. When he speaks again, his voice sounds stronger.

'She's with Gina.'

Jess feels herself stop, as if Ed's words had tripped a switch. The phone bounces off the centre console, into her lap.

'Jess! Did you hear me? We don't have much time.'

Ed's words are an insect buzzing in the distance, joined by a slow thudding as her blood begins to flow. The adrenaline hits and everything looks preternaturally sharp. She picks up the phone with her fingertips.

'Where are you?' Her words sound like

gravel.

'Do you know the old iron mine on the Clearwater Road? Tourist trap. You can get there in fifteen minutes from the house.'

'Make it ten.'

Lucky she chose this route—the mine is no more than three or four miles away, if she can only remember the right turning. Compared with the Jeep, the BMW is virtually silent. The last time I was in here, she thinks, was when Pav drove me to the morgue.

'I've seen too many bodies,' she says out loud, and the sound of her voice surprises her as it fills the car.

After ten minutes she checks the mirror and turns the car back the way she came, moving slowly to look for the side road that she must have missed. Since she left home she's seen no more than two other cars.

This time she finds the turning, and after a quarter of a mile her headlights pick out the painted sign: 'Clearwater Iron Mine—Open 10 to 4 Daily.' She pulls into the small car park; there are no other cars, no sign of anyone. The ticket kiosk has a broken window, sealed with polythene and tape, and a padlocked door.

Jess turns off the engine and sits for a moment, looking around. There's no doubt that this is the place Ed meant. Set back from the clearing are the silhouettes of various pieces of machinery, like a collection of modern sculpture. When Jess opens the window she can hear the wind playing notes through the rusty iron, an animal sound. There's no moon now, the clouds have thickened and although she can't feel them, heavy raindrops are kicking up from the puddles around the car. She turns on the headlights but the wedge of light only makes the rest of the scene darker.

For all the time she's lived here, Jess has never been alone in the forest at night.

The mobile rings again, and she locks the doors before answering.

'Is that you Jess? Turn the bloody lights off.' The rain is hammering on the roof of the car now, enclosing her in another layer of sound.

'I can't see you.'

'I'm by the entrance, straight in front of you.'

Through the curtain of rain and the darkness, Jess can see nothing. She realises that she is trembling and grips the wheel with one hand, squeezing until it hurts.

'Ed?' She doesn't know what she's asking.

'Please, Jess—I need your help. They'll be here in a minute—we don't have much time.'

Her sweatshirt is soaked in seconds as she stands outside the car trying to work out which button will lock the car. The wrong one. The alarm siren is so loud that Jess takes several steps backwards, and the hazard lights strobe amber across the clearing. She presses another button at random and the silence is so thick she could touch it.

'I'm sorry, Ed, I'm sorry, I'm sorry,' she shouts into the darkness. There's no reply. She half runs, half stumbles through the puddles towards the machinery by the entrance. The rusty metal smells like blood.

'Ed?'

Still no answer. All she can hear is the sound of the rain drumming on the sheet of corrugated iron that serves as a roof to the mine entrance. Standing under its shelter, she wipes the rain from her face. A large padlock is hanging open from one of the double doors, and the other has been pushed half open.

The trembling has come back and her legs feel unsteady. She stands in the doorway, leaning in but not letting her feet cross the line. The damp smell of blood and rust is even stronger here.

'Hello? Ed?' She expected an echo, but her voice soaks into the walls. If she thought it was dark outside, this is a place that's never seen daylight.

A torch. Maybe Annie keeps one in the boot. And maybe she should phone Pelham or Pav. She hesitates under the shelter of the roof for just a second or two, before running out into the rain in the direction of the car. As she crosses the clearing she looks for the shape of the BMW, but sees nothing except the sheet of rain. She stops. The hissing of the rain is broken by a rumble of thunder in the distance, but there's no lightning to illuminate the scene. Behind her the iron sculptures and door to the mine have disappeared. She is surrounded by nothing but a featureless wall of water, the sound of it isolating her still further.

Think, she tells herself. Maybe I ran in the wrong direction. She turns ninety degrees and begins to walk, counting her steps. After twenty paces she stops again, another turn, another twenty paces. Each step squeezes water from her sodden trainers, and her clothes hang from her body like a suit of chain-mail.

This time there's a brief flash of light a few seconds before the roll of thunder, and she sees the mine entrance about twenty feet away to her left. Now she runs again. Under the roof, out of the rain, she hears a sound, but it's her own voice muttering 'stupid, stupid bitch.'

How could she have missed the car? Could someone have driven it away? No—surely she would have heard. But in this rain? She reaches out to one of the iron struts supporting the roof. The dark metal is cold and pock-marked, but comforting.

Damn! She left her bag in the car. And her mobile. Jess thought she was used to isolation, but this is different. Yet, unless she imagined it, Ed is here somewhere.

'Don't turn round!' The voice is male. Familiar. Not Ed.

Close.

She knows that she'll never forget his smell. The cologne has faded but the stale musk is like a signature.

'Powell.' She says the name to herself, but loud enough for him to hear.

'Correct! Well done, Jess—or is it Chad?' His lips are so close now she can almost feel them against her ear. 'Or maybe, just maybe, little Jennifer? I feel I know you all.' His breath is hot as he chuckles quietly and deliberately. 'Which is more than you do!'

Jess senses him pull away and takes the chance to push herself out into the rain, forcing her legs to start running. Just go straight, she tells herself. Get to the road and keep on running. In the millisecond it takes for these thoughts her arm is grabbed from behind, spinning her around so that she topples and falls onto the mixture of gravel and mud. The grip on her arm hasn't lessened and she's jerked upright, a burning pain in her shoulder.

I should scream, she thinks. But she's become mute, a voiceless child.

'Time to stop running,' says the voice.

There's a new smell suddenly, sharp and medicinal. Even as it registers, Jess feels a damp cloth pressed over her nose and mouth. For a second there's a sense of drunken spinning, but her struggles barely start before they end and she collapses in Powell's arms, her last small sigh lost in the sound of the rain.

CHAPTER EIGHTEEN

Although the rain has stopped, the wind remains to bend the trees lining the road down to the old bridge. Pelham sees no other cars as he reaches ninety, and then brakes sharply for the roundabout.

'Be open, you bugger.' He hears his own voice and thinks—I'm getting old.

His prayer is unanswered—the diversion signs are lit and the bridge is closed because of the wind. Twenty miles at least, down to the new crossing and back again. Too far. He ignores the sign, pulls over at the control centre and shows his ID.

'Sorry, sir, it's really not safe. You'll have to go down to Uskmouth.'

'I'm not asking. There's been an incident and I need to get to the scene, now. It's my risk—look, I'll even write you a disclaimer.'

He scribbles on the back of a form lying on the official's desk, and ignores the shouts that follow him out of the door.

If anything the wind is even stronger, threatening to pull the car door from its hinges as Pelham gets in. As soon as he reaches the main section of the bridge, hundreds of feet above the water of the estuary, a gust pushes the car sharply towards the central barrier. Before he can correct the steering he feels the impact and hears the tearing sound of metal on metal—and then he bounces back across the empty carriageway, towards the edge of the bridge. The whole car frame is juddering as the automatic braking kicks in; Pelham feeds the wheel back until he reaches the middle lane, and completes the remainder of the two-mile crossing at a careful crawl, the buffets of wind sucking air out through the ventilation grilles.

*   *   *

The lane down to the disused ferry quay is narrow and overgrown. Pav is waiting for him at the end, backlit by the portable floodlights illuminating the white-suited team waiting around the dumped car. Annie's car.

'Why is it always three in the morning when these things happen?'

'We were waiting for you before anything was moved,' says Pav.

The tide is out, and a couple of feet behind the car, the grass grades into a strip of reeded marsh before the mudflats begin. The damp air is sweet with the smell of rotting vegetation. Pelham looks through the window at the body behind the wheel, sprawled back in the seat, the mouth slashed into a clown's grin.

'Have you called Liz?' asks Pelham.

'Not yet—we don't want her seeing him like this. There will be time enough.'

'How long has he . . . ?'

'Six hours, give or take.'

Ed's face is sunken and grey, as if the flesh had drained away with his blood and his last breaths, but a broken tooth glistens, untainted by blood, caught on his shirt like an oversized button. He seems too small for the car—how quickly death shrinks us, thinks Pelham.

He walks to the edge of the grass and looks across the channel at the lights opposite, on the coast of Wales. For some reason the wind seems calmer here although he can hear it in the trees and the cables of the bridge. He takes out a cigarette but leaves it unlit, rolling it unconsciously between his fingers until it cracks and he throws it into the reeds.

'John . . . ?' He hadn't heard Pav move up behind him. 'I'm afraid there's more—did you see the passenger seat?'

Pelham walks to the other side of the car where the door is hanging open. Neatly arranged in the middle of the seat is a severed hand, pale in the floodlight in contrast to Ed's grey face. It looks unreal, an object that has never beckoned or stroked.

'It's not Ed's,' says Pav. 'He's still . . . intact. And Marty was only missing one.'

'So some other poor bastard's been a naughty boy.'

'The hand doesn't look fresh but it isn't decomposed. I'd guess it was kept in the fridge until tonight—we need forensics to take a look.'

'So this was planned?'

Pav shrugs. 'I'm a techie, not a doctor, but this doesn't fit any pattern I know about for paedophiles. It's completely atypical. So far, BestFrendz have acted like any other group of child abusers. Secretive, obsessively so.'

'And bloody violent,' says Pelham.

'True. But that fits within normal boundaries, if there are such things.' Pav turns away from the mutilated body and, unconsciously, traces the line of the scar on her cheek with the tip of her finger, almost caressing. 'So what's changed?' she says, as if to herself. 'It's like someone's crossed the line, or been pushed over.'

'Unwin?'

'We've seen his obsession with Jess, but that doesn't make sense either. There's no connection between them.'

'The man's a bloody psychopath!' says Pelham. 'What other reason does he need?'

'Come to think of it, they *are* connected,' says Pav. 'Jess worked on the original Perry Stiffley case. If Unwin was involved with that . . .'

'But why should he target her? He pursued her, he stalked her. You'll be telling me next that he wants to be found,' says Pelham. 'All that shit about a cry for help.'

'I'm not saying that,' says Pav. 'But there's a link somewhere, we just need to find it.'

Pav signals for the teams to start their deconstruction of the scene as she and Pelham lean against the bonnet of his car.

'There's one last thing,' says Pav. 'We tried Jess, she's not answering her phones. We also sent someone up to the house—the computer was left on, the alarm wasn't set but there's no sign of her.' She shows Pelham a plastic bag containing a mobile. 'This was in the car, on the floor under the passenger seat. It's Jess's. The last call she took was just after nine yesterday evening—from Ed.'

'Tell me this isn't true. After everything we said, and she still goes to meet him.'

'We don't know that.'

'You taking bets?' He tries not to yawn, and fails. 'Three murders—a young boy and two paedophiles, one of them a cop. And three missing females—two young girls and a woman who should have known better. I can't believe she'd be so stupid.' He sees the expression on Pav's face. 'Sorry, it's been a long day.'

'Don't worry, I feel the same. If it's OK with you I'll get a couple of hours' sleep, then I'm off to Suffolk to see Jess's . . . friend. His number is on her mobile—she was meant to go there last night.'

'You spoke to him?'

'Anton. Works in a residential unit for autistic children.'

'Jesus—it's like a bloody infestation. Aren't

295

there any ordinary people out there?'

'You should get some sleep, too. There's nothing either of us can do until we get the forensics back tomorrow.'

*   *   *

The first thing Jess notices is the taste, as if she's been sucking a piece of metal. She works her mouth, trying to swallow, but her throat feels like sandpaper and her tongue is stuck to her teeth. She sleeps again.

*   *   *

Her shoulder begins to burn, and she wonders if hot blood is leaking under her skin, filling hidden cavities. She shivers and realises that her whole body is damp, as if from a fever; she smells old earth, deep clay. When she opens her eyes there's no difference in the darkness.

There's another pain in the small of her back and she realises that her hands are tied behind her. Her feet are bound as well, and she rolls her weight like a walrus, shifting onto her side. The ground is gritty, and the sound of small pebbles skittering away is unsettling until she recognises the sound, like the soft patter of mice at night inside the cavities of her house.

Another noise. At first she thinks it may be an animal, but then she hears the sniffing and sobbing of a child. She can't tell how close it is;

the quiet cries have no echo, no direction.

'Hello—who's there?' Jess means to whisper but her voice fills the space around them. The sobbing stops for a moment and then continues.

'What's your name?' says Jess.

The sound dies away, but there's still no answer.

'My name's Jess—is that you, Rhiannon? Bryony?'

Silence.

'I came to your house—do you remember?'

She can hear the child breathing, somewhere near. Jess senses a wall behind her and inches herself up until she's propped upright against the rock.

She tries the child again; wanting not to be alone, wondering if there are more than the two of them—but all she can hear is the watchful breathing. How far away; six feet, ten?

'Where are you, sweetheart?' She moves towards the sound but as soon as she begins to scrape across the rocky ground the breathing becomes a frightened whimpering.

'It's OK—I won't hurt you.'

It's hard to move with her legs and hands tied; at one point she falls on her shoulder and can't hold back the shriek of pain, but the echoing cry of fear from the child tells her she's close.

And all the while Jess murmurs to herself as

much as to the child; it's OK, nearly there, you'll be fine.

She feels the heat of the other body first; whoever it is is holding her breath. And then they're touching. Jess feels the long hair like a spider's web on her face; a girl for sure.

The child must be tied up as well; neither of them can hold the other, and they nestle together for comfort like beaten pups.

Jess keeps talking and eventually the girl answers, repeating the same few sounds over and over, but it's a language Jess has never heard before and within a few minutes the girl is quiet again.

Now that she's become accustomed to the space, Jess can hear dripping in the distance. She counts the seconds between each sound, a single echo muffled into silence. The burning in her shoulder has died away, but it throbs dully like a second heart. She forces herself to blink; once, twice, again, in case her eyes have been injured and she's somewhere full of light, but she can feel nothing and the darkness remains.

Only now does she let herself think.

Gina. Ed said that Gina was here. How did he know her name? I never told him her name. I never told Ed about my daughter.

She tries to remember her conversation with Powell at the station in London. She talked about her daughter, but did she say Gina? Did she tell him her name?

How easily they caught me, she thinks. One word, one name and I act like a fool, straight into the web.

Another feeling forces itself into her consciousness. A full bladder. As soon as she becomes aware of it, the discomfort becomes almost unbearable and the distant sound of dripping is like an invitation. Amongst the smells of wet earth and rock she picks out the scent of urine. Probably the child.

Although the cold air is still, it sucks heat out from Jess's body under her wet clothes, and the shivering reminds her of her fear.

The child's breathing seems to be more regular, and Jess wonders if she's fallen asleep. She has no idea of the time, how long she's been here. Not long, she guesses, by the dampness of her clothes. Even in this atmosphere they would dry out before too long. Her left foot is numb, thick and spongy, and she tries to move her toes to get the circulation moving. They feel clumsy, as if she's working them with levers.

*   *   *

A sound, far away. Voices? The child has heard them too, and whimpers softly, curling into Jess's body. The sounds are indistinct, and as they get closer the voices stop and all she can hear are footsteps and their echoes. For the first time since she can remember there's the promise of light, nothing more to begin with than a jerking glow that could come from anywhere. Then a small sun explodes, so bright that she can see nothing else. She scrunches her eyes shut and instinctively tries to cover them with her hands, forgetting that they are pulled tight behind her. Even with her eyes closed she can feel the light playing across her and then moving elsewhere.

'Smells like a cesspool down here. Some people have no control.'

Powell.

'Come along, *Jess*.' He stretches her name, drawing out the sibilants. 'Open your eyes, admire your environment. We went to so much trouble.'

The torch beam moves away from her face and Jess squints at the man in front of her. At first he is no more than a shape, edges in the darkness, but as her eyes adjust Jess sees the features on his face resolve themselves into something familiar. She wonders if he ever looked any different.

The child has been pulled away and lies curled up on the ground about six feet away. Her face is smeared with clay from the floor and her hair is almost black and matted as if it hasn't been brushed for days. There are embroidered flowers on her flared jeans but the light is too dull for Jess to make out the colour; everything is dusted with red.

Maybe twelve, maybe thirteen years old.

300

Although she hasn't moved, her eyes are open and unblinking.

Jess has never seen her before.

'Part of our latest consignment—we had her delivered yesterday. Should wash up well enough, before we ship her on to her final destination.' Powell reaches down and lifts the girl's chin with the tip of his forefinger, then lets her drop.

The roof of the tunnel is so low that Powell can barely stand upright. Must be part of the mine, thinks Jess. The rough walls are covered with a film of water, shining red in the torchlight, and the floor is a mixture of muddy clay and fragments of rock. The shadows are thicker behind Powell, but Jess can make out the shapes of two other people, like dark reflections of the man in front of her.

He's carrying the torch in one hand and a child's colourful backpack in the other. He reaches in, pulls out a can of Coke and drinks noisily before placing the empty tin carefully on the floor. Jess runs her tongue across her lips, unconsciously.

'I hope you haven't become too attached to your surroundings,' says Powell. 'We have places to go, people to see.' He bends down towards Jess, shining the light directly into her eyes. 'We're going to make you a star!'

One of the shadows behind him moves forward and takes the torch, while Powell reaches into the bag and pulls out a roll of

301

silver tape. He looks over at Jess as she tries to back herself further against the wall.

'No, no, my dear. We have something else for you.' He bends over the girl on the floor, who continues to stare at Jess even as the tape is wrapped around her mouth and hair, again and again, until Jess wonders if her whole head is to be encased. The girl barely struggles, as if this is something that has happened before.

Powell puts the tape back in the bag, stowing it carefully in its rightful place, and then takes out a plastic bottle of Coke. He shakes it a couple of times, takes off the top and puts the bottle to Jess's lips. Bitter, like an infusion of cloves. She forces her mouth shut and turns her head to one side, feeling a small dribble of liquid running down her chin.

'I thought you'd be thirsty, my dear. Coke and roofies—Rohypnol—kids pay good money for this. And let's face it, you are part of the chemical generation.' He sighs. 'Or we could leave you here. Bit of a shame, after all the effort we've gone to, but I'm happy to let you make the choice. Just remember, no one will be back here for a very long time. This isn't Hollywood. Come to think of it, cowboys aren't your thing. You're more into sugar and spice, from what I gather, or maybe you're not even sure about that. Whatever, no one will find you; there are no miracles.'

The person holding the torch plays the light away from Jess for a moment, and in the red reflected glow from the walls his face looks familiar.

'Ed?'

'Your friend Ed has gone to a better place,' says Powell. 'But he played his part, just like you will. This kind gentleman is part of our medical staff. I don't know what we'd do without him.'

The man behind him hasn't spoken and blends back into the shadows as he shines the torch across Jess's face.

The bottle moves towards her again.

'Why me? I'd never heard of you, I never met you.'

'But I know about you,' says Powell. 'Bit of a disappointment, by all accounts. Bit of a dreamer. And selfish? Oh dear me, yes. Only one person matters to J. C.'

'You're talking bullshit.'

The bottle is in her mouth and her head is tipped backwards as Powell pinches her nose shut between his fingers. She tries to struggle but her throat works against her will, swallowing the bitterness. She expects an instant reaction, as if it were going to burn its way through the wall of her stomach, but there's nothing except relief at feeling liquid in her mouth after so long.

Powell cuts the tape around her ankles and pulls Jess to her feet before reaching down for the girl. The only sound she makes is a soft exhalation as he throws her over his shoulder, but her eyes are still open, watching Jess.

They walk and stumble through the tunnels. Jess follows the man with the torch, conscious of Powell behind her carrying the girl and behind him the other shadowy figure. From time to time they pass side passages, some still with the remnants of railway tracks. In one opening an open trolley sits on the rails, half full of rubble, abandoned. Then the tunnel opens and they pass a dark pool, its surface unmarked and reflecting nothing.

Whatever Jess drank earlier is having an effect; she's finding it harder to walk, tripping over the smallest pebbles. I should have left a thread, she thinks. That's what you do, like Ariadne. To find your way back. Ar-i-ad-ne, Ar-i-ad-ne. Like a train, chatter chatter chatter. Chattering over the rails. Chatterton, Chatterton, Jennifer Chatterton.

She sings the words to herself, in time to her steps, turning them into a dance. No one else speaks.

They're standing outside the entrance to the mine; Jess can't remember how they got there. The half moon is bright in the clear sky peppered with stars, and Jess starts to count them until someone pushes her towards the car standing a few feet away, a large four-wheel drive with the tailgate open. Without being prompted she climbs into the back, stretching out along the floor. The girl folds in next to her as if they were back in the mine.

Then it's dark again, and there's a new smell of oil and wool as a cover is thrown across the two bodies.

*   *   *

This time Jess wakes into the light. She tries to move but nearly topples the chair to which she is lashed. The room seems familiar, but it takes her a few moments to remember where she's seen it before. And then she knows what it is to feel true fear, as if her limbs were dissolving, her lungs could find no air to breathe. It's the barn, out in the Beacons. Not the same though. The other room had been stripped and desecrated, but this is fully operational. In one corner, near the window, is a computer rack, higher than a man. Just like the ones in Denny's workshop. The rack at the barn was a stripped carcass, but here it is alive; behind the smoked-glass front, green lights wink on and off in an unreadable pattern, and the air around her is filled with a soft hum. High on one wall is a large flat screen, and the table in front of her is a replica of the one in the barn, with dark leather straps around the legs. Everything is pristine, unused. There's no smell of bodies, nothing but new paint, incongruously hopeful.

A sudden rush of sound rocks the room, a plane flying fast, rooftop high. For a moment Jess is confused, thinking she's back at home and watching Harriers erupt from behind trees as they race down the valley, following the line of the river.

She finds it hard to concentrate, as if the drugs from earlier are still clouding her thoughts and she tries to focus on herself. Someone has removed her trainers and her feet look soft and puffy. The same tape that she saw covering the girl's mouth in the cave has been wrapped around her body, fastening her to the chair. As she realises that her mouth has been sealed, Jess feels her tongue beginning to swell, blocking her breath and she panics, works her jaw, tries to free the tape, hears herself grunt.

Behind her, a key turns and a door opens. Her muscles tense and with an effort of will she forces herself to stay calm. The man in front of her is a stranger, a big man in a blue shirt that barely stretches across his belly. He avoids her eyes. With a single movement he rips the tape from Jess's mouth; it burns as if the skin from her lips had been peeled away and she can't hold back the cry of pain; and then she's too thirsty to struggle as the man forces her to drink from a plastic bottle. She closes her eyes with something like relief as she feels the liquid soaking through her body and softening it. She doesn't notice the man go.

*   *   *

'Wake up, Jess.'

The first thing she sees is Powell perched on the edge of the table in front of her, grinning like an overexcited dog.

'Thought you might like me to fill you in, so to speak, on what's happening. Hello, are you there?' He leans forward and slaps Jess hard on the cheek. The stinging clears her mind for a moment and she forces herself to look at Powell.

'You should pay attention, Jess, stop dreaming. Remember what I told you? I'm going to make you a star.' He slips off the table and walks around to the window opposite. From where she is, Jess can see nothing but a blue sky.

'Some of my clients are looking for a little girl-on-girl action, and the customer is always right. To survive we must evolve, and to evolve we must diversify. Wouldn't you agree?'

He turns away from the window and looks at her, appraising. Jess tries to focus on him, but every few seconds she feels her head jerk upright, like someone trying not to sleep in the front row of a theatre, and her eyelids have almost swollen shut. Her nose is filled with the smells rising from her clothes, a mixture of clay and urine and stale sweat, and a scratch on her face is beginning to sting.

'You're not looking your best, my dear. Don't worry, we'll clean you up before your

307

appearance. "Lights! Camera! Action!"' He pulls a tissue from his pocket, spits on it, and rubs at the dirt on Jess's face even though she tries to pull away.

'Quite the tomboy, aren't you? Always getting into scrapes.'

'Fuck off!' The words are blurred, the best she can manage.

'That's better. You need to get your voice back—the punters like a bit of noise while we're filming.'

'Won't be any filming.'

'Oh, but there will. I even have a title for yours—*A Family Affair*—very fitting.'

He's back on the table now, swinging his legs slowly.

'You don't think I do this for fun? Payback, Jess—I've waited a long time for this.'

'Payback for what . . . ?' Jess's tongue gets in the way of the words.

'We never actually met, the first time round. But I know all about you, oh yes. Darren told me about you, while we were still speaking. Until you twisted him round to your way of thinking.' He takes a tube of handcream from his pocket and massages a little into the backs of his hands. It smells of lavender. 'He betrayed me, for you. Do you have any idea what that cost me? My career, my family. My name. Everything. All because of you.'

Darren—she's heard the name recently, somewhere else, but it's as if her memories have become thick and turgid. Not one of her current clients, she knows that. She goes further back, before she moved away from London; and then it comes: Chana. She talked about Darren when she stayed with Chana; the little boy who confessed what had happened to him and helped to break a paedophile ring.

But that was five years ago.

'Aah—you remember now; I can see it in your eyes,' says Powell. 'You can always trust the eyes.' He's still rubbing his hands together, as softly as if he were touching a lover. 'But I never forgot, never. Not once. So there's a lot to pay back; aren't we lucky that we have the time?'

Like a hyperactive child, Powell is off the table again, pacing up and down in front of Jess, unable to stop himself from reaching out and touching everything he passes.

'Would you like to know the order of play? We found a delicious chap to service you.' His voice drops to a whisper. 'Hung like a bloody elephant. Might be a bit of a squeeze but he'll fit it in somehow.'

Even as he speaks she can feel the pain, and twists and turns on the chair as if she could move out of the path of the words.

'All too much is it, this anticipation? Don't worry, it'll soon be your turn.'

She hears somebody else come into the room, but can't turn her head far enough to see who it is, and her muscles tense again, tight little spasms in her shoulders and legs.

Powell stops moving and lets his leg brush against Jess, hands on hips, head on one side.

'I thought it would be best to warm you up first with a good seeing to before moving on to the main action. What do you think?'

Jess has shut her eyes. It's a family affair, it's a family affair. She can hear the tune, but can't remember the words. Concentrate. Don't listen to this bastard.

A sudden pain shoots through her neck as Powell snaps her head back and pulls one eyelid open between his thumb and forefinger. She can smell his breath, as sweet as the body in her car.

'Look at me when I'm talking to you! Always look at your audience. Or the camera. Do you realise how many people will see you? More than you ever dreamed of.'

It must be a woman behind her; cheap scent, thick and flowery.

'I found you a lovely partner. Unique. A sweet girl—she's been very cooperative over the years. Some of them really take to it, you know—you can always tell. Of course, there are tears at first, the odd scream, but they soon get used to it. Enjoy it. *Ask for it.*'

Jess thinks she hears something behind her, a stifled, back-of-the-classroom laugh.

'We have a few things to prepare,' says Powell. 'But don't worry, we'll be back soon. Oh, and I've arranged some entertainment. As

310

you'll see, we service many markets. Sex has nothing to do with it; you're intelligent, you know that. It's power, control. Making the puppets dance.'

Jess knows about control. She remembers when she was young, waiting in the dark for steps to stop outside her room. She remembers how she couldn't speak or call out, her voice frozen, the way it is in a nightmare of paralysis.

The door clicks shut behind Powell. Jess tries to flex her wrists, but the tape is wound too tightly. At least her mouth is free, but her lips are sore and cracked and she runs her tongue over her teeth; they feel pitted, etched.

The large screen on the wall flickers without transition from darkness to bright images. She can't see the speakers and the sound is thin, but the pictures are clear enough. Carwen, but looking different from any time that Jess has seen her before. The video was shot in this room; no, it must have been the one at the barn, before it was stripped. Over the tinny music Carwen half dances across to the table and allows herself to be strapped down. Playing a part. But as a naked man joins in and begins to work on her body her expression stays the same, a kabuki mask.

Jess turns away from the screen, disgusted and heartbroken, wishing she had known. What was it Pav called them? Procurers? Not Carwen; she tried to save her children by

311

giving herself. She failed.

And now, Jess thinks, it's my turn.

The door opens again. Jess expects Powell but it's a woman she doesn't know, maybe her own age, carrying a small knife. She cuts the tape around Jess's feet, then moves behind her and releases her from the chair.

'Time to get you sorted out.' She sounds like Carwen, even looks like her. The same stretched skin, the same miasma of cigarette smoke lifting from her clothes.

Jess tries to stand but her legs have no muscles. The woman catches her before she falls.

'Stamp your feet, that's right. Get the blood moving.'

Leaning on the woman for support, Jess hobbles through the doorway and along a short hall to a bathroom.

'You got ten minutes to sort yourself out. Don't worry 'bout your hair, they'll make you wear a wig. And don't look for anything sharp 'cause there ain't nothing.' As the door is locked behind her, Jess collapses slowly onto the floor, and begins to sob.

1986—5

It's always afternoon in this room, the daylight slow and round as it lights the shelves of books, the surfaces of furniture and mantelpiece untouched by dust. Nothing in here is placed by accident—Jax wonders if there's a code hidden in the patterns made by the arrangement of chairs, the anodyne prints hanging on the walls. The man sitting opposite is barely taller than her but older, maybe thirty, his white shirt and jeans pressed and spotless.

Obviously gay. And he pretends not to smoke, but she can trace the tobacco under the incense he burns before she arrives. He takes up as little space as a woman, never coming too close, and seems comfortable with the silences that punctuate her visits; sometimes, he said on her second visit, you say more when you don't speak.

As soon as she arrives, she hands him the envelope of money from her father; as always, he places it on the coffee table next to his chair. Relativity established, the ritual begun. She knows enough now not to wait for him to speak and starts talking as though picking up a conversation from a few minutes ago, although it's a week since they last met.

'The mornings have been better.'

'Less nausea?'

'Some—but it doesn't last as long.'

'And how about eating?'

She shrugs.

'I put on a couple of pounds this week—me, not the baby.'

It took a while before she was sure she was pregnant, with no guidance from her periods which stopped and started to a rhythm of their own.

'Have you thought any more about an abortion?' His face is more neutral than expressionless, as if any feelings balance themselves out.

'I told you before—I got pregnant because I wanted to. It wouldn't have happened otherwise.'

She doesn't care if the therapist hears her frustration or watches her eyes flickering anywhere but at him. He's the third she's tried, been sent to. Jax had described the others on her first visit: the psychoanalyst who sat out of sight and smelt of cat food; the person-centred woman—what the fuck does that mean? said Jax. How can I talk to a woman in a cardigan?; the cognitive behaviouralist who gave her exercises to stop her vomiting after every meal.

But she comes back to this man, this enigmatic creature in his stage-set room. At every session she looks for clues, something he overlooked and forgot to hide away. She wants a trophy. Something private, something intimate.

The man takes care never to touch her.

One day she waits outside his flat, a hundred yards or so down the street, hidden behind a car. She uses her father's camera, takes a series of photos without him seeing. In one of the frames he appears to be smiling directly at her; she keeps one copy in her bag, another in the Labrador tin.

I want to work with you, not your labels, he says the first time they meet. Labels are temporary, you wear them by choice, even when others use them. What do they mean? he says. Obsessive? Bulimic? Stalker?

Remember the choices, he says.

She always does.

Why Chad? he says.

Because she's not me.

Jax hasn't said this before.

This is hard, this takes time. Through the weeks and months, while she swells and bloats and changes, his voice is her anchor.

Why the baby? he asks. She never talks about motherhood.

Call it education, says Jax. I'm giving my parents a new experience, the pregnant teenage daughter. I don't think it will go down too well at the golf club. But she looks away as she says this, and places both hands on her swollen belly.

She decides, near the end, that the baby should go into care. Be adopted straightaway.

It's the right choice, everyone can see that. No encumbrance; no reminders of a bad time; an obsession, an illness. They never talk about who was responsible but her father no longer brings Fabrice to the house; it's a poor assumption but an unexpected win.

*   *   *

After the birth, Jax sees the therapist for another few weeks, a winding down. She doesn't tell him how it hurts, this new separation.

'Have you decided what you'll do next?' he says.

'My father found me a flat, up in Crouch End. I'll move in there until next year, then I go to uni.'

'To study?'

'Social sciences—maybe I'll end up as a therapist.'

He laughs, and shakes her hand—it's the first time he's ever touched her flesh, except in her imaginings. A small success.

She hasn't looked in the Labrador tin for months.

'You've done really well,' says Nic. 'But why change your name? And why that one when there are so many to choose from?'

'We all find ways of adjusting, you told me that. I couldn't be Jennifer any more, not even Jax. And I've given up so much, let me keep this one thing. It's so small, just a label. My last little crutch, my last little memory. I'll throw it away when I don't need it any more. Promise.'

He sees her to the door and watches her walk towards the corner; a queer, thin creature, depleted after the pregnancy. He knows she won't look back.

CHAPTER NINETEEN

Pav doesn't sleep, after all. She arrives at the cottage soon after sunrise, but then dozes in the car until seven-thirty.

Anton looks familiar; Jess described him well. Pav feels the attraction in his quietness, the way he listens, the way he looks into her eyes. A plausible man, the kind of man you trust.

She asks when he last saw Jess, when he last spoke to her; there's no reason not to believe him. If Jess were here she would sense her presence but the building is empty except for the two of them. All the same, she asks to look around the cottage, conscious of searching. Something is missing, so familiar that it takes her a few minutes to place the gap.

'Your computer,' she asks. 'Where do you keep it?'

He smiles, for the first time. 'I'm not too good with machines,' he says. 'I use the one at work when I need to.' A pause. 'Are you going to tell me what this is about?'

Pav watches his face as she tells him that Jess is missing. It's hard to read his reaction, so many people can act these days.

'I told you last night that Jess wasn't here,' says Anton. 'She said she was on her way, but never turned up. You didn't need to drive for hours to find that out. Why are you really here?'

'You met her through work, is that right?' says Pav. 'Is there anyone she's mentioned to you, someone she might have gone to see last night?'

There's a pause before Anton replies. 'She's a loner,' he says, 'I saw that the first time we met. Doesn't like to talk about herself. There was a guy, way back, but she hasn't seen him for years. Must have been a strange relationship, but she didn't really talk about him or what was wrong. I think maybe it was a bit of a fantasy; most people are a little bit in love with their therapist. It's not the done thing at all.' Another pause. 'To be honest, I thought she might have gone to see you. Last time I saw her she talked about you, a lot. Now I've met you I understand why.'

'Jess and I have been working together; a difficult case.'

'She told me about that too—the missing girls. But when she blew me out I realised that there was someone else in her life.'

'I thought I was here to question you.'

'I'm trying to be helpful,' says Anton. 'I've only known Jess a couple of weeks and I've thought about her a lot. She seems so strong at first and then you realise that she's like a fallen sparrow. Part of her is broken and she doesn't believe anyone can help.'

'You thought you could?'

'When we first met I told her that she reminded me of the children I work with. Sometimes they seem normal, and then you realise that their worlds have different rules from ours. It's hard for them to live with us. But inside they're clever and beautiful and vulnerable—and they need love more than anyone.'

'I know,' says Pav, quietly. 'I felt that too.'

'But I wasn't the right person to give her that love; you are,' says Anton. 'And because of that, maybe you're the right person to find her.'

He walks Pav out to her car. 'If it's any help, there's a woman in London, someone she used to work with. You could probably find her, the name is Chana. A nurse, works for Social Services; maybe Jess went to see her instead of me. Though I don't know why she'd do that. I guess I don't know her too well.'

*   *   *

As she drives towards London, Pav has Chana

traced, makes a call, arranges to meet at her flat at lunchtime. She drives carefully, light-headed from lack of sleep, thinking about Anton's words. The last time she was in bed was with Jess, trying to warm a body as cadaverous as a tom night-walking the city streets.

*   *   *

'You worried me, girl, when you called. What's up with Jess? She ain't answering her phone. Is this something to do with the murdered boy? She told me about that, last time she was down.'

'How long have you known her?'

'Since she came to work here—it was her first job after she qualified. '91, '92 maybe. Skinny little kid, never did eat properly. Didn't talk much about herself, never mentioned her folks. She used to say, the only reality is what there is now, right now. The past don't exist. Therapy talk. She really believed it.' A pause. 'The band though, she talked about the band. Not that I ever believed her, not really. Went along with it though. What else could I do? We all have our little dreams. And then, screw me, but it turns out to be true.'

'How do you mean?'

Chana tells Pav about the club, about Jess singing with Jamie.

'I couldn't believe it when he asked her up

on stage. Don't think she could, either. She's got a good voice—not my kind of music, but the crowd liked it.'

'Did you meet him, this Jamie?'

'No. Funny thing—they haven't spoken for years, they perform a song together, have a quick kiss and then Jess wants to leave. You'd think they'd arrange to see each other again. Catch up.'

She makes more coffee while Pav looks around the flat.

'That's a pretty good computer in the spare room—didn't think the NHS could afford machines like that for its staff.'

'You kidding? One of Jess's buddies got that for me. Didn't she tell you how she trashed my old machine?'

'You tell me.'

'Well,' says Chana, 'I'm no expert, but I never heard of a computer virus that knows somebody's name.'

*   *   *

'Nature or nurture,' says Powell. 'Do we inherit characteristics? Do we inherit sin? Or is it all behavioural? Some ghastly old perv of an uncle fiddles with a boy's prepubescent parts, and when the little chap grows up he feels constrained to do the same.'

Jess feels as if she's waking after a heavy night of drinking. The screen on the wall is alive again, but this time it's showing a shot of the waiting table in front of her.

'But where does that leave you?' says Powell. 'Just a link in a chain, like that lovely tattoo on your shoulder. What did you pass on to your offspring, the fruit of your sullied loins? An obsessive character, a penchant for the carnal? Self-deception?'

Jess still has no strength to lift her head, and focuses on Powell's shoes as he walks slowly around her chair.

'Mutability. A good word, don't you think? The ability to change, to become something different. What a gift, what a burden; something we've both experienced. Of course, you had a choice. I had none.'

He stops in front of her, lifts her chin with one finger as he did with the girl in the mine.

'Well, my dear, time to party. We decided to go for the warm-up after all—get you in the mood. Perhaps it will help you empathise—a good, therapeutic word.' He nods at someone behind Jess and she feels herself lifted out of the chair and bent forward over the table. The leather straps are pulled tight around her ankles, and a hand on her back keeps her pushed down onto the surface.

'I do hope that the buckles aren't chafing you. One of my colleagues suggested Velcro but that seemed so . . . common. It's these little touches that make all the difference, don't you think?'

Her mind is clearing by the moment, sensation returning to her limbs. She pulls against the straps and tries to lift herself but the pressure on her back is too great.

'I see that you're feeling more frisky. Very good. We had to choose whether to keep you on Rohypnol or allow you to express yourself *au naturel*. Perhaps we should have asked your preference; then again, perhaps not. I always think that there's a lot to be said for uninhibited reactions. And, please, don't worry about making a noise—we're used to screamers.'

He leans down, his lips brushing Jess's ear.

'Remember, you're an Englishwoman, so "play up, play the game!"'

She hears the door open, somewhere out of sight. Closes her eyes. Tenses her body, as if it would do any good. There's an undercurrent of voices on the other side of the room, and then Powell is back by her side.

'I was going to leave you to one of our special studs but then I thought about your eyes, your beautiful eyes, and I thought—why let some functionary spoil you when I'm available? You're honoured, I hope you realise. I'm confident your performance will match my expectations. But don't take poor Carwen's efforts as your model, oh no. She was a peasant; no fire, no panache, no imagination.'

There's the sound of a zip, the rustle of

clothing falling to the floor, and then Powell's body is moulding against hers, his hands steadying her hips, his lips against her ear.

'How many ways, Jess? I guess it's time to find out!'

*   *   *

Pav and Pelham park on the gravel outside Jess's farmhouse, disturbing the cat and the half-eaten rabbit kitten under his paw.

They check the study first; Pav notices the card on the corner of the desk. She examines the photograph, looking for signs, then logs in to Jess's email and reads the messages; from Gina, from Spider, all of Jess's replies.

'Don't know about the girl,' says Pav, 'but if Spider's a teenager I'm still in nappies.'

'Trust me,' says Pelham, 'all those emails are from the same person. He was grooming her, like she was some fourteen-year-old kid. Playing mind-games; how could Jess have been so blind?'

'So why send the last email?' says Pav. 'That would really have blown it if he was grooming her.'

'He could afford to,' says Pelham. 'He knew she couldn't back away now.'

Something pricks Pav's finger as she uses the keyboard, a splinter from the broken mug, and she notices the coffee stain on the wall above the monitor, a perfect sequence of flattened droplets, motion made static.

They continue to search the house. Last time they found the clothes, now they're looking for a note or signs of a struggle.

A reason to leave, maybe, a reason to run away.

Something incriminating.

In Pelham's jacket is the solicitor's letter they found here, the day Marty's body was discovered. Jennifer Chatterton. There's no record of the name on any of their databases; so far she's nothing more than words on a page.

The solicitor had been cooperative, in the end. The client, he'd said, was Mr van Renwyck, a senior partner with one of the major accounting firms in the City. Maybe he bought the rights to Hacksaw's music. It happens. Didn't Michael Jackson buy the Beatles catalogue? Strange business, the music scene.

What were his instructions, they'd asked? Not much, he'd said, just to send a standard letter, a frightener. It usually works.

'How long have we got,' says Pav.

Pelham checks his watch. 'Another ten minutes, then we have to leave. That gives us two and a half hours to get to north London.'

'How was van Renwyck when you spoke to him?' says Pav.

'He wasn't around—I spoke to the wife. Didn't say much—she was on her way out, but happy enough to see us this afternoon.'

Upstairs, Pav finds the long brown box pulled out from underneath the spare bed, the lid already open. She kneels beside it and handles the folded clothes carefully, lifting each piece and laying it on the bed, keeping the piles in order. She hears Pelham behind her but ignores him, working in silence until she finds the unsent birthday cards, each one signed with love, and she keeps her face hidden from the man by the door as she replaces each item in its rightful place.

*   *   *

The boundary between terraced suburb and green belt is as marked as a border. This is a part of London that Pav has never visited: a couple of minutes after leaving a crowded high street dotted with kebab shops and burger bars, they could be back in the country. It's like something from an old film; a village pond with ducks, a red telephone box, no cars parked on the street. A stage set for the rich.

The houses are set well back from the road, mostly hidden behind walls and hedges and railings, with name signs at each entrance to a drive. Pelham turns on the hazards as they slow to a crawl, not wanting to overshoot.

'Couple of million at least, these places,' he says. 'What was the name again?'

'Narth House—there, on the left,' says Pav.

It feels as if today is the only day there has ever been in her life. Cross country twice in one day, after a sleepless night—at least Pelham did the driving this time, letting her sleep on the motorway.

The high, iron gates to the drive swing open as they turn off the main road, and Pav notices a small camera mounted high on the wall, covering the approach. As they stop in front of the house, a woman is waiting at the top of the steps between the neo-Georgian pillars.

'You don't get many like her in the Forest,' says Pelham before they leave the car.

The woman could be any age between twenty-five and thirty-five, the product of careful tailoring, an expensive hairdresser and a personal trainer. Pav wouldn't have recognised her.

'Mrs Renwick?'

'Van Renwyck, with a "y" not an "i". My husband is most particular.' She smiles as she shakes their hands. 'You wouldn't believe how much things like that matter, back on the Upper East Side.' Her accent seems at odds with her appearance; American-lite with London vowels. She leads them into a formal drawing room; Regency stripe and dustless surfaces, lit by windows that stretch from floor to ceiling with views over a rolling green countryside.

'Actually, you're lucky to catch us. We'll be spending the next few months in the New York apartment and won't be back until after Christmas. My husband apologises, by the way—he wanted to be here when you arrived but he's a little delayed.'

'What is it that he does?' says Pelham.

'They call him a rainmaker, although I always think that sounds rather spiritual for someone who buys and sells companies. If he were in the middle of a deal now, he wouldn't be home at all.' She sighs. 'Lawyers and accountants—they seem to think there's something macho in working through the night.'

'How long will he be?' says Pav.

'We don't have to wait—it's down to me really. I understand this is all to do with the website? One of my friends noticed it when she was browsing the Internet. I would have left it, but my husband is rather hot on these things even though he'd rather forget my old life.' She spreads her arms to take in the room. 'As you see, I have embraced conventionality.'

'Your old life?' says Pelham.

'I promise you, five years at that pace and you're burnt out. I always tell my husband, he's got it easy. But that was a very different lifestyle, and I was very young. My husband, though, does *not* approve, and we never talk about it. As he will no doubt tell you within minutes of his arrival, his mother is a "Daughter of the American Revolution"! Very grand, very puritan. To be honest, very dull.'

She fingers the pearls around her neck.

'I still don't understand,' says Pelham.

'There was a girl, just after we started to be well known. Scrawny little thing. But then, weren't we all? I suppose she had a resemblance to me—dressed the same, dyed her hair the same colour.' She smiles at the memory and fusses with her pleated skirt. 'You know, she even copied my tattoo. My husband keeps trying to persuade me to have it removed, but I guess it's a small reminder of the old days.'

Pelham tries to suppress a coughing fit.

'You're right to laugh, Inspector. It is quite incongruous.'

'You keep talking about the old days, your old life . . .' says Pav.

'Never believe someone who tells you that they don't like fame. It has its downside but it's the best drug around. Even now I get a buzz when someone remembers me. No—don't apologise. No reason why you should.'

The realisation breaks over Pav and Pelham at the same moment, like a cold shower washing away the last remnants of sleep.

'What happened to this girl,' says Pav, 'the one who looked like you?'

'You have to remember, there were a lot of them around. Guys as well. We weren't people, we were objects of desire. You soon learn not to be flattered, at least not too much.' She goes over to the window and stands framed against the light with her back to the room, no more than a silhouette.

'This one went further than most. She was a clever little thing—had Jamie right where she wanted him. Actually, I could never quite work out who she was most obsessed with, me or Jamie. Me, I think, but maybe it didn't really matter. I was easier to copy, he was easier to screw.

'She began messing us about; cancelling hotel reservations, making up stories about us to the press. Our agent, Freddie, wanted to take out an injunction, but her father smoothed it over and promised to send her for treatment. Funny, all the stuff I have now, all of this, she had then. A little rich kid who wanted somebody to love her—I think that's all it was. If she had treatment of any kind, I hope it worked.'

'Did you ever hear from her again?' asks Pav.

'No, nothing, not until this business with the website.' She walks back slowly and joins them. 'Did you know we recorded one of her songs? Before we knew all about the nonsense, of course. She was a damned good musician, better than me.'

'You say she looked like you, copied you,' says Pav. 'Did she actually impersonate you?'

'Not that I can remember. Even on the website, the only song recorded by Hacksaw is the one she wrote. From what I could see, when I looked at it, the rest are all new. But my husband, he blathered on about copyright and trademark and intellectual property and God knows what else, and so the lawyers sent off a letter. To be honest, I wouldn't want to take it any further.'

'You seem remarkably . . . calm . . . about it all,' says Pav.

The woman shrugs, smiles again, looks around the room.

'You remember what she was called?' says Pelham.

'Jax—we all liked punchy names. I think they were taken from her initials; I mean, where's the street cred in Jennifer Chatterton? No wonder she changed it.'

'And now she uses your name—isn't that a bit strange?' says Pav.

'Why should I care? Since I married I have a new name of my own—she's welcome to the old one. Anyway, I'd have killed anyone who tried to call me Jessica.'

She walks them back to the car.

'Thanks for your help, Mrs van Renwyck.'

'No need to be so formal, Inspector. My friends still call me Chad.'

CHAPTER TWENTY

This is not a time to be mindful. Jess remembers herself as a child, lying in bed and trying to project her soul outside her body. Sometimes she made herself believe that she had succeeded and was floating by the ceiling, separate and unfettered.

It doesn't work now. She lies with her eyes open, barely conscious of the slick polythene sheeting that blurs the green and white stripes of the mattress. The room is windowless, barely larger than a cupboard.

She wants to sleep, to become unconscious but every time she closes her eyes the sensations from all parts of her body have fused into one burning centre, as if the pain has reached a high plateau from which it can neither rise nor fall. A wave of nausea hits her, and she retches dryly. Her last meal was—when? The cereal that Pav left for her yesterday morning? Or was it the day before, maybe? Her watch has gone, she has no sense of time.

Her mind is shutting down. She can't feel in more than single sensations: bruised, cold, shaking. Even fear is too complicated an emotion. Her body smells hot and sweet, like something rotting from the inside out. Each time she closes her eyes, her body ratchets forward involuntarily as if she's back across the table, causing her to grunt with pain. So she sits upright, unblinking, staring at the floor, out of time.

She comes to with the sound of the door shutting, and when she looks up there's a young woman standing in the small room. At first Jess doesn't take her in, just another teenager in jeans and trainers with her hands in her pockets, a crop top showing the gold ring through her navel. But there's something else; Jess wills her brain to work faster—this is important—and then recognition. The card Gina sent; this is the same girl, motionless in front of the door, silent. But she's somehow different without the sun to light her; reduced.

Jess pushes herself up from the mattress but it takes all her energy and she sways precariously, as if the slightest movement would throw her off balance.

The girl moves away from the door towards the far corner of the room, keeping her back to the wall, as if she were confronted by a wounded animal about to strike out. Jess follows the girl with her eyes. The silence has been there for so long now that it seems neither of them know how to break it, until another spasm of pain deep inside doubles Jess over. She rocks backwards and forwards with her arms wrapped around her body, as if to stop herself from breaking into pieces.

The girl moves forward a few steps, takes

one hand from a pocket and drops a couple of tablets on the mattress before retreating to her corner; Jess feels the warmth of her body in the second it takes for the girl to brush past.

'They're only aspirin—sorry there's no water.' The flat Midland vowels are unexpected and out of place.

'Gina?' At last Jess understands what Powell meant by 'payback'. 'Are you OK? Has he done anything . . . ?' She's suddenly conscious of how she must look, like a drunken whore after a violent punter, and wishes there was something she could use to wrap around herself. The girl is still silent and watchful.

Jess tries again. 'How did he get you . . . ?' But the girl shakes her head in frustration and looks away.

'I guess you don't recognise me,' says Jess. 'I must look . . .' This time the girl interrupts.

'I know who you are.' She sounds dismissive; and then, 'I thought you'd look older.'

Jess props herself against the wall by the end of the mattress. She holds out a hand to the girl standing so far away.

'Gina, please . . .' Her throat feels too dry, and then without warning she belches up a mouthful of bile, spitting it onto the floor.

'Fuck's sake,' whispers the girl. She pulls a used tissue from one of her pockets and holds it out for Jess to take.

'This isn't how I wanted it,' says Jess.

'I know what you didn't want,' says the girl. 'You didn't want me.' She's found her voice at last. 'You gave me away like I was some crappy present you wanted rid of.'

'It wasn't like that.'

'Don't even try.' She starts rocking backwards and forwards. 'When I was little, they said I was going to have a new brother or sister. But when the baby arrived, they said, "Well, actually, this isn't your new brother. You're different." Really fucking different. Like I was last year's fashion.'

'But they didn't need to tell you . . .'

'Didn't need to tell you!' Gina mimics Jess's voice. 'You think I wouldn't have found out I was adopted? Given away by some cow who was too stupid not to get pregnant? You crack me up. And don't try to tell me you did it for my sake, or it was all for the best, or any of those other crappy phrases.'

'You don't understand. I was sick.' Her voice sounds small.

'Right—and getting rid of me made you better, something else to vomit up. Why didn't you just abort me, have me scraped away into a dish?'

'Whatever happened to you . . .'

'Shut up!' There are tears in her voice. 'You never wanted to talk to me before. I used to cry myself to sleep wondering what I did wrong before I was born. So now you listen!'

335

But before she can say any more the door opens and Powell walks in.

'And I so wanted to witness the grand reunion. You see, Jess, I'm a very fair man. I always pay my performers, and an exquisite performance deserves an exquisite prize. What, aren't you pleased to see each other? Gina been shouting at you, has she?' He puts his arm around Gina's shoulder and she nestles her head against his body, smiling like a cat after a kill.

'I know she can be difficult, but isn't that your forte? Or are you only understanding nine to five? I suppose that's the difference between having children of your own, and simply interfering in other people's lives, like you did in mine.' He starts to stroke Gina's hair. 'I haven't seen my daughter for five years, because of you. So I did my research into Miss Chadwick, and what a cornucopia I found! Quite the little caterpillar, weren't you? Fixated, obsessed, a very tenuous grip on reality, and pregnant to boot. And then you became a butterfly and left it all behind like an old, unwanted body. Even your daughter; some might call that selfish. And to think people call *me* sick!'

As Jess sinks down onto the mattress Powell squats in front of her, his head on one side like a bird.

'You really don't look healthy. Still not eating properly? You should take better care of yourself.' He takes the folded handkerchief from his breast pocket and dabs at Jess's face. 'It seems so unfair, doesn't it? After all the pain, all the detritus you've discarded, you look at yourself one day and realise that, whatever you call yourself, nothing has changed. Nothing, except that little voice that never stops.' He leans even closer. ' "Fraud," it says. "Cheat." So it was an easy equation, an eye for an eye. My daughter had been taken, you had one you didn't want. Fair exchange, don't you think?'

He rises slowly, one hand on his back. 'I should take more care of myself, at my age. Can't keep up with the young studs any more.' He holds out his hand to the girl. 'Come, Gina, we should leave your mother to reflect, rest and recuperate. Regrettably, I have been called away again this evening—some urgent business elsewhere. But don't be too disappointed. Showtime starts again tomorrow morning.'

*   *   *

Pav realises she must have fallen asleep as Pelham takes one hand from the wheel and shakes her shoulder again.

'Your phone, woman.'

She listens carefully to the voicemail, and smiles across at Pelham.

'Have they found the girls? Jess?'

337

'It's not that good,' says Pav. 'But they've been rechecking Ed's contacts. Turns out he has a cousin, a GP. Lives in Clifton—I've got the address. Seems that he was "severely reprimanded" by the General Medical Council a few years back—an over-liberal policy on supporting Class A drug addicts. Probably a user himself. Heroin was his thing—one of the drugs in Perry's body.'

'And they still let him practise?' says Pelham. 'No, forget I said that. I'm sure he promised to be a good boy in future.'

*   *   *

The large Victorian house is set behind a high hedge and the woman who opens the door to them matches her home, tall and narrow. She holds her left arm stiffly, at a strange angle. When she sees the warrant cards her eyes show no surprise. The house is quiet; no voices, no music, no television.

'Have you found him then?' she asks.

'Found who?' says Pelham.

'My husband, Leslie. Isn't that why you're here?'

'We came to see him.'

'You'll be lucky! He hasn't been home for days—which isn't unusual. But he hasn't been into surgery either. Why they keep calling me, I don't know. As if I could do anything about it.'

338

'You don't have any idea where he is?' asks Pav. That expression on the woman's face, she's seen it before. When she was in uniform, investigating domestics, praying that one of them would press charges.

'I don't ask.' She holds up her arm. 'He taught me not to. He always sets the breaks himself, but this time he thought I needed a reminder so he set it crooked.' Her voice is slightly slurred and at first Pav wonders if she's had a stroke, then smells the gin on her breath.

'Have you reported him missing?' says Pelham.

'Missing?' The word is a hiss. 'I hope the bastard's dead. Every time he goes I pray he won't come back, but . . . sometimes I wonder whose side God is on.' She looks around the large hallway and then wanders off into a living room to find her drink, with the two officers trailing her. When she's sunk into one of the large, old-fashioned armchairs, Pelham tells her about Ed, leaving out the details. She listens without interrupting, drains her glass when he's finished and refills it from a bottle on the coffee table. She doesn't look at either of them.

Pav explains; there are other lives at stake, some of them are children. They need to find her husband. The woman seems unsurprised, as if she hears this every day. Pelham takes a breath as if about to speak but Pav catches his eyes and shakes her head, gently, and he subsides.

They wait while the woman sips the gin like a bird pecking at a puddle and then drops the glass back on the table so hard that they all recoil.

'I knew you'd turn up one day, but never *today*. It's like imagining your own death.' She pauses again but only for a moment. 'Sometimes he stays away for a night, sometimes for a couple of days, but this time it was different. Usually he gets overexcited; that's how I know he's about to go off.'

'So what was different this time?' says Pelham.

'He was so quiet, I don't think he even knew I was here. Usually he just disappears, doesn't take anything except that stupid wooden briefcase, but this time he packed a bag and took the little computer from his study.'

'Show me,' says Pav. They file upstairs to a room at the back of the house and the doctor's wife turns the handle tentatively, as if she expects it to be booby-trapped. The room looks like the aftermath of a burglary, with papers spilling from open drawers on to the floor.

'So he really has gone this time. The door—he always keeps it locked. I haven't been in here for years.'

Pav moves around the room, checking the skirting boards, shifting filing cabinets, peering behind cupboards. 'There's no phone point in here.'

'He used one of his mobiles, unless it was a call he didn't mind me hearing. Then he'd use the phone downstairs.'

'What about the Internet?'

'One of his . . . friends . . . gave him this gadget, like a credit card with a tiny aerial attached. He was so pleased he even showed me. It went into the side of his laptop; he said it meant that he didn't need a phone line to get his emails or look at the Internet. I said to him, why don't you just get another point put up in the study but he looked at me as if I were mad. I'm lucky he was in such a good mood.'

'Did he file things like phone bills—would they be in here?' says Pav. The woman shrugs.

'Where are you going with this?' asks Pelham.

'The doctor has more than one mobile,' says Pav. 'He'll have one for work, a public number if you like, but standard practice in BestFrendz is to use pay-as-you-go, changing the numbers every few weeks to prevent calls being traced. We won't get any joy there. But that little card in his laptop includes a mobile SIM card. If he sourced it from a stolen phone, then we're buggered, but it's just possible that he's using one that he pays for. You know how much trouble the people in BestFrendz go to in order to stay above suspicion.'

It takes ten minutes of working through the papers left in the filing cabinets before Pav shouts, 'I think I found them!' She runs her finger down the pages of itemised calls. 'Look, two different mobile numbers. One's used to make ordinary calls, but the other only ever calls one number! That's the one he'll be using for Internet access.'

'How will that help you find him?' asks the doctor's wife.

'Every mobile phone, or phonecard like the one your husband's using, connects to the network through radio waves connecting it to a base station. Whenever a mobile is switched on, it sends out a signal every so often, and we can trace that signal. In London, you could get within a few hundred metres of the phone, but out here the area will be much larger. Still, it's better than nothing.'

As Pav leaves them to set up the surveillance, Pelham starts checking the other upstairs rooms.

'You've got teenage children, right?'

They're standing in a bedroom. It feels unused; two pairs of boy's shoes are neatly lined against one wall but there are no clothes to be seen, no posters on the walls. The air smells stale. Pelham turns to look at the woman behind him; she stares back with something like pride.

'I don't know what you think of me, but you'll never understand what it's like to live with a man like my husband. When I realised what was happening it was too late. I was in a trap, a bloody, bloody trap. But I made a deal; as soon as the boys were old enough, they went away to boarding school. Yorkshire—I'd have chosen Australia if I could. It was the best I could do for them.'

*   *   *

Pav checks her watch as they drive away. 'Jesus—it's only five-thirty. Feels like midnight.'

'We should make one more visit, if you're up to it. The last piece of the jigsaw.'

'Do I have a choice?'

'They're expecting us.'

They take the motorway east from Bristol and then head up to the suburbs of Oxford. So many houses, thinks Pav, so many little universes.

This time there's no gin, only a frightened couple and the honeysuckle air freshener that just fails to mask the smell of tonight's supper.

'Our daughter's upstairs doing her homework. Do you have to talk to her?' The father's voice shakes a little.

'It shouldn't take long. She knows she's adopted, right?' Pav does the talking.

'We told her when she was very young—we couldn't lie to her. It's never been a problem.' He pauses. 'She's our princess—she wouldn't do anyone any harm.'

'Did she ever ask about her natural

mother?' says Pelham. 'Has she ever tried to find out?'

'We talked about it, all of us. We said to Alison, we don't mind, we'd understand, but she wants to wait until her exams are finished, until she's eighteen. She's very single-minded, doesn't like distractions.'

'What about hobbies?'

The parents look at each other as if this is a trick question.

'Films,' says the father. 'She goes to the cinema in the retail park with her friends.'

'And CDs,' says the mother. 'She loves her music.'

'Does she play any instrument?' asks Pav.

'There was the recorder when she was little, but she gave that up. They all do, don't they? Not very cool.'

'I think we'd better have a word with her now, if you don't mind,' says Pav. While the father goes upstairs, she asks the mother, 'What about boyfriends?'

The woman smiles for the first time. 'Poor Davey—she leads him a merry dance. They've been together, if you can call it that, for nearly a year now. She's only sixteen you know.'

'What's he like?' asks Pelham.

'Davey? He's in the year above Alison, lives round the corner. He'll be head boy at the school next year, I shouldn't wonder.'

The girl that comes downstairs is slight but unmistakable, her mother's daughter. The hair is different, long and dark, tied behind, but this could be Jess at sixteen. She winces as her mother introduces her.

'Everyone calls me Ali except Mum.'

Pav shows her the photo from Jess's study, but the girl shakes her head. 'I've never seen her before.' She checks again and Pav watches carefully as she looks at the photograph, but there are no signs of recognition.

'Her name's Gina,' says Pav.

'No—sorry. What's she done?'

'What about the name Jess? Jess Chadwick?'

The girl shakes her head again.

'One last thing,' says Pav. 'What about chat rooms on the Internet? Do you ever . . .'

'Do I look stupid or something? You have to be really sad to do that. Go upstairs, check my computer if you want.'

'No need for that,' says Pelham. 'It's obviously a case of mistaken identity—sorry to have bothered you.'

*   *   *

They find a half-empty wine bar in the high street nearby.

'You were right, John. Unwin really caught her.'

'You'd think she would have realised . . .'

'We believe what we want to,' says Pav. 'You saw the box of baby clothes in her room.

345

Getting that first email from her "daughter"—
it must have been like a dream come true.'

'So who's the girl in the photo?'

'Gina? Probably not even her real name.
And I doubt if she wrote the emails—that was
Unwin all along, drawing Jess further in.'

Pelham drains his glass, rubs his eyes and
checks his watch. 'Jesus wept—look at the
time. Another day gone and we're no fucking
closer. But at least we know that Gina doesn't
exist.'

'Oh, yes she does,' says Pav, 'she exists for
Jess.'

CHAPTER TWENTY-ONE

Jess puts her ear to the door but the corridor
outside is silent. She can still feel the straps
around her thighs; no matter how hard she
massages her skin she can't rub the sensation
away. It hurts to sit and she feels nauseous
when she lies on the thin mattress, so she
stands with her back to the wall, watching the
door. She's lost track of time, feels as if she's
moved into a different world with different
rules.

I didn't choose this, she thinks. Nic used to
tell me that everything that happened to me,
happened because I chose it. When did I
choose this?

It must be a couple of hours since Powell and Gina left. She remembers the tablets that Gina gave her and scrapes one with her teeth, suspicious. It has the bitterness of aspirin, but if not, what the hell. She works up some saliva and manages to swallow the tablets, and wishes she had some water to wash them down.

The room feels colder than ever; she hasn't slept properly since the night before she found Marty's body. She tries the mattress again, but every time she closes her eyes she's either back in the room, strapped across the table, or looking at the smile on Gina's face as she rests her head against Powell.

Why couldn't Gina still be faceless, the way it used to be? The girl she saw earlier was a stranger, someone she thought she knew who turned out to be an impostor. But then, she thinks, I never knew Gina. She was something I made in my mind. Jess remembers the brown box, the sets of baby clothes; they belong to a dream, not a person.

Why did Powell pick on me? she thinks. I did my job, that's all. Why blame me; he's the criminal, he's the pervert. But she knows the reason, always knew it, from the moment her baby daughter was taken away; one day someone would come along to make her pay.

Her thoughts are interrupted as the door opens without warning and clicks shut behind Gina. Jess stumbles to her feet and faces her daughter across the small, bare room.

'Powell . . . ?' she says, for the sake of breaking the silence.

'Gone out, like he said. He won't be back till late, maybe tomorrow.' Her eyes are red and swollen, and she dabs at her nose with a sodden tissue.

'Whatever you think I've done,' says Jess, 'neither of us deserves this.'

No response. Jess wonders why the girl has come back. She can see her more clearly now; smaller and younger, with bad skin that's too pale and poorly dyed hair. She looks like any teenage mother from the estates, could even have a baby of her own.

My daughter; a stranger, thinks Jess. Free to come and go while I'm a prisoner. One of my judges, one of my jailers.

And she's afraid of this girl with her relative freedom and unknowable mind and wonders— how much does she hate, how badly does she want revenge? There's some hope, though; when she looks at Gina's face there's no sign of triumph from earlier.

'I never knew before, about Powell's daughter,' says the girl. 'He never said. I thought he liked me best.'

'I don't think Powell likes anybody,' says Jess. Another silence, and then, because she has to know, 'Were you there when—in the room . . . ?'

'I don't remember. Maybe. Powell gave me

something this morning. It's easier when I'm out of it, but then I forget what happens. Sometimes.' Jess wants to believe her.

'This place we're in now—where is it?' she asks.

'This? I don't know. Some industrial estate; I don't know where. We were staying in an old place out in the country, but something must have happened last week and we had to get out quickly.'

Jess doubles over suddenly as another wave of nausea attacks her, and she lowers herself on to the mattress. Gina takes a couple of steps towards her and then stops.

'You're not well.'

Jess doesn't mean to sound angry but can't help herself. 'I'm hungry, I'm tired, I hurt! You don't know how much I hurt! I've just been raped in front of my daughter who I haven't seen since the day she was born. And I'm scared. No, I don't feel well.'

Gina unconsciously works the tissue between her hands, and small white clots fall to the floor.

'Those girls are here,' she says. 'I think he's planning something special.'

Jess wipes her face. 'What girls? Bryony and Rhiannon?'

Gina nods. 'And the other one they brought in with you.' Her voice is almost defiant. 'I'm not stupid. I know he's cracked.'

'So why did you get involved with him in the

first place?'

'My mum met him somewhere—I don't know. She was always bringing different blokes home since Dad left.' She pauses and looks up. 'You know my dad, don't you? My real dad.'

Another stab. What does she use for memories? thinks Jess. How many empty spaces where there should be histories? And who made her what she is?

As if it would help she takes refuge in the present. 'Tell me about Powell.'

'When Mum wasn't around he used to take photos, like it was a game, a bit of fun. Sometimes we made videos at his flat. Then some of his friends started coming round and joining in.'

If Powell were in front of me now, thinks Jess, I'd strangle him, I'd crush him, I'd turn his grinning face to pulp.

'I didn't like that.' Gina pauses, remembering. 'That's when he started giving me pills to make it easier. And he was nice to me afterwards—he always bought me clothes or CDs.'

'Did he ever talk about me?'

'He said he knew who my real mum was. Said you hated kids, that's why you gave me away. Said that's your job, taking kids away from their parents.'

'He lied, you must know he lied! I try to help children, not hurt them.' She doesn't say—I know what it feels like to lose a child.

Gina shrugs. 'He said we should teach you a lesson, me and him and Doc.'

'Doc? Who's Doc?'

'Just some guy Powell knows. He gets all the drugs, and he does the cutting.'

For a moment, Jess sees Marty's slashed mouth and the raw stump of his wrist. Fallen angel.

'There was this Russian guy the other day, one of his suppliers—he got cut. Powell said he was cheating on a deal.'

'A deal? What was he supplying?'

'What do you think! The girls—*kuritsas*, he calls them. It means chicken in Russian.' She says it like a child showing off after a lesson.

'How do you know all this?'

Gina sits cross-legged in the middle of the room, hugging her knees with one arm. Her voice suddenly sounds very young.

'Doc likes to talk about it. He tells me everything that happens.'

'Where does he do this . . . cutting?' asks Jess. 'How does he do it?' The fascination of abomination; she can't let it go.

'In the studio, where you were earlier. They use the same table for everything. Doc has this weird wooden case, always carries it with him. It looks really old . . . and inside there's knives and scalpels . . . and two small saws.' She'd describe ear piercing with more emotion, thinks Jess, just like the other children who've seen too much. Children who've learned how

351

to survive by breaking the connection between an act and its emotion.

Must run in the family.

'He hasn't touched me yet, though. I belong to Powell.' It almost sounds like pride.

'But Powell won't keep you for ever.' Jess tries to keep her voice calm. 'You know what he is, you said it yourself, he's cracked. He's a paedophile, a torturer. What happens when it's your turn?'

'Powell says we're all little sluts, we all get what we deserve.' She takes her left hand from the pocket of her jeans and holds it in front of her face, turns it to see every angle. She could be checking the quality of something in a shop. 'When we were in your house and we found the baby clothes—I guessed you bought them for me. I told Powell I wanted to stop messing with you. Told him I wasn't going to carry on. He called me a fallen angel. Said if I carried on like that he'd get Doc to teach me a lesson.'

'Oh my God . . .' Jess can't stop herself; she kneels in front of Gina and takes the girl's hand as if picking up a wounded bird. And in her mind all she can hear are Powell's words, asking what traits she passed on to her daughter, and she wonders—Where does the guilt stop?

'Gina—I'm sorry. I'm so sorry . . .'

The girl pulls her hand away, slowly, as if reluctant to break the contact. She shrugs. 'Whatever. I'm lucky—Doc had someone else to see to, then I guess they forgot.'

Jess looks at her own hands. Under the fluorescent light they seem paler than ever, the fingers long and slender. Musician's hands, Jamie called them.

Gina suddenly checks her watch and jumps to her feet. 'Shit. I have to make food for Doc and I'm not even meant to be in here.' Before Jess can move, the girl is out of the door and the lock clicks behind her.

I should have asked the time, thinks Jess.

*   *   *

There are no curtains across the glass that stretches from floor to ceiling, looking out over the old docks and new galleries. Pav slides the door open and stands on the balcony, sipping a glass of wine. Dark by nine o'clock, and the breeze is on the cusp between cool and chill. Few sounds make it up this far. A motorbike accelerating, an ambulance siren, a single burst of laughter. The apartment feels empty with Annie away, and for all that Pav is tired she can't sleep. Her scar is angry tonight and she fingers it unconsciously, tracing the crescent across her cheek.

The breeze strengthens and she goes inside. Ten minutes since she last checked with her team, and still no trace of the doctor's computer. He might never use it again, might have changed the number. Might be nothing to do with Powell, or Jess, or the missing girls. Could all be a coincidence. Could all be a mistake.

The wineglass is just about to tip its contents over her lap when the phone jolts her awake.

*   *   *

Pelham sits at his usual table in the Thai restaurant in Lydford, a few hundred yards from the police station. The noodles in his bowl are congealed and cold, the ashtray is full and the wine bottle empty. The waiters choose paths that avoid his table; no one asks if the food is OK.

How can you find someone, if you don't know who they are?

His phone lights up and judders across the tablecloth.

'Sir—we've got contact. Leslie Murchison, and he's still online.' Pav's voice is sharp with excitement.

'Location?'

'Edge of Uskmouth.'

'How far can you pin it down?'

'A few kilometres.'

'That's worse than useless!'

'Maybe not. I'm on my way in—meet me at the station and I'll explain.'

Pelham snaps a credit card at the waiter who follows him to the door.

'Keep it—I'll be back.'

*   *   *

It's maybe twenty minutes before Gina reappears with a cheese sandwich wrapped in newspaper.

'It's what I gave the girls.'

The smell of food; eat or throw up? Eat, Jess decides, if only for strength. The cheese sticks to the roof of her mouth and she wishes there was water. She's conscious of her daughter watching every action, every movement, hand to mouth, as if fascinated by the habits of some strange, new species.

'Why did Powell want to teach me a lesson? Why did you join in?'

'I didn't know what he was going to do. It was all a game at first—the emails, the photos, messing up your website. Looking round your home. Just a game.'

So Powell and Gina had been in the farmhouse. They must have taken the child's sock from the long brown box and used it as a shroud for the dead animal that Wagner brought in. Of all betrayals this feels like the greatest.

It's almost funny, how willing she was to be deceived. Begging for it. How many other tricks had they played? The Gina emails, luring her to London; she'd been right all along; Gina must have been watching, laughing as Powell taunted her.

'He said you were a sicko, a crazy woman. I didn't think you'd be so fucking ordinary.' Gina moves slowly towards the door, someone who doesn't plan to return.

'Don't go—talk to me.'

Anything—just stay.

'How many people are in this building?'

'I dunno. Depends what's happening. There are always more when he's making a video but none of them stay. And sometimes he keeps the *kuritsas* on site.'

'What about you?'

'We used to stay in his flat—what a hole. But we haven't been there for weeks; we're staying here for now, and Doc. It's really crappy.'

'But now, right now. Who's in the building at the moment?'

'You, me, Doc. The girls.'

'And Powell? You said he wouldn't be back for a while.'

'He had all this hassle with the Russians so he's gone out tonight, to see some Albanian guy who charges less.'

He threatens to mutilate you and you stand there talking about the economics of abuse. Whatever happens next, Jess thinks, Powell's already won.

'You said Bryony and Rhiannon are here. Have they been . . . ?'

'Not yet. The older one—Bryony—I'd seen

her before she got taken. And the little one wasn't meant to be here at all—Powell went really apeshit. And the third one, the one that came in with you, she's like a trial run from the Albanian. But there's something going on now.' A pause as she looks away. 'Another film.'

A family affair.

The thought of it helps Jess to make a decision. 'How many exits does this building have?'

'You can't get out, no way!'

'We have to,' says Jess. 'You know what's going to happen. Powell used you to get to me. He doesn't need you any more.' She wonders if this is too much, too fast, but Gina simply says, 'You think I'm stupid, but I'm not. Like I said, it's what I deserve.'

'No one deserves this—not you, not me. What I did when you were born, that was so wrong. But if we help each other now we'll make it through.'

No answer.

'Gina, please. Tell me how we can get out of here.'

'There are two doors—one at the front, one at the back . . .' She speaks slowly, almost reluctantly, and then without warning takes two steps towards Jess and clings to her, sobbing into her neck.

Jess takes a moment to react, then wraps the girl into her body, holding her until the sobbing dies down, stroking her hair. 'We don't have much time, we have to get out tonight.' She thinks quickly. 'You said Doc likes you. Why don't you tell him you want to go outside, just for a while? To get some air, anything. Then you could go for the police.'

Gina wipes her eyes with the remaining shreds of tissue. 'No way. I don't go anywhere outside by myself.'

Jess thinks for a moment. 'Doc's in the building. What if we knocked him out somehow, took his keys?'

'No, no—you don't understand. Powell's nuts about security. There's a security guard, and both of the doors are watched by cameras. And there aren't any keys.'

'So how do the locks work?'

'All the doors inside have keypads, you put in a code to open them. But the main doors, they have these fingerprint readers. Only Powell and Doc can use them.'

'If he was only keeping kids here why did he go to so much trouble, so much security?'

'It was all here already, when Powell got the place. The building used to belong to a computer company that went bust. Powell said they used it for something called "disaster recovery"; really made him laugh.'

'Maybe it's easier for us, not having to find a key. The two of us could drag Doc to the door while he's unconscious—hold his hand up to the fingerprint reader.'

'Dream on! The guard would see us on the monitor. And what would we do even if we got outside?'

'Call for help. You said this was an industrial estate, there must be other people around.'

'It's just car parks and buildings like this. And this time of night, it'll be empty.'

'Whatever. It's better than waiting to be cut. Where will Doc be?'

'Further down this corridor—all the rooms are there; mine, Powell's, Doc's and a store room where they keep the kids. Then there's the studio, a wall, and at the front there are stacked boxes to make it look like this is a warehouse.'

'And that's where the door is?' says Jess.

'Plus one at the back, next to where the security guy sits.'

'I don't understand. This guard, he must know what goes on.'

'They're all part of BestFrendz; everyone here is.'

Everyone.

'Where's Doc now?' asks Jess.

'As Powell's away he'll stay doped up in his room. Guy's a real smack head.'

'What about knives? If you make food, you must be able to get hold of something.'

'Like, they're gonna let me have a proper knife? Dream on—they're all plastic.'

'There must be a way. There's always a

way.'

Gina joins Jess on the mattress. 'You know I told you I'm Powell's special product? Doesn't want—didn't want—to use me up? He never lets Doc touch me; always makes him laugh, watching Doc watching me. But if I go to Doc's room now, maybe he won't be able to keep his hands off. Then you come in, you know . . .'

'And what? Hit him with a shoe? For God's sake, Gina—even if we manage to hold him down, which I doubt, he'll make a noise. The guard's bound to hear him.'

The girl's smile comes straight from Eden. 'I know what Doc likes. I promise, he won't be able to make any sound. As soon as he sees me, he'll want another hit. I'll do it for him, make sure he's well out. It's the only way.' She plays with a silk scarf, green and gold, tied around her waist, then undoes the knot and offers it to Jess. For a moment she's a child again. 'I always knew that Doc would cut me, one day. Maybe today, maybe tomorrow. He can't make it easy, but he can make it hard; maybe now I won't have to find out.'

Jess works to control her breathing. She takes the scarf from Gina and the cool silk warms instantly to her touch, flowing over her skin.

'Go now—no, wait—tell me where his room is.'

Gina is by the door. 'Turn left, go to the end

of the corridor and then right. Doc's room is the third door on your left—I'll make sure it's unlocked. Give me ten, no, fifteen minutes.'

They stand awkwardly, as if the earlier touching never occurred.

'Gina . . .'

'Fifteen minutes.'

Jess starts counting.

CHAPTER TWENTY-TWO

'Make an assumption,' says Pav. 'The doctor is with Powell, possibly at another location like the barn. If they're using it for the same purpose, they'll need broadband connections.'

'Like that big satellite dish? There can't be many of those.'

'Not quite that easy. This area isn't remote—they'll get broadband via a phone line. The guys have already checked the local service providers—the list just came through.'

Pav runs her finger down the sheet of paper. 'We're lucky. Only forty-eight connections. If this were Bristol or Birmingham it would be four times as many.'

'You think forty-eight is good? Fuck's sake, woman.' Pelham throws the empty cigarette packet across the room.

'Of these forty-eight we discount all those in built-up areas. People would notice something going on. No residential areas or office blocks. That brings us down to ten.'

'Ten teams on a night like this?'

'Look . . .' Pav runs her finger down a line of figures on the paper. 'This is the traffic—the amount of information—on these connections in the last three months. All of them have regular, predictable patterns. All except two, from two different suppliers. And they go to the same building. Although the connections have been there for some time, there was no traffic until last week.'

'Don't tell me—the day after we found the barn. We need . . .'

'All sorted. A team is on its way and there's a car outside—we can be there in half an hour.'

The rain has returned. Thick, heavy drops explode on the pavement outside the station doors, creating a layer of spray so thick that Pelham's feet are invisible as he runs towards the kerb, and he has a momentary sense of wading out to sea.

*   *   *

The industrial estate is like a small suburb waiting to be populated, the landscaped verges more earth than flower, the empty roads glistening black and orange in the rain. Although some units have windows, most are blind with pastel coloured walls of corrugated metal. A large direction board at the entrance to the estate shows the location of each building but few are allocated to companies, the whole project a mistimed venture left stranded by a receding tide of failed dotcoms. The names are unreadable through the rain.

By the time Pav returns to the car from checking the board, her hair and clothes are already soaked and shapeless. They drive on, past car parks that never fill and buildings whose only function now is to define a boundary between inside and out. The estate roads curve and cross in a Celtic pattern that has them lost within minutes, and they pull in only when Pelham sees a solitary car parked near the entrance to one of the units; a Jaguar, last year's model, its colour indeterminate under the sodium lights.

'That look like a doctor's car to you?' says Pelham.

Although the area is deserted, Pav keeps low as she runs close enough to check the registration.

'Murchison's,' she says, back in the car. Her skin has darkened in the rain, all except for the scar which seems luminous in the light from the street lamps. 'Careless or what.'

'Can they see us?' says Pelham.

'There's only one security camera, at least on this side, and that's trained on the door. Doesn't seem to be on a scan cycle.'

The only sign that differentiates this

building from most of the others is the small light over the main door, showing that someone pays the bills. Apart from the doctor's car they've seen no other signs of life anywhere on the estate.

'This could be a wild goose chase,' says Pelham.

'Or a plant,' says Pav, 'like the barn. They knew we were coming. Maybe they led us here deliberately.'

'We still need backup,' says Pelham.

'I didn't use the locals in case they were compromised. Our own team is on its way.' Pav checks her watch. 'Should be here any time now.'

The rain muffles all other sounds and Pelham checks the rear-view mirror every few seconds in case someone is stalking them from behind. He checks the locks.

'The girls could be in there. Jess could be in there,' says Pelham. 'Or whatever her name is.' He sounds cheated, the victim of a cheap trick.

'We all try to fit in, one way or another,' says Pav. 'This was her way.'

'And you're not judging . . .' Pelham checks the time. 'Where the fuck is the backup?'

'What do you want to do, John? Walk up and knock on the door?'

'We could check for other exits.'

'The guys will do that when they arrive.'

Pelham finds a shop receipt in the pocket of his jacket, and begins to fold a tiny peacock

364

with a tail that fans open at the touch of his finger. When he's finished he places it carefully on the dashboard.

'I wonder if Jess knows yet, about Gina,' says Pav.

'You still think she's real?'

'I think Powell covers all the bases. Think about it—he has access to a lot of kids, and the writing on the card we found in Jess's study—that was never Powell's.'

'So he got some teenage girl to pretend to be Jess's daughter? I don't think so!'

'Maybe she's not pretending,' says Pav quietly. 'Maybe he fooled her too.'

As they fall silent again the building in front of them seems to sway and shimmer like a mirage through the sheets of rain rolling down the windscreen, and the air sticks to their skins.

*   *   *

The walls of the small room appear to be advancing and retreating like waves on a beach, moving in rhythm with her own breaths. The fluorescent tube has started to hum, but when she turns off the switch the darkness is even louder and she clicks it on again within a couple of seconds. The only movable objects are the mattress and her shoes, the spike-heeled sandals someone strapped on while she was unconscious. She weighs one in her hand;

the dull red leather is scuffed and stained and torn away around the bottom of the heel, exposing the fish-white plastic core. The fluorescent tube would be better but there's no way to reach it, even wearing the shoes and balancing on the mattress.

Then there's the scarf, collapsed on the floor where she let it fall when Gina left. Jess bends to pick it up but stops before her fingers make contact with its surface, impregnated with millions of dead skin cells; and for the first time in years she remembers the Labrador tin.

You could strangle someone with this. How hard would you need to pull; how long does it take?

And she begins to wonder about Gina; woman one minute, child the next. 'I'm just product,' she'd said, but maybe she has more freedom than she pretends. Maybe no one is going to cut her. Maybe it's all a trick.

But there was the hand at the barn.

She's stopped counting, lost track of time. It could be five minutes, or fifteen.

Gina, her sixteen-year-old daughter, alone with a man who mutilates people without a thought.

Barefoot, with the scarf stuffed into her top and a shoe in her hand, Jess half expects to find Powell outside the door, but the corridor is empty and silent, the air warm and stale. This is an anonymous space. The floors and walls are plasticised, aseptic; nothing will take hold here, not even emotions. There are other doors and Jess hesitates at each, expecting whispers maybe, or crying, but they are mute. And blind—there are no keyholes, just numbered keypads next to the handles.

The corner of the corridor is thirty feet away. She doesn't want to make the turn, leave the safety of this space which she already owns. For a moment she sees herself; dressed like a drunken teenager at a club, clutching a worn-out shoe like a talisman, prepared to kill a man. She has a sudden urge to laugh; don't go there, she thinks, not yet.

One step at a time.

Part of her mind registers that her body no longer hurts. Adrenaline, she thinks, must be a great painkiller.

The next corridor is as anonymous as the first but one of the doors is ajar. She pushes herself against the wall and moves as close as she dare, puts the ridiculous shoe on the ground and prepares the scarf, wrapping it around her wrists. Too early; the voices are low but it's conversation, not sex. A girl and a man, and Gina promised that the doctor wouldn't be able to shout. How can I do it, she thinks, if I hear his voice? And then—They're waiting for me; Powell's in there too, this is all part of a game. She looks up at the ceiling, searching for hidden cameras; maybe this is just another performance.

She tries to work out where the main door is from here. Perhaps it would be easy to get out; the story about fingerprint readers suddenly seems ridiculous; a fantasy, part of their sick practical joke.

The voices have stopped, and then there's a sound halfway between coughing and choking. Before she can move, the door opens and Gina is there, holding a hypodermic.

'It's done.' She looks at the scarf. 'You won't need that—come in, quickly.' She smells of alcohol.

It could almost be Ed stretched out on the camp bed, motionless, with his eyes shut, but the hair is lighter and sparse, the scalp mottled pink and brown. He looks ridiculous with his trousers pulled down to his knees and a tourniquet around his thigh. As she gets closer, Jess notices flecks of white foam around his lips.

'What have you done?' she whispers.

'He can't hear us.' Gina points at the almost empty bottle by the corner of the bed. 'He's pissed most of the time, especially when they're doing a video. But he usually lays off it for a few hours if he thinks there's a chance of doing some gear—says they don't go together.'

'He's not just drunk.'

' 'Course not. But with Powell away he couldn't resist the chance.' She drops the hypodermic on the floor. 'I gave him more than he was expecting, but I didn't think he'd react like this. I don't think he's breathing.'

Jess forces herself to touch the body, her fingers to his neck, feeling for a pulse. 'I can't tell.' Her own heart is racing so hard that she's not sure where the beats come from. 'What if he isn't dead, what if he wakes up?'

Gina takes a roll of silver tape from the small chest of drawers and works efficiently, tearing a number of short strips with her teeth and covering his mouth. Before she binds his ankles, Gina removes his shoes and socks and lines them up next to the bottle of Scotch, and then wraps the tape around his bare skin, five or six times.

'Powell says this looks crappy. He prefers leather straps, but the tape works better.'

It seems to Jess that Gina has done this a hundred times or more. 'How far to the main door?'

'I don't know—a few hundred metres maybe.'

'OK—we have to get him there so we can use his hand to open the lock.' Jess takes the legs and tries to move the body. 'Jesus, he's heavy. You have to help—take his arms.'

Gina ignores her, reaches under the bed and pulls out what looks like a wooden attaché case.

'What are you up to?' says Jess. 'Just take his arms—we have to get out of here.'

Gina flips open the engraved brass catches, but leaves the case lid shut. 'I already told you.

If we try to drag him to the door we'll be seen.'

She opens the case. 'Doc calls it his toolbox. Never lets it out of his sight.'

Jess recognises forceps, scalpels with handles of ivory and bone, a curved clamp-like object, and two small saws. Antiques. She lifts one of the saws, a thin blade about six inches long set into a solid wooden handle worn smooth with use. The blade is dark and pitted as if diseased itself, infected by the rotting flesh and bone through which it has passed.

'You wanna be careful with that—it's sharper than it looks.'

'You don't expect me . . .'

'He's meat. A dead pervert. For fuck's sake, at least he died happy. He won't feel anything now. You wanna get out of here or not?'

Jess lifts one of the doctor's hands a couple of inches from the cover and lets it fall. His skin already seems cool, the flesh tones modulating to blue; or is that just the effect of the light? Maybe there's no choice. 'Which . . . which finger do we need, for the locks?'

Nothing.

'Gina—which finger? Is it just one?'

'I'm trying to remember.' Pause. 'His first finger.'

'What do you mean, first? The index, next to the thumb?'

'I'm sure.'

'The left or right hand?'

'Shit!' Gina shuts her eyes, does a dumb

370

show of reaching out, touching something. She opens her eyes. 'I'm sure it's the right hand.'

'How sure?'

'I don't know. Why can't we take both?'

'And I'm supposed to cut off his fingers using this?' She holds the saw like a dagger.

'You need something hard to cut on; use the case. Doc always starts with a scalpel and saves the saw for the bone—not so messy. But why should we worry?'

Jess watches, fascinated, as Gina splays the doctor's right hand over the top of the closed case, palm upwards.

'Don't go through a joint. And make sure you don't cut me.'

How much blood is in a finger, thinks Jess, how hard is the bone?

The saw falls to the floor. 'I can't do it, Gina, no way.'

'If we're still here when Powell gets back and sees what happened to Doc . . . trust me, you don't wanna know. We got no choice.' Gina picks up the saw. 'You want me to do it?'

'No!'

We're all here because of me, thinks Jess. My fault, I have to put it right. 'Cover his face with something; use the scarf. And give me the saw.'

She keeps her eyes closed, says to Gina, 'Talk to me. Tell me about your house, what music you like.' Say anything to stop me thinking about what I'm doing.

371

And when she's finished, Gina picks up the two fingers. They seem ridiculously small, the edges ragged and raw.

'We'd better go; Powell could get back any time.'

There seems to be blood everywhere. Jess looks up from wiping her hands with a shirt that she found draped over a chair in the corner, then rips off a piece of cloth and hands it to Gina. 'Wrap them in this.' She feels cold, remote, as if the hands that did the cutting belong to someone else.

'We've got to find the girls; they must be terrified.'

Gina stops by the door. 'Like that's really gonna help when we get picked up on camera. You haven't seen them, have you? I don't know about the Albanian kid but Bryony's out of it most of the time, like she's brain dead or something. But at least she's quiet—the little one does my head in.'

'We'll take our chances. You want to run off, fine. But I can't leave them here.'

'Fuck's sake!' But Gina leads Jess to a door in the first corridor just down from her own cell, punches a code into the keypad.

Inside it looks like a makeshift dormitory, maybe the size of a suburban living room, but empty except for six mattresses pushed against the walls. Six children at a time. There are no windows, just the same dead light that casts no shadows on the three children. Jess recognises

372

the girl from the mine, hugging her knees on one mattress, her clothes still smeared with red clay; Bryony lies stretched out on another, furthest from the door, her eyes wide open while Rhiannon strokes her sister's hair with an obsessive rhythm as if trying to wipe away some obstinate dirt.

As Jess runs towards them Rhiannon gives a little scream and pushes herself further into the corner, but Bryony and the girl from the mine watch her with so little expression she wonders if they're drugged.

'It's OK—no one's going to hurt you. We're going to get you out of here.'

She can't help but look at their hands; all the children seem undamaged but soiled, as if the dirt had burrowed into the skin.

'There's no way we're taking them as well,' says Gina. 'It's going to be hard enough.'

'We can't leave them here—there's the guard . . .'

'If we get away, you think he's gonna wait for Powell to come back? Or the filth? Dream on.'

Jess hears an edge of hysteria in Gina's voice, and tries to keep her own level and calm.

'We're all going together.' She reaches for the two older girls and helps them to their feet, praying that they can still move.

'You've got to stay with us, understand?' She picks up Rhiannon and holds her tightly, the child limp and heavy in her arms. 'OK, let's go.'

Gina leads them back, half running, half walking, past Doc's room, through another security door and into a high area stacked with palettes and boxes. 'That's the main door, over there. Once we get about halfway the guard will be able to see us on the monitor.' She points at a winking red light on the camera mounted over the door.

'Give me a moment,' says Jess, breathlessly. She untangles Rhiannon's arms from her neck and lowers her gently to the ground, but holds on to the little girl's arm. 'Which way do we go when we get outside?'

'It's just car parks and other buildings like this. I've only seen it a couple of times.'

'We'll need to find a phone box, or at least get to a main road.'

'We gotta get out first, and quick.'

'You know which finger to try?' says Jess. 'The right hand.'

Gina unwraps the stained cloth and holds up one of the fingers. 'This looks like it bends the right way.' She starts to giggle, stops abruptly and then, with Rhiannon clinging to Jess like a monkey, they all run for the door.

CHAPTER TWENTY-THREE

The headlamps arrive from the wrong direction and pull in next to the Jaguar, nose to tail. Although they can't hear whether the engine is running or not, the lights stay on as if the car has come to a temporary halt and will be moving on at any moment.

'Not one of ours, then,' says Pelham. His back already aches from crouching on the other side of one of the spindly hedges that border the parking areas, a quarter of a mile from where they left their car outside one of the few other buildings to have been let. The rain has become softer and silent but the ground around their feet is already a muddy pool that overflows into Pelham's shoe as he shifts his weight.

'Tomorrow morning I want a list of everyone on the backup team,' he whispers. 'They're all fired.'

'They'll be here in the next twenty minutes—there's nothing we can do until then.'

'Wrong estate, my arse. We should have used the locals.'

'Too risky—you know that.'

As if a decision has been made the headlamps suddenly fade into darkness. The driver stands by the door for a moment, a coatless silhouette in the misty rain, scanning the car park.

'Two against one?' says Pelham.

'And whoever's inside. He's calling someone on the mobile.'

He seems barely to notice the rain, this stranger, his only concession an upturned collar on his jacket. He seems in no hurry, pacing up and down beside the car, trying another number or maybe the same one, listening but not talking.

'What do you think? Is it Goodwin/Unwin, or whatever he's calling himself today? I need new glasses.'

Pav swears under her breath as she tries to get a clearer view through the bush and a thorn catches in her finger. She sucks the blood away before replying.

'Impossible to tell from here. Right build, right height—and whoever he's calling isn't answering.'

The man pockets his phone, hunches his shoulders and breaks into a jog towards the building, as if he's noticed the rain for the first time, but after a few yards he slows to a walk, then stops, then turns back to the car.

'He knows something's up. If he leaves now we'll lose him.' Pelham begins to straighten up but Pav pulls him back down.

'I don't think he's leaving—look!'

The man opens the passenger door and pulls something from the glove compartment.

Pelham squints into the darkness. 'Oh fuck—the bastard's got a gun. This just gets better and better . . .'

*   *   *

Halfway towards the door, Gina stumbles; one of the fingers rolls across the floor and under a tower of palettes.

'I knew we should have cut off the whole fucking thing.' She drops to her stomach and reaches into the narrow gap, sweeping the floor with her good hand. 'It's no use, it's gone too far.'

The sudden cacophony of alarm bells is so painful that Rhiannon screams and tries to bury her head in Jess's shoulder as the camera above the door rotates like something alive, staring at them. Gina scrabbles to her feet. 'Shit—the guard's picked us up on the monitor—he'll be here any second.'

Rhiannon seems to be heavier by the moment as they dash the final few yards to the main door. When the alarm bell stops they hear footsteps echoing from the corridor, getting louder. For a moment they stand mesmerised and then Gina takes the remaining finger and presses it against the pad by the door.

Nothing.

'Try again,' says Jess.

Still nothing.

377

The echoes flatten as a man runs around the palettes towards them. Jess recognises him; the man with the bottle when she was strapped to the chair. He no longer looks fat, just mountainous.

'For Christ's sake—hurry!'

'Must have been the other one,' says Gina.

'No time now.' Jess lowers Rhiannon to the ground and turns to face the guard, now only a few feet away.

'Come on, you sick bastard. Come and try!'

The guard stops at the same moment as Jess feels a sudden draught of damp air. She turns towards the open door, but even before she sees who's there she catches the faint scent of lavender.

Both the man in the doorway and the gun in his hand are slick with the rain. No time to think. Powell looks surprised as Jess throws herself at him and as they topple to the ground the gun slips and skitters away.

Powell's stronger than he looks. He's punching her head, her throat, rolling her over and kneeling on her stomach, stopping her from breathing. Jess can see Gina's struggles becoming fainter in the arms of the guard a few feet away, and with the last of her breath she screams at the girls standing mesmerised by the doorway.

'Get out—run!'

She clings desperately to Powell as he tries to get up, holding him for just long enough to see the girl from the mine grab the hands of Bryony and Rhiannon and drag them outside, towards two figures running through the rain. Maybe it's imagination but Jess thinks she hears Pav call her name even as Powell slams the heavy door shut, the grey steel surface channelled with rain.

It's suddenly quiet. Someone bangs on the door once from outside, a frustrated echo, and the voices are no more than a low drone. Jess is on her knees, winded, and then pain burns through her head as Powell pulls her upright by her hair. His suit is sodden, colourless, clinging to his narrow frame.

'Don't worry, bitch, we still have a little time. I guessed something like this might happen so I arranged a short diversion for the peelers; the only people out there are your two friends. Skulking in the bushes, they were, like frightened rabbits; lucky for us that they play by the rules.'

'Leave us behind—you could still get away.' The words come out slurred; during the struggle Powell had punched her face and her jaw feels semi-detached.

'Who said anything about leaving? *Götterdämmerung*, Jess, the twilight of the gods; you understand what I mean. I don't want you to have any false hope.'

He kicks the severed finger across the floor.

'And look at this! I never expected you to be so inventive—very good. I imagine that was

Gina's idea; she was always keen on medical procedures.' He nods at the guard holding Gina's limp body. 'Bring her—there's no time to lose.'

*   *   *

This could be yesterday all over again, or was it only this morning? From where she's been forced to sit on the floor Jess can see the table still waiting with its empty straps, like an altar. Although she's untied, the guard is standing over her, quashing any thoughts of trying to escape.

Gina seems to be conscious again but hasn't moved from where the guard left her, propped under the large TV screen on the wall. It was Carwen on show last time; Jess doesn't want to think who will star today.

She tries to catch Gina's eye, but the girl seems focused on Powell, following every movement he makes.

The room comes to life as Powell turns on lights and equipment, and checks the video camera pointing at the table.

'A live webcast. A little sooner than I'd anticipated but a real "must see".' Another adjustment and the TV screen comes to life, a wide-angle shot of the room with the table as a centrepiece, every grain of wood in focus. 'There's such a delicious freedom when today is all there is. Don't you agree?'

380

'You're mad,' says Jess. 'Let Gina go, you've got me. That's what you wanted.'

'You have no idea what I want.'

It's the first time she's heard him speak without a sneer.

'The police are already outside,' says Jess. 'It won't take them long to find a way in.'

'No doubt. But not to this little sanctum. We all come to the same end, Jess, the guilty and the innocent. I leave it to you to decide which category you fit. And I long since decided to order my leaving of this world. To orchestrate it, if you prefer.' He looks around the room with pride. 'No creeping away for me, no dying like an animal under a bush, alone. That's why this room is so perfect. My ark, my bunker. Short of explosives it will take hours for anyone to break in here. And we need just a few short minutes. They'll be the most important minutes of your life. And the last, of course.'

The guard behind Jess is so close she can feel his heat, smell his sweat, sour with fear and excitement.

Powell points at Gina with the gun. 'Get her over here!'

The guard shuffles slightly but makes no move towards the girl, and when he speaks there's a tremor in his voice.

'Why don't we leave them? We could get out the back way, before the others arrive.'

'You want to leave before all the fun starts?

But of course!'

The sound of the gunshot is deafening as the bullet passes over Jess to smash into the guard's face, and Jess rolls out of the way just in time to avoid the body as it collapses, trying not to look.

'He always was so dull.'

Jess watches as Powell turns his back and moves towards the screen. Forgotten, she thinks. He's forgotten that I'm free. She tries to get to her feet but Powell hears the sound, turns and fires another shot. This time Jess feels the bullet as it barely misses her face, and she drops to the ground again.

'Don't be so eager to leave us,' says Powell. 'Young people—so impatient.' He pulls Gina upright; Jess expects her to struggle but the girl seems resigned to whatever Powell has planned.

'Camera's running, Gina. You know how this works—should do, by now. It's showtime—which script shall we use?' He circles the girl as he speaks but she shows no reaction even when he reaches out to touch her, as if she was something precious but unknown.

'To be honest, girls, I've had a little crisis of conscience over the past few days. Yes, even me. You see, I haven't been entirely truthful with either of you. Call me an old softy, but I tried to give you each what you most wanted. A mother for one, a daughter for the other.

But I always had this niggling doubt—had I made the right match? And when I see you together . . .' He looks from one to the other, and back again. 'Maybe the nose is the same, but maybe not. And the eyes . . .' He shakes his head. 'Who can say?

'But we still have a decision to make; who shall leave and who shall stay. You see, I've changed my mind. I'm minded to leave a witness behind, someone to keep my memory alive. But which of you shall it be? Perhaps I should let you decide.'

*   *   *

'Bit bloody cramped in here,' says Pelham. He tries to shift his weight in the back of a van lit by nothing more than a bank of computer screens.

'I could bring the car round,' says Pav.

'Forget it. Where's the negotiator?'

'On his way. It's my fault; I should've arranged to have one with the first team.'

Pelham tries to stretch his legs again. 'It wouldn't have been like this in the old days. We would have had that door off in ten seconds—all be over by now.'

'And bodies all over the shop. You watch too much TV.'

'At least the girls are out. What about the third one; we know anything about her yet?'

'I'd guess Eastern European,' says Pav. 'She

still hadn't said anything when the paramedics took them to hospital.'

'Albanian, any odds you like. Bastards.'

The third officer takes a call on his mobile and immediately starts tapping at a keyboard in front of one of the screens.

'What's up?' asks Pav.

'One of the bulletin boards we monitor—they just announced a live webcast. BestFrendz.'

They cluster round the monitor, watching the scene inside the building as Powell paces up and down, waving a gun at the two women, smiling and mouthing silent words.

'What is this,' says Pelham. 'A film, what?'

Pav shakes her head. 'Webcast—this is live, broadcast over the Internet. It's happening now—almost certainly inside that building. He's got Jess in there.'

'Where's the sound; why can't we hear what he's saying?'

'Sorry, sir—the fault's their end. There's nothing I can do.'

'Well, fuck negotiation. I want that door down—now! Blow it off if you have to.'

As they jump out of the van Pav calls back, 'And get a wireless laptop set up—have it brought in to me.'

They find Doc's body first, half on, half off the mattress as if he collapsed trying to get up.

'Murchison,' says Pelham. He points at the mutilated hand. 'Someone getting their own back?' And then he notices the bloody saw on the floor. 'Will you look at that! Bastard—I hope it was agony.'

'I doubt it.' Pav is peering closely at the body. 'Fresh needle marks; smells like he was drinking as well. And look around his mouth; I'll give you ten to one he died the same way as Perry Stiffley. You'd think a doctor would know that alcohol and heroin don't mix.'

'But he didn't amputate his own fingers.' Pelham picks up the silk scarf. 'And this doesn't look like his colour.'

*   *   *

At last there's just one door they can't open. Pelham batters at it with his fists. 'Bloody thing's a foot thick or more. That's where the bastard's got them.'

One of the other officers comes over. 'We tried all the other walls—this is like a self-contained module. Never seen anything like it before—we won't be getting inside in a hurry.'

'I don't care how you do it, just get me in there.' He turns to Pav. 'I'm going back to the van—at least we can see what's happening from there.'

'No need.' Pav sits on the floor and takes a laptop from the case slung over her shoulder. 'If the signal's good enough I can connect to the Internet from here.' The screen lights up as Pelham kicks the door once more and then, with a sigh, sinks heavily beside her.

*   *   *

'On second thoughts,' says Powell, 'I'll make the decision. Already made it. You're not fit to judge the poetry of death, the elegance, the irony. And what a show, no hiding away, not now, all in the open . . .' It's as if Powell is talking to himself while he paces round the table, waving the gun like a baton.

Jess can barely hear the words. She manages to sit upright and looks over at Gina, lying on the table, but the girl's gaze is still fixed on Powell.

The man has heard her move and he comes to stand in front of her, but just out of reach. 'Well, my dear, goodbye at last. I hope you appreciated the entertainment over the past few weeks. Too short a time, I know, but think of it as a distillation, the very essence of your reward.'

There's a sound, somewhere outside the room, a reminder of another world. The sound of steel on steel, echoing up the corridor.

Powell goes back to Gina and runs his fingers across her face, a blind man reading her features. 'It sounds as if your friends have caught up with us. *Tant pis*. The doors will hold them for a while. Long enough.'

The red light on the camera is winking with impatience.

Outside the room Pav watches the little screen on the laptop. Even without sound, she can see that Gina knows what will happen, has known all along. The girl's eyes are closed as Powell climbs up beside her, brings the muzzle of the gun to her temple.

And then, without warning, Gina's whole body arcs as she knocks the gun away. Her legs and arms are wrapped around Powell, trapping him like a fly in a web. Jess rolls out of shot and when she reappears it's with the gun aimed waveringly at the two writhing figures on the table; she's shouting silent words, looking for the shot.

Pav watches as Jess moves closer, the gun steady now, pointing at Powell's head. And all the time she's shouting and screaming, and only when the stream of silent words ends does Powell stop struggling and look up into her eyes, her beautiful eyes. He could almost be smiling as the gun kicks in Jess's hands and the back of his skull explodes into a mist that floats towards the camera lens in slow motion, blinding them all at last.

CHAPTER TWENTY-FOUR

Autumn can be grey in Venice but today is sharp and bright, warm enough to drink brandy and hot chocolate outside the café next to the Accademia bridge.

Jess wears the camera like a pendant, and Pav and Jess's mother watch while she focuses on tourists walking by, shooting frame after frame until they turn to stare; and then she turns to a seagull, or a crowded vaporetto at the jetty. A skeletal cat is washing a kitten under one of the tables, and Jess lies on her stomach on the damp paving, snapping each movement of its paws.

'She takes a lot of photographs,' says Pav.

'Ten rolls a day, on average. She packs them into boxes and stores them in her father's old room. The films, that is. She never has them developed. I offered to get her a digital camera, but . . .' The older woman's eyes are invisible as she watches her daughter from behind dark glasses, even though the sun is pale in the sky, and then slowly gets to her feet. 'I'll see you back at Ca' Priuli; don't keep her out too long.'

As her mother walks down to the vaporetto stop, Jess joins Pav at the table.

'John sends his regards,' says Pav, reaching across to straighten Jess's scarf. 'He often talks about you.'

'He was very kind. Everyone was very kind.'

'I came here as soon as I could; things were pretty hectic back at home. We wrapped up a huge part of BestFrendz—a result.'

Jess turns slowly. The roots of her hair are a dark band cradling her head, and the blonde spikes of eight weeks ago are already softening into curls. 'You phoned every day. I'm not used to that.'

'You went through something . . . I can't begin to imagine what it was like. And it's because of you that the girls are safe, and Gina.'

'Ah—Gina. First you have a daughter, then you don't. But I couldn't have done it without her help.' Jess cradles the mug of chocolate in her hands. 'How is she?'

'OK, physically. Still in the hostel.'

'She won't stay—they never do.'

'Don't be so sure. I meet up with her, once or twice a week; coffee and a pizza. And she's still going to the counsellor—you didn't have to pay for that.'

'Her life's been shitty enough so far. And she was my daughter, if only for a few weeks.'

'Gina fell through the cracks,' says Pav. 'We can't catch them all.'

'But we have to try.'

They both watch the traffic on the Grand Canal. A working boat passes in front of them, full of crates of food, and one of the men calls up something but the breeze takes his words away.

'I told Denny I was a fake,' says Jess. 'I told him to destroy my website, all my songs, everything. Bastard refused.'

'You're not a fake, and neither are your songs,' says Pav. 'They're your poetry, your life. No one can take them from you whoever you are, whatever name you use.' She takes a deep breath. 'You haven't talked about your daughter, your real daughter.'

Jess laughs. 'There is no "real", Pav, not in my world.'

'I met her.'

Silence.

'She exists, Jess, she's real.'

Jess finishes her brandy before replying, sipping slowly. 'I have no daughter. I have no one. All I have is me, and even I'm a fabrication.'

'You're so wrong! Look at me; I don't do fantasy. I'm here because of you, because I care for you. And your daughter—no, don't shake your head. She'll be in touch. Give it time. And when she does, I promise, you'll be proud of her.'

Eight weeks ago, as they watched the ambulance take Jess and Gina away, Pelham had said, 'I don't understand why Powell didn't kill her when he had the chance.'

'That's easy,' Pav had replied. 'Why kill her once when she can die a little every day?'

A small bird lands on the table and starts pecking at a half-eaten biscuit in Jess's saucer; she carefully breaks off a piece and crumbles it onto the table.

'What's happening about your flat?' says Jess.

'We're selling—or rather, I show people round and Annie shouts instructions down the phone from New York.'

'So where will you stay?'

'I'll find somewhere; can't afford Annie's lifestyle, though.'

It sounds like a question.

'I'll be going home in a couple of weeks,' says Jess, 'but the farmhouse is going to feel pretty empty. Just a fabricated woman and her noisy cat; you could have a room of your own . . .'

'I'm not used to sleeping alone; far too cold at this time of year . . .'

It no longer matters what people think, and even the cheers and wolf whistles from a passing boat can't stop the first kiss that neither of them wants to end.

They finish their drinks and Jess takes Pav's arm, leading her down to the private water taxi. The Gothic palaces lining the narrow side canals loom over the boat like cold, white sepulchres, and when they leave the shadows of the buildings and cross the empty lagoon, Jess sits at the front of the boat, sometimes reaching over the side as if trawling for something hidden below the water. Her fingernails are now all the same length, too long to hold down the strings of a guitar.

The solitary island coalesces out of a bank of mist, and they follow a concreted track from the jetty alongside a deserted canal. The few boats tied against the bank look tired, patterned with fallen leaves. There's no grandeur here, nothing more than a few isolated buildings and scrubby grass. No people, no life.

They come upon it suddenly, the old cathedral, a Byzantine relic sprawling like a monastery a mile or so inland. 'It's the most lonely place in Venice,' Jess had said, and she was right. She pulls herself free and runs ahead to enter the building.

The memory of incense; a phrase she heard once. Perhaps that's the scent hidden under the dust of the interior, the memory of chasubles and chanting and certainty. Jess waits at the end of the nave until her eyes have adjusted to the gloom, and then looks up at a giant mosaic that covers the apse; a faded blue Madonna holding a child, framed in gold.

Pav watches from the doorway, unwilling to intrude until Jess turns and beckons her in, and they stand together for a while under the ancient dome before making their way back outside into the bright afternoon.

They find a worn stone bench and sit in silence while the mist ebbs and flows, until the dampness in the air invades them. Then Jess takes Pav's arm and the two women lean towards each other, walking slowly back along the path to the jetty where the boat is waiting.